In a Place Like That

By the same author and available from Quartet

NIETZSCHE IN TURIN: THE END OF THE FUTURE

In a Place Like That

LESLEY CHAMBERLAIN

QUARTET BOOKS

First published by Quartet Books Limited in 1998
A member of the Namara Group
27 Goodge Street
London W1P 2LD

A catalogue record for this book is available from the British Library

ISBN 0 7043 8070 6

Printed and bound in Finland by WSOY

In a Place
Like That

IN A PLACE LIKE THAT

We
don't know, you know,
we
don't know, do we,
what
counts.

One
and the same
has
lost us, one
and the same
has
forgotten us, one
and the same
has –

Paul Celan

1

WHAT'S THE MATTER?

'You sure you'll be all right, Harry? What about the children?' Maria always created her own send-off by flapping.

'The children are with Sin, dear.' Her husband, familiar with these panic scenes, spoke in a tone of borrowed weariness. He had to indulge her. Otherwise she would have a breakdown and they would have to leave Muzeb.

'Is that supposed to console me, that my lovely little children are in the sole care of a pro-Bezzakonian witch? Now you're joking, Harry.'

But Harry choked with real laughter. Neurotics were very funny when they put their mind to it. 'Sin's a perfectly good au pair, Maria. Anyway, you employed her.'

Maria, when she thought of Sin, failed to create a stable picture. Sin was a university graduate from Britain who liked Bezzakonia, yet kept shouting about the terrible personal cost of taking part in the Bezzakonian experiment, which made Maria all the more depressed. Also she suspected Harry was attracted to her.

'Make sure she doesn't forget to feed them while she's telling them the history of the Revolution.'

'I'll sit in myself.'

'No, Harry, no.'

Sin was quite young, quite pretty, and did not lend herself to the description 'sensible'.

'I am joking, dear. I've got the whole weekend mapped out. We must get on now.' The car engine had been running for several minutes while they talked. 'Do your seat belt up. I don't know why you're fussing anyway. After all, you're going to the West for the weekend. The land of the free.'

Maria needed only have replied that there were times when everything connected with Bezzakonia, even getting out of it, seemed uncomfortable, like a woolly jumper on bare skin, but she fell back on what she thought Harry would better understand.

'I'm just sorry Pat can't come.'

'Pat is ill.'

'Yes.'

'In that case nothing can be done.'

'No.'

They pulled out of the ghetto and waited to join the ring-road traffic. Harry had to execute an official U-turn in order to head in the opposite direction. He aimed for just in front of a rumbling bread van with only one headlight and rammed his foot on the accelerator.

She wailed, 'I don't like this filthy road. But at least you can't see it at night.' Maria preferred all of Muzeb in the dark. In the daytime, except in summer, when the trees softened its open spaces, it blew a Snowland draught into her soul. After a while she added, 'Sin's right. We do live in a ghetto,' then she sat thoughtfully, letting him concentrate on the driving.

'At least we've got a nice place to live in,' he said.

She let it go. Pat was ill with the vague Muzeb malady which every so often felled people. Maria wondered if she was really sorry Pat wasn't coming after what had been said. They told her at the Wives' Circle Pat said Maria doesn't know what she wants.

That's why she's difficult. Not true. Not true. The point is travelling alone anywhere is not much fun, and especially not in Bezzakonia. It's not restful, for one thing, when you can't share responsibilities and jokes and problems.

Still, the tickets had been booked. Moreover, the shopping list written in Maria's small, uneven hand suggested the Blanchflower family's daily lives were punctuated by such glaring omissions to necessary comfort and convenience that they would not survive their hardship posting to the capital of Bezzakonia if Maria did not from time to time place bulk orders with foreign department stores. So there was no question of her not going on the R and R excursion. There was no question of a change of plan, even though without Pat beside her she had no more than three words of Bezzakonian. She fished in her bag and wondered if by some miracle she had managed to leave her passport behind.

'Darling, you'll hardly see any Bezzakonians. You'll be in the train asleep and when you wake up it'll be the West.'

Harry, who was omitting all the shunting and passport checking, visits to the lavatory and ticket inspections which made real journeys less smooth than their ideal counterparts, not to mention the long border stop at Bezbez, seemed suspiciously keen not to unmake long-standing arrangements. What was he up to, then? Whatever it was she couldn't do anything. Perhaps he just wanted a weekend alone. Everyone did from time to time.

They arrived at the Bezumgrad station just before six.

'I'd see you on to the train, darling, but I must go to this damn reception for the Duke of Edinburgh.'

He was weak, she thought, so weak, but she loved him.

Getting out, she held the passenger door open and leaned in.

'Harry, I know you're always honest with me. Sweetheart, is it true that the ambassador is on Valium? I mean, Dr Denman told Ursula, who told Pat, and you know how Muzeb gets people down.'

Harry's laugh looked and sounded false.

'I wish you'd take me seriously.'

'Maria, how can you say that? It would be more than my job is worth to come to Muzeb with a frivolous woman.'

Harry had this way of speaking, she thought, and this way of laughing that gave her no reassurance at all.

'What will you do over the weekend?'

'Go with Sin to the GASTRO in the morning and stock up on frozen pike and a case of that Chianti if they've got any left. Otherwise it'll have to be Bezum's Mucus Ani. Soften the passage of our time here.'

'Oh, Harry!'

Giving the Bezzakonian wine a Latin pronunciation was a piece of Harry's original humour, though now everyone in foreigners' Muzeb repeated it. It was one of those jokes which kept people alive, Pat said. Ursula, the keep-fit addict, said Harry deserved a medal for it and that it would last long after the Blanchflowers had moved on to an easier life. Harry, seeing the immediate effect it had on people, could hardly believe he *was* the author. Better cash in on his luck while he could.

He went on, 'Then in the afternoon I propose a walk with the children on Bezum Hills, followed by an early supper of burgers at the American Embassy snack bar. Sunday morning I'm playing broomball. Then lunch at the English Pub. After that I'll be whacked and sleep the afternoon away with a good conscience.'

'Oh, Harry, it sounds like the perfect weekend! I wish I were staying.'

Harry, whose hair at forty was already receding, leaned over and kissed his fussing wife. Funny pair they made, he thought, he not tall and turning to fat, she long-bodied and rake thin. Like Jack Sprat and his wife, only the other way round, or was it?

'Harry, I wish —'

'Maria, I must go. Prince Philip and the Olympic Equestrian Committee await.'

She couldn' t contest it. She kissed him back, pushed the door shut, patted the car roof, slid the brown Gucci bag with the gold motif over her shoulder and finally set off across the poorly lit square.

He let the engine of the Volvo tick over till he thought he saw her disappear into the vast main building of the station. It's not the right place, he thought. She should go down the side, straight on to the platform. Still, never mind, someone will direct her.

Harry was fundamentally cruel to his wife, and had become more cruel in Muzeb. That he didn't speak any more Bezzakonian than she did was one reason for his decline. The others included his age and the fact that the young turks in the embassy, who smoked pot and slept with each other's wives, were gunning for him. He wondered about the ambassador and Valium. Perhaps they were gunning for the ambassador too. He would try to find out.

Well, that's his problem, that he's not always nice to me. Ours is to get on the train, Maria told herself, passing through that extraordinary moment of transformation by which habitually chaperoned women realize that right now they are as alone as anyone else in the world and have to find their place.

She arrived at the platform the long way round, via the big overhead noticeboard which listed arrivals and departures.

'Bezbez? Arcadia?' She looked expectant. Passing men were more helpful than passing women, but only just. One with a cigarette in his mouth finally growled, '*Tuda*.'

'Over there?'

He pointed.

'Oh, thank you. You're so kind.'

The stream of heavily wrapped people carrying boxes and bundles propelled her along. Everything in this country was bundled. It either did or didn't have legs and a voice. The scale of things was also enormous. The train stood four times the height of a man. Alice-in-Wonderland syndrome, a sarcastic member of the Wives' Circle had once called it, and now this idea was imparted to every new member, to help her deal with expatriate life.

It is difficult for wives, Maria thought. Their men work hard. Well, they have to, if the world is not going to be blown to smithereens by misunderstandings between Fortress Muzeb and the White House. In her mind she saw the two sides constantly lined up like black and white chessmen, ready to start the game if the diplomats dropped their guard. We mustn't give the Boomies an inch, or let them take one. If stalemate is the price of peace, let's keep the stalemate.

But it was only when she came to Muzeb, after three months' Foreign Office preparation, that she first encountered the analogy between the Cold War and marital war. In truth, this was the Cold War more often discussed in the Wives' Circle. Many a marriage went from decline to fall in Muzeb. It was possible that Muzeb showed up what was wrong with the marriages in the first place, like one great lie detector.

Maria strode five minutes up the platform till she came to a man in uniform. Seryozha the conductor had seen the *foreignka* coming but pretended he hadn't.

She held up her reservation. 'I just thought I'd check with you. All right if I get in here?' Words were necessary to accompany her smile, she decided. It didn't matter if he couldn't understand.

'*Net,*' he said wheezing. '*Nelzya bez platskarty.*'

'It's not all right?' Pressing her lips together, Maria made a move towards the steep iron steps of the carriage door, but the conductor barred the way.

'*Net.*'

'Look. I don't understand. *Ya* –' she indicated herself – '*ne ponimayu bezzakonsky.*'

He shrugged.

Other people were now boarding the train. He checked their tickets and let them pass. Through the lighted windows with curtains still undrawn, she watched those privileged travellers who had been allowed to pass enjoy the full satisfaction of finding their berths. It was not at all unpleasant, settling in for an eleven-hour journey. She had never really thought about it before, but clearly this was a moment of human satisfaction, getting settled in a train.

'Oh dear, you don't understand, do you?'

She looked at her gold watch, an elongated hexagon with Roman numerals showing off her pale freckled skin and slim wrist. The train was due to leave in fifteen minutes. Harry had told her Bezzakonian trains always ran on time. Indeed, transport didn't seem to be one of Bezzakonia's problems, give or take a dozen people spilling out of every closed concertina tram door and all those air passengers whose official seat was the aisle or the lavatory. He expanded like a schoolboy on every subject, bumping up the numbers, and the horrors, and called it wit. Dear Harry.

'Look. I need to know what to do. Tell me what to do.'

But Seryozha the conductor just stood, as if the entire effort of his life went into breathing. His chest rose and fell audibly. '*Platskarta nuzhna, madame.*' He waited. She did nothing. Finally he seized her right hand, which was holding the reservation, raised it up, moved his grip from flesh to ticket and then said, pointing his finger to the far end of the platform, whence she had come some ten minutes ago, '*V byuro!*'

His muffled voice wasn't easy to understand. Already he was saying it again, louder this time, breaking up the syllables and slowly enunciating: '*Vam nado v byu-ro! Tuda.*'

'*Tuda*' again. Evidently some kind of direction.

'Right –' Should she leave her overnight bag? She could nip back faster without it. On the other hand, perhaps she'd better take it. He might not understand. Indeed, it might be stolen. Then she'd have no toiletries, no towel, no book, no fruit for the journey. 'You want me to go to some kind of office? Off I go then.'

He looked at his own watch, with a hammer and sickle on the face, and sighed.

With the Gucci bag over her shoulder, she broke into a clumsy, long-unpractised run, dodging the human bundles coming the other way. At school she'd been good at athletics. She hadn't been bad at French either. It seemed she had given up everything when she got married. Still, she wasn't in bad shape. They ate a healthy diet, despite Muzeb difficulties. I mean, she heard herself saying to the latest Circle recruit, we import milk and fruit, and French cheese, but who doesn't who cares for their health? And especially with children you have to be so careful. Also Harry and I fast once a week. People always gasped when she said this. But they had

9

decided firmly not to get fat, or, in his case, fatter. So, encouraged by Ursula, who had been here ages, they just drank juice, usually on a Wednesday. Now she thought about it, it seemed like a peculiar sort of training for being in Bezzakonia, a sort of keeping fit that was both physical and mental.

Entering the booking hall, she stopped and took a breath. She looked to the right, where the man had pointed, and found the word '*Byuro*', along with another much longer one. The door was closed. On it was a sign which obviously meant that too.

Hell's bells. She ran round the perimeter of the vast hall, checking no other service point was also called '*Byuro*'. The station clock shifted a minute even as she stood there, its loose minute hand plummeting through sixty seconds of space in one second of time. Oh no, this isn't true.

But there he is still. I'll have to go back. She could see her man in the distance, up the platform, and broke into a more accomplished run towards him. The second sprint left her breathless and hot.

'Closed.' The word tumbled out, and she let it, as if that was all there was to the matter. It wasn't her fault. '*Zakryto*.' She handed him the toy word in his own language. Adults were collectively responsible for broken toys. Children were simply vulnerable.

He shrugged. And wheezed. And nodded. '*Da. Pozdno.*'

She smiled. 'So, if you don't mind, I'll get on now. The train's about to leave and I have tried.'

'*Net.*'

She felt cold. Harry would have said, had he been looking, 'My dear, you've gone white.' It was his version of solicitude. No, mustn't be too hard on Harry. He was kind sometimes. Sometimes he did notice things. And it would have been nice to have him here now for moral support.

'But I've bought a ticket. What else do I have to do? I don't understand. *Ya ne ponimayu.* And whatever it is, if the blessed office is closed, how can I do it?'

The words stuck in her throat. Hold on, Maria, don't lose control, don't, please. This matter can be talked about calmly, that's one thing I'm sure of. Harry's voice had internalized itself in her head. That realization brought her even closer to tears.

The conductor pointed to his watch. He seemed to be indicating when the office would open.

'Eight o'clock? But the train will have left by then.'

He shrugged. He ran his eyes along the train. All the doors were shut but one, and the open one wasn't his. Accompanying parties were already walking away. Through the one open door a young couple were holding hands.

It was an uneventful life Seryozha led. He worked six days a week, and once every month, when there was a compulsory voluntary labour day, he worked seven. That was when they painted railings or cleaned windows or mended broken fittings and replaced light bulbs. His wife had long ago gone off with another man. Of his two grown-up children, one was clever and lived in the boffins' colony in Novobezumsk, all luxuries and expenses paid, and the other had married a collective farmer in Riograd. Neither kept in touch. He bought his sausage and onion and buttermilk and tea in the GASTRO under his block of apartments. He shared facilities with a married couple who called him uncle and regarded him as inferior. But he thought they were lucky. For one thing he didn't drink much and for a second he never cooked, because he could get a hot meal here in the works canteen. If he had a weakness it was that he liked sport. He watched ice hockey on television. And he read newspapers. People said they were full of lies, but he wasn't bothered, so long as there was something to read. He read from *The Bezzakonian Truth* pasted on boards at the bus stop, while waiting for a tram.

The news gave him something to think about. The news was in South-East Asia, where Bezzakonian troops were helping in the struggle against imperialism. It was in Washington and Muzeb, where sincere people on both sides were trying to help the psychotic Americans negotiate the strategic arms limitation treaty. The news was in Iran, where the people had overthrown the Shah, and in Georgetown, where the suicide of hundreds of believers in a false religion had once again revealed the malignity

11

of Western decadence. The news was where Bezzakonian cosmonauts orbited in space.

Seryozha felt he had long ago made his own home in that pure and infinite space. From there he watched the world go by. He saw its badly-oiled machine in motion, like a train travelling in a circle. Every time the wheel came round to him he knew the contraption had turned through another cycle. He logged the world on its way who knew where and for what purpose. He might just as well have been the recorder of passing sputniks as a railway guard.

'Oh, please.' The *foreignka* was crying now. Her make-up was smudged. She looked older, less elegant, less composed. She was worried. She was unhappy. It mattered to her to get on the train, it seemed, and not just because she was supposed to travel to Arcadia tonight. It mattered.

'*Prokhodite.*'

That sounded different. 'What?'

He repeated the magic word, gesturing with his arm. He even held open the carriage door for her, then climbing in behind he combed the compartments for an empty seat. She hadn't confirmed her seat reservation; strictly speaking he shouldn't have let her on, and the train was crowded, even in first class, but the only remaining seat was bound to be hers. He picked up the flight bag and offered silently to put it on the rack.

'No, no, I need it here, but thank you. *Spasibo.*'

He noticed her tear-stained, bloodshot eyes. He couldn't remember the last time he had come so close to another human being.

He began speaking in a huge, low, heaving voice which betrayed real breathing problems. 'I don't know how it is in your country, *madame*, but you know we are not all scoundrels here. It would make me happy if you remembered that when you needed him, Uncle Sergei helped you. He helped you. Yes, he did.'

He got off then without turning. She heard the door slam and almost immediately the train glided into motion. With her heart hammering, she got up and pressed her face against the window, trying to see, but he was out of sight. Something her au pair had said about life here being a treasure hunt passed into and out of her mind.

The other people in the compartment stared at her. All seemed, like her, middle-aged. A woman was crocheting. A dark-haired man in a blue track suit asked, in a language she understood, 'What's the matter, capitalist lady?'

'I don't know what he said.'

'No, what's really the matter?'

The woman put down the mink-coloured crocheting, which seemed to be shaping into a beret, and gazed sympathetically at Maria, still standing. The man was leaning against the window. The glass made him feel the absence of the window blind. He reached up and pulled it down until it clicked in place.

'I feel so useless.'

'But that's what he was trying to tell you about himself. He wanted to give you something you needed. That's how life works here. We have to need each other. Don't you see? Sit down now and join us. Tell us about the West. We certainly need you.'

'You need us but . . . I've been sent . . . to say we're not good enough.'

2

RULES OF THE GAME

The notion prevailed officially for a short while in Bezzakonia that if men and women shared hygienic facilities, no unnatural desires would occur between them. The language students the British government sent to Bezzakonia in '72 encountered this ambitious cultural experiment.

'The washbasins are communal and there are no showers, though we do have separate dorms,' said Antonia, reporting back from the introductory briefing.

'That's crazy. We can't not wash,' said Natasha and Jem.

'Of course not. We'll just have to be sensible and civilized. Just the right use of rules if you ask me.' Eamon rubbed his hands.

'You are vulgar, Eamon.'

'I will be if I get the chance.'

The next morning the English girls got up at six to wash and took it in turns to guard the door. They went for a stroll round the block till breakfast began at eight.

Three hundred students crammed into the enormous canteen.

Seeing the tables were set in fours, Jem and Natasha pushed two together, so their group of five could sit without a squash. Dave appeared just as a waitress came over, scowling and rattling off something in Bezzakonian.

'It's not allowed to move the tables,' he translated. He had the best command of the foreign language.

The waitress in a black skirt and white blouse nodded in self-justification, arms folded, surveying the damage to her sector.

'Also we have to leave one place on every table for a stranger from another country. To be friendly.'

A thin young Oriental man with bad skin loitered as the domestic monitor to the English-speaking group, Vladnina, bustled over. The expression on her face said minding children was impossible. 'Never mind, waitress. I'll be responsible. It's the Empire, you know, the English are so used to doing things their own way. Sit!' she barked, setting the young man between Dave and Jem.

'Ngip,' said the young man hopefully.

The cheese slices were already sweating and curling. The students waved away wedges of baked omelette before the waitress had time to set them down. The same fate befell a cabbage and marrow stew.

Jem said, 'I can't bear to see all this waste.'

'Imagine being force-fed and then you'll bear it,' said Natasha.

Antonia shook her head. 'It's just a peasant diet.'

Eamon arrived late. He was a rather handsome young man from Belfast, with lovely brown eyes, but he was so childish the women had all already dismissed him as a prospect. He went about with a jaunty air of deserving more success with women than they had so far granted him.

'It couldn't have taken you twenty minutes to shave,' Antonia reproached him.

'Leave the poor man alone. You're beginning to sound like a bossy Bezzakonian.' Natasha cast a deprecating glance across at the staff table.

Antonia, who didn't like herself for being bossy, decided she should talk more to the stranger. 'And where do you come from, Ngip? Ah, *North* Vietnam. How interesting!'

Eamon began, 'You know what the Bezzies have done in the last half-hour? They've put a guard on the communal facilities and posted up a timetable. Because there was this French girl this morning showing off her breasts. Half the men in the building came to watch. That's what alerted that old bag in the housecoat and that's why I'm late, Aunty Tony. From now on it's women only from eight to eight-thirty.'

'Shsh! She's only over there.'

'Eamon's lowering the tone as usual,' said Jem.

Eamon waved an empty cup at the waitress and tackled some cold omelette.

Eventually Dave said in a sarcastic voice, 'The Bezzakonians were probably trying an experiment to see whether they could trust us and apparently we've already failed.'

'Trust? Trust us to do what?'

'To be observers of a new way of doing things. To play our part as privileged guests.'

'Tosh. If they herd us all together, men and women, half-naked, maybe not you, but most of us will find a way of enjoying it, because we're human beings. I know you like it here, Dave, because it's pure and all that, but that's because you're screwed up.'

'You're a sex maniac,' retorted Dave, draining his tea. 'You should shut up.'

'Are you going to make me?'

'I am a human being,' said Ngip, which was a blessed intervention.

The five-minute bell for lessons rang.

The classrooms were located in the bowels of the great building, and though buildings rose up above the earth with the ugly impudence of skyscrapers everywhere, much of what was important about Bezzakonia appeared to be housed underground. The students called the thick-walled classrooms dungeons. The only redeeming feature was high ceilings. Each room was crammed with a blackboard and desks, which gave the impression every last educational opportunity in this country was being seized.

'Sit near me, children!' cried Mrs Galina Smirnova, as Eamon instinctively led the others to the back row. 'We are not so many.'

He grimaced and gave in. Galina Smirnova had enormous winged and spangly butterfly spectacles. She looked to be in her mid-thirties, with just a hint of grey hair under the spectacle arms.

'All the women here look sort of bossy and motherly at the same time,' whispered Jem.

'A model to be avoided,' Antonia whispered back.

The students, who were being financed by their countries to become Bezzakonian specialists, repeated phrases and did exercises round the table. The teaching involved a lot of rote learning, which reminded Antonia of collective chanting at school prayers. Jem whispered something again to Antonia.

'Would you like to share your insight with all of us?' demanded Galina.

'Yes, certainly. I said language doesn't work like that. It's about communication, and improvisation, not about being theoretically right.'

'This is not correct,' said Galina. 'Now pay attention.'

A surprised silence followed her dismissal of Jem's point.

'"How shameful of you! How shameful of him! How shameful of me!" Say the phrases please, Eamon, Natasha. Good, Dave. You sound like a Bezzakonian already.'

Dave brushed his dark forelock anxiously out of his eyes. Eamon said in English, 'I wonder what's Bezzakonian for teacher's pet.'

'What's it got to do with you? Just because you don't know anything.'

'Children!' Galina clapped her hands.

'How shameful of us!' giggled Natasha, and a tiny smile escaped from the corners of Galina's mouth.

'Can't we learn normal language?' grumbled Jem.

Dave interrupted. 'I think all of you should shut up and give Bezzakonia – and Mrs Smirnova here – a chance. They do things

17

much more fairly here than at home. Everyone is equal. And when everyone has been trained to work hard and put in his or her little bit, it will be a great place to live.'

'Dave, for God's sake. With armed guards on the bathroom door?'

'That's only because of people like Eamon.'

'You don't think there's something wrong with the master plan? You're crazy.'

'None of you understands.'

'What makes you think you do?'

'Children, please! We are speaking Bezzakonian!'

Over meatballs and potatoes for lunch, Antonia tried again to get conversation going with the compulsory alien. 'From *North* Vietnam, eh?' She decided to avoid reference to the war in progress. 'How nice. We're from England.'

'Have you been learning Bezzakonian long, Ngip?' asked Jem.

'That's Vietnamese for "too long", I recognize the gesture,' said Eamon, and everyone laughed, including Ngip.

Vladnina wanted to be part of the pleasant gathering, so after the plates were cleared she drew up a chair with all the enthusiasm of one who had been invited. 'You know, I feel privileged to watch over you individualistic English. I know you feel homesick. You see, I have read Dickens, so I can imagine how it is for you, at home on your damp and foggy little island. I know that you treat your pets more kindly than your children and that every-where you suffer great unemployment, and the working class is repressed.' As she leaned across to address the girls directly, her shelf-like bosom pressed against Eamon's sleeve. He raised his eyebrows and mouthed the word E-NOR-MOUS. But it was Antonia's response, 'Which Dickens novel was that, Nina?', which provoked stifled giggles.

In the afternoon they took a trolley bus into the centre of Bezumgrad and walked down Bezum Prospect, where the neo-classical façades of the stately city buildings were crumbling. There was hardly any traffic, just a few buses and trams, and the pedestrians who passed showed no sign of recognizing, still less welcoming, foreigners in their midst.

The students reached a bridge over a gloomy canal which had shrunk in the summer heat, leaving a green tide mark.

'I thought this was supposed to be a beautiful city.'

'It was!'

'Reminds me of our bathroom when my mum's not there. Perhaps we can wash in it,' said Eamon.

'You have this irresistible urge to take your clothes off, don't you?'

'You're so sensible, Aunty Tony. The Bezzakonians could do with someone like you.'

'I get the impression canals aren't part of the plan any more. The world's moved on,' suggested Jem, who had been hanging over the side, trying to divine the truth in the opaque water.

'I wish it would move back. Look!' cried Natasha, as three women walked by arm in arm. 'The Bezzakonians even walk in chains.'

Dave wasn't amused. 'Oh, for heaven's sake! You're so hung up.'

'You're saying that to me!'

'I didn't mean it as a sexual thing.'

'I didn't mean it as one either. There are other things in life.'

Eamon tried being the peacemaker. 'When did your mother leave, Nat?'

'Don't call me that, Eamon. She left in 1950.'

Natasha's mother was a Bezzakonian exile who had married a British diplomat. It seemed like a special qualification on which no one could comment.

'Shall we have an ice cream? There's a stall over there,' suggested Antonia. 'I believe it's something the Bezzakonians do well.'

'I doubt it.'

The students plunged their hands into the tub.

'Which one? Which one?' snapped the *vendeuse*, standing behind her metal barrow in a white coat.

'Why is she shouting at me? They all look the same.'

'They're the same but individual. She's trying to make a

philosophical point.'

'Oh, God, I think I'll go mad here. Why is everyone defending them?'

'Just choose, Nat. Otherwise she's going to slam her barrow shut right on your fingers.'

'Another bossy mother,' observed Antonia, after they had been instructed not to discard the wrappers on the pavement.

'As I keep saying, they have a thing about rules here.'

They walked along licking.

'They're good rules. You're all anarchists. This is a nice clean street and this is the best ice cream I've ever eaten!' Dave was happy.

There was another meal in the dining hall around six in the evening, after which Politeknikum No. 31 imposed a ten o'clock curfew. The rule was redundant; if the students went out again, past the bust of Bezum in the entrance hall and into the dusty street, invariably they came back sooner. The city centre, where they could always return, had one café, but there were never any tables free, so they gave up trying. As for the few unnamed bars, their aura was uninviting. The smell of alcohol was detectable from yards off and every now and again drunks staggered out into the street to be reproved by the abundance of mothers passing by.

'Have you noticed?' said Eamon. 'There don't seem to be any normal men about, only drunks.'

'There must be some men in the army,' said Antonia.

Natasha scoffed at what she considered a ridiculous conversation.

So the students gathered in the dorm in the evenings. No portable music existed in those days. Eamon drew cartoons and made jokes. He used variations on the shame phrase over and over: 'Oh, how shameful of Natasha to be so picky with her food.' 'Oh, how shameful of Dave to be so clever.' Everyone roared on cue, leaning back on the beds. After passing round a bottle of whisky he had bought on the plane, Eamon drew the French girl's breasts too, to prevent them slipping from memory. 'I wish to evoke that marble whiteness which teasingly suggests women's breasts are hard as stone, whereas we all know that really they shift and fill out to the male touch.'

'I think that's enough, Eamon. We are rather stuck here, you know.'

'If that is your wish, Aunty Tony, so be it. I will say no more.'

He went back to sketching and passing his drawings round. He drew himself asleep with two people conversing over him in Bezzakonian: 'He's asleep.' 'You don't say!' Then around eleven-thirty he and Dave went back to their male dorm.

The girls were astonished to hear a tap on their door just before midnight.

'Vladnina!'

'Shsh. Since you are good girls I wanted to show you where the showers are. As a special privilege. Come.'

The students followed in their night things to the end of the corridor, down five flights of stone steps and through two doors, where Vladnina located the right entrance and turned the long key.

'Absurd just for a shower, isn't it?' She laughed. She was only a couple of years their senior and so much wanted to be friendly. 'That's the way things are here,' she said.

Inside the warm white-tiled basement the institutional showers were just a row of nozzles, but out of each thundered the soft heated waters of the Gulf of Arcadia.

Antonia led the way. They stood for a good five minutes, together with Vladnina, letting water and soap slide off their young skins.

'My mother says luxury is what allows human beings to be truly human.'

'I heard your mother was a film star, Natasha. Is this true?'

'Certainly not. Incidentally, why do we have to go through this great rigmarole to get a shower, Vladnina?' Natasha had the body of a Cranach Eve, whereas Vladnina could have been her grand-mother.

'You really want to know? We believe in Bezzakonia that to withhold good things, and then return them as rewards, is a sound educational principle.'

21

'What?' The running water persuaded Antonia she hadn't heard properly.

Natasha, wrapped in a towel said, 'It's not a sound educational principle, it's the wisdom of peasants. Only peasants would make such a thing of privacy. Only peasants would use it to bribe people.'

'You are like your mother, Natasha. I'm sorry. We try to make something new here. The bourgeois heritage of England makes it difficult for you to understand the ideal.'

'I don't see what that's got to do with showers.'

'You will, my dear. As I say –' she looked from one of her charges to the next – 'in your situation a shower like this is a privilege. I want to help you.' Vladnina finally put on her glasses. 'So I'll see you tomorrow. And don't forget to come to me whenever you want the shower key.' The blue nylon housecoat billowed out behind her.

'We are a bit stuck up,' said Antonia, as they climbed the stairs.

'I like being stuck up.'

Jem turned to Natasha crossly. 'Well, no one else likes you for it. Vladnina's got a hard job. She wants to be friends with us. We should be nicer. Though wasn't it funny she thought of your mum as a film star? I suppose that's the only way they can conceive of decadence here, now that they've done away with the aristocracy.'

'They're all absurd little peasants.'

The class had been under way for an hour and goodwill was flagging.

'Excuse me, can you tell me the way to . . . '

Natasha said in English, 'No one would tell you even if they knew.'

Eamon added, 'How shameful of you, Nat. Everyone knows this is the land of peace to the world, the country of international friendship.'

'For God's sake, you two!' shouted Dave.

The class was dividing. Dave was Galina's star pupil and she couldn't help concentrating on him. He validated her existence.

She got into the habit after every difficult question of putting her head on one side and purring, 'Maybe Dave knows, maybe,' while she waited for the thrill of finding out.

'I wonder who she washes with,' whispered Natasha.

'She'd like it to be Dave,' giggled Antonia.

'Yuk!' yelled Eamon in the corridor.

'Fuck off! It's not my fault.'

'You could at least admit everyone's *painfully* repressed in Bezzakonia. One of these days the lid will lift off the whole place.'

'No. You're just a sex maniac. You can't see things any other way.'

The waitress was already taking back plates of warm cheesecake from the next table of French students. She shook her head. 'Girls, you need to eat.'

'No!' they shouted.

The sixty tables in the refectory were beginning to provide entertainment for each other with their little protests about this and that, though everyone had showers now, provided they were willing to walk.

'Mm, no, I'll have my cheesecake. I quite fancy breakfast this morning.' Natasha stretched out a hand towards the food while eyeing a blond Dane whom Antonia had found to supplement Ngip.

'Jens.' He shook her hand.

'Natasha.'

Dave looked sick at the absence of repression around him but said nothing.

Antonia was already getting up to leave. She had packed two rock cakes in paper napkins. 'Well, I'll leave you to it, then. No, Jens, I must go. Jem's ill. One of our group.'

'Is it serious?' Eamon asked.

'Yes, she was up in the night.'

Vladnina came over. 'No Jem?'

'No jam, no, Vladnina, sorry. Aunty Tony's eaten it all.'

Antonia, ignoring Eamon, held her stomach in demonstration of what ailed Jem.

'Ah. Too much of our lovely Bezzakonian ice cream. This fate often befalls our foreign visitors.' Vladnina looked pleased with her diagnosis.

Antonia exploded. 'It's not Jem's fault, it's the city's fault. Yes. How shameful of the dull and grimy city of Bezumgrad to give us a bug. It's the water. Some of the French have got it too. They told us.'

The French alongside started a slow handclap.

Vladnina looked grave. 'This slander on our hero city does not correspond to reality. I think it is very likely the ice cream.'

'Believe what you like. You're wrong.'

'A discouraging start to another day of international under-standing and co-operation,' pronounced Eamon gleefully.

The Dane clapped him on the shoulder. 'She's good, isn't she, Antonia? I like strong women.'

'Well, you've come to the right place, pal, wouldn't you say?'

Towards the end of week two a heart appeared on the classroom blackboard linking Dave and Mrs Smirnova. Another was inscribed on a card and hung round the neck of Bezum in the Politeknikum entrance.

Eamon proudly owned up in his lovely Ulster tenor to his misdeeds. 'It's only a joke.'

'You have no shame,' said Vladnina sorrowfully. 'You will get me into trouble. Besides, how can you do this to Bezum? We would not defile your Winston Churchill with cheap amours.'

'He probably had a few cheap amours himself. People do in our country. Anyway, are you going to take my shower hour away because I've been naughty? I shall pong if you do. Bezzakonia will be the loser, not me.'

Vladnina shook her head. The rules didn't work very well in practice. But there were one or two other standard punishment procedures. She decided to remove him from his group.

With this news in his head, he swaggered into breakfast late, waving his cup in the air. As the waitress reluctantly poured him coffee, Vladnina sat down beside him.

'I don't see why you should mind, Ay-mon, going to class with the Vietnamese. It is just a little change.'

'No, I don't like it. You're just trying to punish me. I'll find another way of learning Bezzakonian. Shit, this coffee's stone cold. Hasn't Bezum invented the hotplate yet?'

Vladina retired, shaking her head.

Eamon yelled, 'Off to class, Dave? Don't get Mrs S. too excited now.'

'Christ, you're a bully. You're as bad as they are. You want everyone to see it your way.'

'Well, they don't, do they?' Eamon indicated Natasha and Antonia. 'The truth is I'm on my own. Defending what it is to be a normal human being.'

'That's not how we see it. We're their guests, after all.'

'Bugger off to class, then.'

Eamon slowly finished his breakfast, then took the trolley bus into the centre.

The women with string shopping bags saw him get on but they had a way of not disclosing their possession of the power of sight, he thought. He punched his ticket in the machine. Maybe it is satisfying keeping rules! Well, yes, but only because it doesn't matter one way or another. As a foreigner I can afford a hundred bus tickets. People can live with rules, even approve of them, so long as they don't set out to confront them. That's what's happening here. There is a kind of invisible line, a limit, and people who want to survive live two paces behind it. When someone like me gets on the bus every Bezzakonian takes two mental steps backwards not to collide with me. I'm a threat to them, out travelling alone. I haven't got the distraction of companions. I might speak to them. And then what? Collision might be taken for collusion. 'Excuse me —'

But Eamon was forced to shelve his selfish ambitions when a disused Manichaean church loomed in front of the driver's windscreen. He and every remaining passenger shoved out of the central door. The Bezzakonians didn't seem to mind *physical* contact. In fact, despite his speculations as to what was happening in their minds, they mainly treated him and each other as inanimate objects.

Eamon took the quiet street by the canal. Somewhere someone was playing a violin. He couldn't name the composer of the familiar piece that escaped from an open window. Damn. I need to give names to things here. To pin them down. I hate to admit it, but I need my education as well as my lust for women. Who would have thought? . . .

Up ahead, over a pretty ironwork bridge, he noticed a class of small children processing in blue, red and white uniforms, with one teacher ahead and another bringing up the rear. You felt there really was a great deal of – what was it? – not so much education but teaching of rules going on in this country. But then underneath the bridge Eamon saw a man shooting his seed into the dirty canal, as if that was what he thought of the Bezzakonian future, and ambition, and shame. Hey, I bet that's against the rules.

Walking on, Eamon tried to list mentally what he wasn't seeing compared with home. For in a way Bezzakonia was *almost* like home, except topsy-turvy, with rules *designed* to be broken and ordinary things turned into privileges, so that daily life became unnecessarily difficult, as if old Bezum had arranged things as a treasure hunt. Eamon laughed out loud and looked around. Well, there were other differences. For instance, he saw no dogs or cats, and he saw no cripples. In that human sense, inhuman rather, the streets were tidy. But it wasn't that. It was the buffer zone he couldn't see, but could feel, which made the difference. It was a deliberate emptiness in the space between people, a space in which nothing could be inferred except the absence of things in contact. Bezzakonia was saying to him, don't get too close. Don't make us touch the invisible line. Behind the line it is possible to live peacefully. 'Like cattle behind an electric fence,' he said out loud, and looked for something to kick along the pavement, but there was no litter.

The men looked around when he entered a street bar. Their wrecked faces showed no more visible curiosity than the women in the bus, but they insisted on staring. Eamon supposed they could allow themselves that boldness because it was their poor health that made them untouchable. He drank a measure of spirits. The tumbler was still wet from being casually rinsed behind the counter. With a frisson of apprehension, he remembered the state of Jem's insides. He didn't fancy being hospitalized. Then the Bezzakonians could do what they liked with him.

He resumed walking, now down the long, straight central boulevard which led him to the railway station. A longing to see a steam train came upon him and, with the inventiveness that solitude invites, he built up the expectation in his mind: of something clean and proud and majestic, full of energy and expectation; of something built by human beings and lovingly cared for with rags and polish. He looked around. The platforms were open. He toured from one to the next. The great green engines standing at their buffers were not steam, of course. They were diesel, with grids for ventilation, not funnels, but he enjoyed inspecting them and their destinations. Carried away by his love of machines, he quickly found himself on the far side of the station.

He was in a siding. The locomotive had only two carriages, and the green-walled steel carriages had only one high window each. A temporary sign hung on the side, in chalky white paint, said: 'People'.

'*Crids*,' whispered a man passing. Eamon translated: 'Criminal detainees'. The man disappeared as suddenly as he'd appeared. Eamon listened. There was no human sound. He left the station and caught the trolley bus back.

It was lunchtime. Antonia observed Eamon looked animated.

'But did you learn any interesting words?' Natasha teased.

'Yes. I've written them down and given a copy to every table in the room.'

'You're joking.'

'Read it!'

Antonia unfolded a piece of lined paper placed between the jug of magenta fruit punch and the ridiculous quarter-size napkins that were daily fixtures.

Eamon got to his feet and banged the table three times with his soup spoon. People nearby passed the word. He banged again. The whole refectory went quiet.

'My friends, I was out in the city this morning. What I saw you will find written on the paper message on your tables. Please read it now if you haven't done so before.'

Antonia looked across at Vladnina, whose face was bloated with fear.

'I'm going on strike against this country's so-called rules and I hope you will support me, brothers and sisters. If there are to be changes to improve the life of the people of Bezzakonia, they must begin here in this Politeknikum. It is our duty to protest. Otherwise, as emissaries of free countries, we are just the servants of Bezzakonia's masters. Let's hear it, then. Ayes in favour of a strike.'

An untidy international cry filled the room. Not all the students had a perfect grasp of English. What they shouted was 'I, I, I . . .' but that was quite good enough. Three hundred students began banging their spoons in solidarity.

Eamon shouted, 'This is how we do things in our country, Vladnina. This is real democracy. You can't just order us about willy-nilly, you know.'

Dave grabbed him by his shirt front and Antonia pushed between them. 'Do you want to cause World War III?'

'Eamon does.'

'*I* do?'

'Stop it!'

Eamon's first winter term as a student in '71 had been spent mostly in candlelight. No coal, no dustmen, no post, no fire engines; one public service was withdrawn after another. The possibility of civil protest had made a deep impression on him, as the means to social justice. It was the means he would implement here. Under his guidance all further efforts to understand Bezzakonia were suspended. It was time to condemn.

The strikers dug in in the refectory. People went out to fetch books.

Jem joined the protesters, looking weak.

'Would you like some rice water?' Vladnina offered.

'Mmm, no, but thank you.'

'*Rice* water? Are you sure they're not trying to kill you Jem?'

'Vladnina's doing her best, Eamon. This whole mess isn't her fault.'

'It is her fault. Rice water is a peasant remedy,' said Natasha. She turned to Vladnina. 'Bloody nation of grannies and peasants! What are you trying to do, kill us all so you can take over the world without a struggle? Seeing that you do everything upside-down and back to front and forget to feed people or let them wash, it promises to be a rotten world.'

Vladnina had fixed wisdom upon her round face. 'I think Jem does this deliberately. A sort of hunger strike.'

'So you do know about strikes, then. You said they didn't exist in your country.'

Vladnina ignored that observation. 'Jem does this because she is weak girl and this is only weapon she has. In Bezzakonia a person must be strong like Antonia.'

'Oh, thanks,' groaned Jem.

'You know what you need, Vladnina, you need un-bloody-brainwashing.'

'I am quite well, thank you.'

'I wonder whose fault this country is,' said Antonia. 'Bezum's?'

'No, it's in some book,' said the Dane. 'They got the idea from a book. Bezum's just an instrument of history. Ask Ngip.'

Ngip pursed his lips.

'Well, it's too late now to find someone to blame. We want change. Bezzakonia must change.' Eamon led a spooning banging chant, until the whole room joined in.

'When students misbehave in your country, what happens?' Vladnina was capable of switching personality, from the supercilious aggressive to the childlike and penitent, and in that way seemed to represent her whole country.

'Nothing much,' said Antonia.

'So what makes people be not criminals?'

'You take your lead from your parents. Then you look to reason, but really it's just something in the air. Tradition, I suppose.'

Vladnina flushed. 'In Bezzakonia we abolished tradition. Hmm.' She walked across the dining room, through the clusters of tables where she had no direct responsibility, and stared out of the window at the housing blocks and scrappy patches of grass outside.

'I think you love your country, Vladnina,' said Jem when she returned.

'You hurt me with your strike. This is all.'

Antonia asked Eamon, 'Well? Are you going to ask people to sleep here?'

It was eleven p.m. and there were already plenty of gaps in the room.

'Don't be so bloody superior with me, Aunty Tony! You didn't see what I did. I'm doing what I think is right. I suggest we reassemble in the morning.'

But in the end the strike was futile, because the students had no power.

In the morning Eamon banged the spoon. 'This is what our governments want us to know, of course. That *they* have no power. This is why they have sent us. So when the Bezzakonians take over the world, at least someone on our side will speak the lingo. Only we have to hope we won't be stuck here when the takeover comes, or we will just be carted away.'

Natasha began to cry.

Eamon took a swig from a bottle of vodka to power him on. 'But at least we've done something these last two days, taken a stand, committed ourselves, made a voluntary gesture. It's the best we can do.' He stopped and pushed the bottle out of his reach. 'Hell, I can't drink on an empty stomach. Have you seen what this stuff does to Bezzakonians? Have a look inside a bar before you go.' He gave a big public shrug. 'Colleagues, fellow Bezzakonian specialists, I'm sorry, but I declare this strike over.'

'For he's a jolly good fellow . . . ' sang Jem, and a hundred or so voices joined in, miming the words, and in their international enthusiasm some confused the song with 'Auld Lang Syne'.

The Bezumians called a meeting. The Director of Politeknikum No. 31, Dr Brzhenev, was a big man of about forty-five, with shoebrush eyebrows and bloodhound jowls, and whose name suggested Serbian extraction. After noting Vladnina's report, detailing the bathroom insurrection on day two and everything that followed, he said they must now decide how to resolve the outstanding problem of loss of face. 'We must approach this matter very subtly. *Tonko, tonko.*'

Vladnina argued that they should have removed the shower privilege at the first signs of rebelliousness, and perhaps brought forward the curfew, and lowered the quality of catering.

But Galina said, 'They won't come back at all if we make it too unpleasant. Then where will we be?' Her personality was less inhibited away from foreigners.

'No treats and no trips,' Vladnina suggested after a few moments. But then she remembered the conversation she had had with Antonia and gasped. 'Oh, but I see that the foreign students care not a fig for trips to museums of the Revolution, of Atheism, of the Working Class, of Bezum, of Egalitarian Art. And in that case we have no discipline that can touch these Westerners, except to send them home, which is where they want to go anyway. Oh, Lord!'

'If they stop coming we'll both be out of a job.' Galina appreciated the tights and books and chocolates the students gave her at the end of the summer courses. You couldn't buy such nice things in Bezzakonia. Certainly not such interesting books. She got up from her chair and laid a hand on the hot, dry brow of her seated colleague. 'There's a stomach bug doing the rounds. The students have it. That's surely the trouble. My poor Vladnina. Mr Director, I move that we adjourn this meeting . . . '

'*Tikho, tikho,*' whispered Brzhenev from behind his plywood

31

desk. 'Quiet! Quiet!' A persistent heavy drinker, he was barely conscious.

'It's all right, darling. Perhaps he will dream it's all been resolved. Let's pray.'

'*Tonko, tonko*,' whispered the director in his sleep. 'Subtly, subtly does it.'

The day of the final presentation arrived. The students took it in turns to file across the platform, shaking hands with a little peasant in shiny shoes and a shiny suit. 'I am Director Brzhenev,' the shiny man beamed, and gave everyone a book of postcards of Bezumgrad and a lapel badge. When Eamon came up, Brzhenev said, 'Ah, here is the young man who likes to see women half-naked. We have a surprise for you.' He pulled Eamon beside him, so there was a clear space in front.

Then Vladnina came on stage. She was dressed up in jeans as a Western girl, for which her figure was ill-suited, but only as far as the waist.

'Come, come, my dear, don't be shy. We must give our guests what they like. What keeps them happy.'

Vladnina's hands were tied behind her back. She hung her head as she walked past, in front of the three hundred students.

'And back again! And back again!'

There was a terrible silence, which Brzhenev took as a mark of respect for Bezzakonia.

3

CAVIARE CHILDREN

Dave and Natasha went out for a walk.

They walked in the residential area near the hostel, far from the city. Anything more scenic and historic involved a trolley-bus ride, and Dave said it was enough just to be here, out and about, and see Bezzakonian life for themselves.

With an affectation Dave had come to admire, Natasha called it doing her Bezzakonian ABCs. 'What can the A stand for? I know. Awful. Now for a bit more awful being and seeing.'

He smiled and even began to look attractive.

The air was dusty in August. A large metalled road supported a few trams and lorries rattling to and from the centre, but all the local streets running between blocks of residential flats were unpaved. A smell of low-grade fuel hung in the air and you could imagine it spreading a thin coating of tar over your lungs. Natasha did a childlike tightrope walk along a huge sewage pipe which further defaced the dirty sand and hardened soil.

'Everything looks behind the times.'

'You must be patient. You must give them a chance.'

'You feel you're on a mission here, don't you, Dave? You feel it's a better place to live than England.'

Huge occasional kerbstones loomed up like relics from another age. Everything seemed misplanned and unfinished in the public gardens designed to gladden the spirits of local apartment-dwellers. This was supposed to be an urban village, with greenery and shops and a children's playground, and all those things could be found, yet where was the life?

'It may be better. In the future. I want to give them a chance, so I'll do what they say while I'm here.'

'But a polite guest is just what they want you to be! To start with. They understand it as some sort of deference you're showing towards your superiors, in this case your Bezumian betters. You're the peasant and they're the aristocrats now, you see? I've talked about this with my father. For hundreds of years in Europe everyone tried to emulate the aristocracy. Ordinary people worshipped self-confidence, and polished manners, and plenty. Then along came the Bezzakonians and overthrew all that. They and their Egalitarianism gave the world a new ideal. That's what we've come here to see, as I understand it. They've taught everyone to think it's great to be rough and pushy and clumsy. The Bezzakonians want to be worshipped because they excel in being rough and pushy and clumsy! Ordinary people have to come over all humble and decent when Egalitarianism's mentioned. If they criticize it, the Bezzakonians call them bad-mannered.' Her mother's daughter, born a fighter, Natasha drew breath. 'Well, that's one thing. Another is what they do here to so-called ill-mannered people, who speak their minds. You remember that trial that was in the papers last year? Those two men got twelve years' hard labour in Snowland. This is a barbarous place, Dave! You have to see that.'

But Dave just thought Natasha was supersensitive about the place, because of her Bezzakonian mother. Her mother fell in love with an Englishman, who took her away. The Bezzakonians thought of it as a kind of treason, which was only like Catholics and Jews disapproving of marriages outside the faith. It wasn't a reason why Natasha should hate Bezzakonia.

'Haven't I just given you my reasons?'

'I thought you were talking about me. I thought you were saying I was low class and that's why I fitted in.'

'For goodness' sake! What I meant was, this is a good place to come for anyone who's got a chip on his shoulder or a guilty conscience about privilege. The Bezzakonians welcome people like that with open arms. All that's required here to be a guest for life is to wipe your feet neatly on the Bezumian doormat and spit at passing rich people. Is that what you fancy?'

Dave wished he could stop breathing. He had never imagined putting up with, even wanting to hear, such things from a woman with Natasha's kind of voice, but now he did. It thrilled him to meet someone so different from himself. He kicked aside a broken bottle on the sun-baked path. The sun could find no surface on which to sparkle, he thought, except on those shards of broken glass.

'I don't know what I want when you put it like that.'

'That's why the teachers here are trying to get you. You're vulnerable.'

'So what are you saying?'

'You should stand up to them. Drop all this hard-working-miner's-son-making-good stuff. You're a member of Cambridge University, for heaven's sake.'

He wanted to wrestle her to the ground and make love to her the way a man should. She was challenging his whole life. But he settled for pointing out a shed-like building, of glass and concrete, to which several paths vaguely led through the dried-up grass. 'Look, it's a grocer's.'

'Right. Let's go in.'

'But we don't need anything.'

'What did I just say about being deferential? Anyway, I do need something. Chocolate. I'd die here without chocolate. We should take some for Jem too. She's wasting away. Her hip bones are sticking out like greenstick fractures. She showed us this morning.' Natasha giggled and felt bold away from home. 'You know what a woman's body looks like, Dave? Hey, don't blush! Just that hip bones should be nobbles, not chicken wings.'

He thought, that's what I need! I need a woman who will talk to me like that the rest of my life. Make me stop deferring to everyone and every bloody thing. He wanted to take Natasha's arm but ended by meekly following her into a shop the size of a small supermarket and smelling pleasantly of sausage and cheese.

'Good afternoon!' she hailed in Bezzakonian the four women assistants in white coats behind the various fresh counters, but they were embarrassed at her capitalist temerity and only one produced a faint reply. Tall, pale and thin, she looked as foreign as her heart was. Two women shoppers gave her a furtive glance but then immediately retrained their eyes on the shelves of identical jars: thirty batches of Bezzakonian vegetable stew, forty tins of Snowland fish. Grain in rough cream-coloured paper packets, overprinted in purplish ink: millet, semolina, buckwheat and barley; and biscuits wrapped in the same paper, printed with a name in green.

'You don't feel they get much pleasure out of shopping,' whispered Natasha. 'It's more like a place you might come to fetch hay and straw and oats for your animals.'

'We don't keep animals. I wouldn't know.'

'I bet you did a couple of generations back. Everyone had a horse and a cow and a pig.' Natasha was ogling a tray of chocolate bars, nestling beneath glossy pictures of theatrical masks and circuses and troikas. 'It's just chocolate they haven't been able to touch. Chocolate advertizing the old life as irresistible. Look, Dave, the Bezzakonians forgot to annihilate the last bourgeois indulgence.'

'Let's pay.' Dave was uncomfortable at the silent commotion their presence had caused.

'You're such a coward!'

'No!' He felt hurt. 'Let's sit down.' Once they were outside he drew her towards a bench beside a small children's playground. Two children in military-style uniform were sliding down a yellow and blue painted slide.

'All right. You want me to go first? Bezzakonia is a simple place. I'll say that much for it. If you didn't mind fitting in, if you had no great ambitions, you could live here. Otherwise it's hell. Just like my parents said. You can't imagine, Dave. I've been raised from the cradle to hate Bezzakonia. When I get here to see for myself, finally I realize that they are right. So it's not a shock so much as a confirmation of what I've inherited. Now that's a problem. What am I supposed to do with it? It's like joining the family business without being given a choice. But it's just my problem. No one else's.' She paused. 'Of course you'd fit in here. You'd work so hard and be so boring they'd put you on a postage stamp before you were dead.'

'Yes, I'd get a medal for my efforts on behalf of the common man.' He felt sick. There was only a small space between them on the bench. He touched her arm. 'Look, do you ever think about anyone but yourself? This country is at least a monument to the virtue of unselfishness. I mean, if you weren't such a snob, if you didn't come from such a privileged background that made you insensitive, you might see how ugly is a world where no one cares about anyone else, except for profit, and some people are considered better than others even before they are born. You could hope and wish these people well like I do, even though they make mistakes. Do you have brothers and sisters?' She shook her head. 'Ah, so you can't know. All your sympathy goes to your mother. Your love goes to the middle-aged survivors, not the young strivers. Right-wing people are always like that.'

'I don't know what you're talking about.'

'Too bad for you, then.'

The bright afternoon was silent. Eventually he said, 'Can I take some chocolate?'

'You may.' He would have said 'can'.

'Do you really not know what I'm talking about? About supporting the Establishment?'

'No.'

The chocolate bar lay between them like a sword of honour. Natasha produced a Swiss Army knife from her Peruvian shoulder bag fringed with tassels and punched two holes in a can of condensed milk she had also earmarked in the shop as useful. Droplets of the palest yellow spurted up on to the metal. She stuck in a finger.

'Here, it's like white treacle.'

They drank from opposite holes.

'You're nice, Dave.'

'So are you. But you're too hard on them. There are many good things. I'm sure it will get better.'

'No. If they weren't people, they'd deserve a bomb.'

'That's an appalling thing to say!' he protested vehemently. But he felt in danger of losing his old self entirely.

'What is your impression of our Bezumian Republic, Dave? Be honest.'

'My first impression, Galina Mikhailovna, is a question: where are all the men? I've not seen a single one here in the Politeknikum, except the bus driver and a plumber.'

'Why, Dave, they are all at work! Some are engineers, some are agriculturalists. My husband is in the army.'

'Some are spies,' said Natasha, 'though maybe not your husband, Mrs Smirnova.'

Galina looked pityingly on such tactless outspokenness. Of course, just as anywhere in the world, so in Bezzakonia, one met occasionally rude people, who said indecent things, just as one met unfriendly peasants, but one day the whole world would be a pleasant place.

'We have a tiny little problem with drunkenness mainly. But this will be overcome. Our society believes in honest work, not exploitation.'

'My father would agree with you.'

'Mine would not.'

'I congratulate your father, Dave. What does he do?'

'He's a miner.'

'This is noble work.'

'Excuse me! So is being a retired diplomat and professor of English noble work!'

Galina leaned forward into the middle of the table where they were gathered. Dave held a finger to his lips behind her back. 'No!' Natasha mouthed back.

'But you know the other reason why you see fewer men, Dave, and Natasha? It is that so many millions were killed in the Great Defensive War.' She stared into Natasha's blue, unprofound eyes and admired her unblemished white skin. 'You know what happened to Bezumgrad –' Tears brimmed in her eyes, so that she had to take off the spangled glasses and wipe the teardrops away and show once again how powerless she was and just like them. 'Which means that we Bezzakonian women are very short of men. Many women struggle alone.' There was a pause, followed by one of those violent psychological switches characteristic of the Bezzakonian psyche. 'Not like your mother, I think.'

Natasha sat up straight. 'My mother misses her country.'

'She could come back.'

'Then she would miss her freedom. When she was here they –' she couldn't say it directly – 'forced her to lead a life which she didn't ask for.'

Dave asked, 'Is that the choice? Would she really lose her freedom here?'

Natasha snapped, 'Yes. You know as well as I do, Dave. For God's sake. So would we if we weren't tourists.'

Galina concluded, 'Well, young people, I am a patriot.'

'So would my mother be, if her country hadn't betrayed her.'

'The war was terrible for Bezzakonia.'

'You are right, Dave, so right.'

'You're both a pair of disgusting liars.'

In the corridor afterwards Natasha roared the way Dave had never heard an upper-class voice roar: 'You're a bastard. I don't want to speak to you.' But he threw his arms round her and hugged her the way he had never hugged anyone. He enjoyed her caring so much, for it meant they had feelings of equal intensity, even if they pulled in opposite directions. There was a chance they could both love this difficult country together.

★

'I'd like to take you out for a real meal.' Dave looked almost handsome that night.

'You're joking.'

'No, seriously. We're reaching the end of the course. At least to be together has been fun.'

Natasha linked her arm in his and they did a crazy double walk to the bus stop, like one of Plato's prelapsarian four-legged happy people.

The trolley bus into the centre was not crowded in the evening because there was nothing to do. Dave reckoned he had seen something calling itself a restaurant near the House of Books, and they had time to call in at that House before making a serious search for food, so they took a long route on foot. As a couple they could not help being more colourful and free than their surroundings, though none of their English peers found them glamorous, Natasha in her old-fashioned knee-length frocks, Dave in his navy nylon jacket. But they stood out in the ranks of restricted lives parading the length of the Bezum Prospect.

The city centre gave off a feeling of stasis, even though traffic and people moved past. It was otherwise indescribable. Nothing was dramatic: not shopping, not conversing, not exchanging ideas, not going out for a meal. Natasha and Dave walked past a cinema. Its billboard had only cheap, saccharine sketches of unreal heroes and heroines, as if the cinema-going public were children who lived entirely in a world of mild fantasy. They were the sort of pictures you could buy anywhere in the world very cheaply and stick on your wall if you had no inkling of what art might be. Dave didn't notice but Natasha had the feeling of something not right. Upstairs in the House of Books they inspected posters as possible presents to take home: posters of drunks neglecting their machines and causing industrial accidents and posters of hero workers exceeding their targets. All this poster-making was done without conflict too, because the drunks were simply drunk. And all the drawing was simplified to make human beings look like cardboard cutouts in a manual of how to live. Bezzakonians were required to live like nineteenth-century children, when childhood was still a state of enforced naïvety.

The café could have been worse. The black table-top and floor were clean and the one room with a sort of interior black and white shiny stucco on the walls might have been cosy. But for an unknown, perhaps unknowable reason the place was empty and only one meal was available. As soon as they said they wanted dinner the waitress nodded and walked away, leaving the lovers to talk. Natasha, in a dress in a gold paisley pattern and a pale pink cardigan, looked frail and elevated and unfashionable, and Dave basked in her company.

The waitress brought back for each of her two customers a grey-gold pork cutlet in breadcrumbs served on a white plate with some tinned mixed vegetables. The food was cooked but cold. The aura of coldness, when they expected heat, was a minor sensation neither of them had experienced before. The bread was cold too, though as good as homemade, with the colour of unbleached flour.

'Maybe the gas is off.'

'No, Dave, they can't be on strike. You told me all the workers were happy here.'

He took a deep breath. 'In that case let's imagine that the citizens of Bezumgrad, all one million of them, have agreed tonight to go without a hot dinner in order that urgent repairs can be done to the city grid. Or the state gas company, BEZGAS, has agreed to provide free heat in hospitals and orphanages all next winter if a million ordinary people volunteer for a single day's deprivation today.'

She toyed with a bit of cold pork. 'But everything belongs to the state anyway, Dave, so they couldn't organize anything heroic like that. All the heroic gestures possible have become institutionalized. Isn't that it? The hero is the system. The final battle has been won.'

He experienced another of those moments when he wanted to stop breathing. 'Well, it hasn't been won at home in Britain,' he said finally. 'There we still have to struggle for the just society. I mean, my dad's had a bloody hard life. If he'd had the education we have, he'd be a different man, he could live in comfort, he could see more of the world, if we had a system like they have here in Bezzakonia.'

'You can't mean that.'

The cold food was unappetizing and heavy to chew.

'I do! Of course I do. I want change. I hate coming from a world which encourages people to be lazy and waste their time and opportunities. Look at Eamon, for instance, just hanging about, and that French girl, picking up men. If she lived in our village they'd throw her out. And they'd get Eamon to work for his keep.'

'And your Bezzakonia's only a glorified village, isn't it, Dave? You really just want to be a peasant. It keeps coming back to the same thing. I'd like to know who first put this idea about it was so great to be a peasant. Someone who never was one, I'm sure.' She took a gentler tone. 'Do you know what I think? You and I have both come too late. You want to believe in Bezzakonia like people believed in it fifty years ago. Now it's too late. There's nothing here worth the effort. As for me, everything happened to my mother and father, so there's no effort I can make either. But because my mother was born here, because my father rescued her, because the great love has already been experienced, the great story has already happened, I can only be an onlooker. I thought if I learned Bezzakonian then maybe I could do something – I don't know what, but something. But now I see the best thing I can do is forget about it and hope it destroys itself soon. It's my version of growing up and leaving home.'

Dave looked across the black Formica table as if he were seeing a different version of himself for the first time in a mirror. 'You shouldn't just take your mother's word for it, you should work it out for yourself.'

'What do you think I'm doing, stupid? My mother was a prisoner in her own country, just because she came from a decent family! I've become your friend, I'm interested in what you say, but even you can't show me anything but vast herds of the downtrodden. No, not herds. How I hate that word.'

The meal was a failure. They left their plates barely touched.

Dave tried to pay and when he could not persuade the waitress to appear he deposited a modest pile of coins on the table. It was a Bezzakonian rule he wished to keep that people who were equals never gave tips.

Natasha drove him deliberately wild as they left. 'You know, the thing I really miss in this country is heavy cutlery. These awful tin forks and spoons. I'm *not* joking. I believe people should have gold knives and forks if it makes them happy.'

They walked along in silence, two colours once more engulfed in grey. The difference was still clearly visible in the half-light which lasted all night through north Bezzakonian midsummer, and they glowed like the horizon because nevertheless they were young and their youth rebelled against any limitation.

'Have you got any of that chocolate left?'

'Mmmm. In my room.'

He took her hand. 'Let's go back, then.'

She planted a clumsy kiss on his lips, more to conquer uncertainty than to lure him into temptation. Then they were strap-hanging, pushed together by a mass of late workers returning home. As they left the bus, he took her hand again and led her along the fortress corridor to the empty classroom.

When they got back to London the airport terminal was so friendly and clean, with smiling middle-aged men in un-threatening black uniforms wheeling suitcases on two-wheeled trolleys. One porter glanced up at the flight origin displayed above the baggage carousel. 'Have a nice time, ducks?' he asked Natasha.

'Not really, no.'

'So it's true what we hear in the papers, then, that things are so bad out there it's like here in the war?'

'Things are bad. The Bezzakonians are very bad organizers.'

'She's exaggerating. Don't believe everything she says,' insisted Dave with a smile.

But then a cloud of confusion descended on Natasha as she was met by both parents. She looked round wildly, like a cat seeking an exit. They were a well-dressed, self-assured couple who looked like two individuals even when they stood close. Natasha's mother was pale, an older version of the daughter, but still thinner. If you suffered as she did when young, perhaps you never quite thrived again. Natasha's father had in 1946, as a young scholar who knew Bezzakonian, spent a year in the service of the British Embassy. Katya was the young friend of a famous poet he called on. She had already spent the war in a camp.

'Goodbye, Dave. It's been nice. You must come round when you're back in Cambridge. There must be a time when we coincide.'

That old voice hit him, the old voice of the spoilt, stuck-up rich girl, as she kissed him on the cheek. The shower of life went cold. He pushed his forelock out of his eyes. 'Yeah, give me a ring, Natasha. College number's in the book.'

The family headed off towards the car park.

'No trains, lad. Where have you been? They're on strike!'

'Oh, hell, how then —' Dave gave a little laugh and a sigh and eventually took the bus to London. He crossed the city and took a coach. When he arrived home it was gone midnight.

His father was waiting up, with the transistor radio playing light music. He looked older and thinner.

'So, son, how was it?' Euan Bevan couldn't claim to have seen the world, but he had once spent a few days in Prague with Mrs Bevan and other members of the local Labour Party. He thought Bezzakonia, as the home of Egalitarianism, must be more vibrant. The satellite countries had less money and less energy. They lacked the power of Bezzakonia's great input into the world.

Dave inhaled the smell of home, with frying in the air and strong soap. The kitchen was so small he felt he could touch opposite walls at the same time. It was just as strange as coming home from Cambridge for the vacation, but somehow he felt more relieved.

'Is that tea?'

'It's a bit stewed now.'

Dave opened the fridge and comforted himself on the sight of yellow butter and bacon and the sweet silver-top milk he poured into his tea.

'I met this posh girl, Dad. Do you know what bothered her most? Bezzakonian knives and forks. The revolution will be a pushover.'

'What are they like, then?' Euan Bevan examined the tarnished wet teaspoon on the kitchen table. 'Like this?'

'Will be one day.'

'I never understood why you wanted to study Bezzakonian, Natasha. It's played such an ugly part in our lives.'

'It's not right to ignore all ugly things. You can learn from them!'

'Tom, for heaven's sake. Natasha's just endured a month of hell.'

Natasha and Kate spoke simultaneously.

'Why don't you have a bath and an early night, darling? Tomorrow, if you're up to it, I thought we might go shopping. Jaeger's still got a sale. You need some new things to cheer you up. Then that boy Zack Windsor rang. He sounded very keen to see you, Nattie. He seems rather nice.'

She listened to her mother without hearing. Her mother the Bezzakonian exile had found this persona, and another life, in a civilized country.

'Wait, Mummy. I have something to say.'

Tom Wynn-Williams watched from the reading armchair and braced himself. Probably his little girl had had a fling with some left-wing boy. His wife went pale at the thought Natasha might have fallen in love with a Bezzakonian. Fear of any return to the past parted her thin lips.

Natasha faced her own reflection in the mirror above the mantelpiece and saw in it a physical duplicate of her mother. She prepared to give vent to her soul, but then subsided. All she said was, casting her eyes around the lovely room, thinking of the whole house, and their way of life, which had so often seemed to her like a high wall to keep other people out, 'Now I understand why we have all this.'

4

THE COLLOQUY

Anatoly Stikh had a difficult decision to make about his future. He wanted two things, both of which were possible: to have an academic career and to marry Marina. The problem was that both involved his willingly staying in Bezzakonia. True, it was difficult to leave, but if he decided to go he would fight to make it happen. If, on the contrary, he stayed he would never again permit himself a moment's yearning. The kind of indecision which sometimes passes for a compromise thus did not appeal: Stikh wanted wholly to want his life and to have chosen it. The Peasants who ran the country had put him for a year in a southern provincial town to decide his fate. So he knew he had to make a decision, but one further problem plagued his sophisticated mind, which sometimes worked against him. That was how to recognize what a decision was. He was still young and felt that if he had a fate, beyond the lies and distortions the Peasants inflicted, then that fate was still pale like the inside of a young chestnut, and malleable. He checked himself. Soft like a baby's cranium, or delicate like a plant shoot? He could think of nothing actually living that was malleable except a foetus, which might be aborted. That troubling comparison had lingered in his mind all through the international conference on 'Form and Fable in Prebezzakonian Literature', whence he was returning. He had been a minor speaker.

August in south Bezzakonia was hot and dry, unlike in the more central capital, Muzeb. Stikh divined that in Bezumgrad it was already raining. He would check later in the newspaper, because he liked to keep track of the weather empire-wide. Otherwise Bezzakonian towns all had the same feel. They even looked the same and sounded the same. The same ground plan kept being duplicated, with the same street names, so Bezum Square led into General Bezpamyatny Street, which ran parallel to BZK Street, and both were bisected by Antinomian Army Street, a continuation of Brumaire Boulevard. (The consonants B, Z and K were the most frequent in the Bezzakonian language, though Bezzakonian was not averse to foreign borrowing.)

Stikh's high, flat forehead was moist, and his glasses stuck to the bridge of his nose while he waited for a bus or car he might hail. His feet sweated uncomfortably in synthetic shoes, but his only alternative, quite unfeasible for a university teacher, would have been to go barefoot. The Peasants would have judged it 'uncultured'. He opened his briefcase, drank half a bottle of warm Bezzak mineral water and threw the rest away. You couldn't buy bottle stoppers anywhere.

A dusty Bezruli saloon passed, whereupon Stikh turned to walk backwards. Any vehicle would stop if the driver saw his white shirt in time. Bezzakonians co-operated because they all needed to live more efficiently than official circumstances permitted. Their spontaneity delighted the Peasant rulers, whose scribes in *The Bezzakonian Truth* wrote editorials about comradeship and citizenship, which irritated Stikh in the depths of his being. They always began with something true, so that under examination they couldn't be accused of lying entirely. He returned his attention to the road. A Brumairich rattled by on the heels of a loose and sturdy Riva, but neither stopped, for a bus followed close behind. It was the usual kind of ill-sprung charabanc used for works excursions. Stikh held out his hand and boarded at the front, the only entrance.

The driver, a slender tanned man with a blue cap and a cigarette, said there were no seats. His faint smirk invited Stikh to look around discreetly: the bus was full of foreigners, Western conference delegates, returning to their hotel. Stikh recognized some of the faces and half-smiled, before lodging his briefcase between his feet and fixing his eyes outside. His wristwatch said just after four.

As the bus picked up speed, dirty green damask curtains flapped at the open windows. To Diana Burke they resembled a flock of trapped pigeons. She transferred her gaze outside and saw several unfinished blocks of flats reaching up meaninglessly above the earth. The rusty iron prongs which should have interlocked the concrete sections flailed unpaired, sometimes pointing skywards, sometimes twisted at unpromising angles.

A few minutes later the bus overtook old wooden bungalows, with faded green and blue painted boards, and fretted gables, and bus stops made out of three swimming-pool-blue concrete slabs, and a skinny cow chained and grazing on parched grass by the roadside. Parallel with the bungalows ran a footworn earthen path, suggesting the citizens of Prairial Blossom suburb communicated voluntarily, though no official pavement had been provided.

Stikh, standing beside Diana, grimaced at the miracle of life taking root at all in Bezzakonia. The bus, crashing against its own suspension, upsetting the balance in the inner ear of every passenger, farted exhaust and staggered on like an old, beaten, still absurdly willing mare. It seemed to be winning the race for civilization, but only because it was in motion.

'I'm Diana Burke,' she said in a pleasant voice. The face looking up at him was somewhere between pretty and severe.

'Yes, you were at the conference.'

Bezzakonia had a lot of international visitors, though that hardly gave the lie to its closed borders. Such visits created problems for Bezzakonians and foreigners alike, for there was the danger, the temptation and the deep embarrassment of the chance encounter: the collision that might be seen as collusion. A streak of elemental fear ran up Stikh's back. And another, more fierce, of envy. How he envied these foreign scholars the lack of conspiratorial clutter in their heads! His moral being broke out in resentment. He was a human being like them, wasn't he? It was chance that caused him to be riding in this bus, though he feared the Peasants might think he had done this deliberately, consorted with foreigners because he was stiffening his will to betray the motherland. He wiped his brow with a handkerchief.

'It is hot,' she said.

The eyes were heavy, like a famous Prebezzakonian woman poet's. A banned poet we've had to wait fifty years to read and even then only her least important works, Stikh shouted silently.

'Ingleesh?' he asked. He was afraid the bus driver would report him.

'That's right. I teach at an English university.'

Diana was a published expert on matters Bezzakonian, but she hadn't really enjoyed the conference. Her paper on sexual metaphor and political revolution had been only politely received. Alan Smithers, whom she had known as a graduate student, as always supported her with a devotion she could hardly bear, though she disliked herself for her coldness. He hung about, and at public gatherings she always ended up talking to him. Possibly that pleased him in a sad kind of way, but it made her feel as much of an outcast and a failure as she perceived Alan to be; the very reason she avoided him. From the decency and sincerity of failure there was, as usual, nowhere better to turn.

Diana's British colleagues professing Bezzakonian literary expertise clung together in social clusters which reminded her of grapes shrivelling on a vine, if she was feeling charitable, or flies on a carcass, if she was not. That they found it hard to open their ranks to strangers, even from their own country, was another charitable view; in truth they were provincial and afraid, and disguised these feelings in odiously loud exchanges of mutual congratulation. Since the Bezzakonians were their hosts for what counted as a free holiday, they had been doubly cautious this weekend in what they said. That there was a lack of progressive political commitment in some Prebezzakonian writers, for instance; that the egalitarian fable was weak; that certain Prebezzakonian optimists foresaw the Bezzakonian future, and the very need for optimism at this stage in world history.

The major British speaker of the whole event had been Professor Peeve. He had finally speculated whether between Bezzakonian and Prebezzakonian literature there even existed any fundamental difference, which had set the room buzzing. The faces of Bezzakonian experts, in suits and shirts but no ties, wrinkled at the mildly risqué but well-informed foreign point of view. Peeve's paper prompted a few jokes about loss of identity and the advantages of timelessness in the final-morning coffee break.

'You don't think there was a difference in that one country was free and the other, the one we are in now, is not, Professor Peeve?' asked Diana, learning to like the bitter black coffee that tasted of something else, barley perhaps.

Peeve had not risen through the academic ranks to be exposed to such crudity. He smiled tightly, the way senior academics had once gagged him, when he was a junior lecturer. A dark beard obscured the lower half of his face, and thick wavy black hair met his eyebrows. The eyes were bright and frighteningly clear, and the nose long and sharp. He could not have been older than forty-five.

'I hardly think that's the right comparison to make, Dr Burke.'

'But you seem to be saying what the Bezzakonians want to hear.'

Peeve looked as if he had been electrocuted. He gave Diana a thunderous glare, shouted 'No!' and strode away. Diana tried to mingle with the other minor speakers, and in order to avoid Alan Smithers ended up talking to a small round Italian with grey hair and, compared with the other delegates, a uniquely jovial expression. His call for literary criticism to remain a liberal humanist discipline she wholeheartedly endorsed. The conference was presumably in everyone's minds as they travelled back to the hotel.

'We have a hot summer, not like in the north. Will you stay on?'

'No, back to Muzeb tomorrow. Then London.'

Stikh conjured with the correct but wooden-sounding Bezzakonian. Further, this woman wore lipstick, and the poet he revered did not. The irrelevant observations steadied him. But what he wanted to know burnt like raw spirits in his gullet. What is your world like? Tell me! Tell me! I must know. He saw her look at his briefcase.

'I teach at the Politeknikum. It's a bit isolated, but I hope to go back to Muzeb in the autumn.'

'I liked your paper on imagery in the late-nineteenth-century Manichaean poets.'

'You are very kind. Yours on Dusheinov was, if you don't mind my saying, not satisfying because it was too complicated. But you have good ideas.'

'Thank you for real criticism. It's hard to come by.'

Stikh, prompted by his underlying confusion, began reciting some verses from Eliot he had quoted to the conference. She joined in.

> Een my beginnink iss, he declaimed – is,
> she said – my end . . . ent
> Now . . . nouww the
> light falls across acroass the openn
> filled . . . field, she held out

He liked the sound of his voice in English making this eerie music with Dr Burke's. 'This for me is very meaningful,' he said. 'I stand alone and have to answer to the world. That there is light means I have responsibility to testify: what have I made of what I see.'

Diana felt a slight tingling on the backs of her hands. 'You Bezzakonians are all so good at reciting poetry.'

'It's our education, yes.'

She recalled her conversation with Professor Peeve, and her disappointment that 'form and fable' had failed to remind anyone that art had more power than political fashion. For herself she believed that art clarified on the eternal plane the tortuous constructs of humanity; that nothing was more valuable.

'You know, I sometimes wish – '

'Stikh.'

'I sometimes wish, Dr Stikh, that your Bezzakonian education was ours, despite the lack of freedom I see here.' She cast her hand towards the bus window.

'Shsh!' He held a finger to his lips. It never did to say anything directly. Even in a bus full of foreign academics you never knew who was listening.

She lowered her voice to a stage whisper. 'But it's true. We have lost our belief in the cultured life as the good life. We academics don't represent anything these days except our own desire to get ahead. Of course, I don't expect an outsider like you to believe me. It sounds too dramatic. Even now, you see, I can't say it strongly enough –'

There had been a moment when she had been working on Dusheinov in the Great Bezum Library in Muzeb. Now she loved Dusheinov, because he understood life through metaphor; he understood how life and literature came together to preserve life from dangerous excess, for the excess went into the safe realm of the metaphor, the great playground of the spirit. The Bezumists had deliberately ignored Dusheinov. His thinking took on the character of a rival and underground philosophical system even while Bezumism was still establishing itself. The handmaiden of Dusheinov's school of thinking was Modernist art, which pictured those 'abstract psychological vectors" Bezumism ignored. 'Oh, lovely phrase!' sighed Diana, embedded in a library which with the degree of concentration and privacy it allowed still might have been anywhere free. They know not what they conjure with, these Bezumians!

She copied derogatory passages from Bezzakonian books, and her own comments upon them, and added the names of Freud and of great artists and poets in the margin. But she knew she was working not only in an unfree world, but in one utterly disillusioned. In the green and brass lamps of the reading room now and again she thought she saw back to the flickering candles of the early Christian catacombs. For her work served no practical purpose other than to worship the invisible spirit of what had died and could not be resurrected. She could do nothing with Bezzakonia, except use it to understand how easily human freedom was won and lost. Thus that realm of shimmering uncertainty which was the fate of enlightened souls everywhere in the twentieth century invited her personally across its threshhold.

'But I do understand,' Stikh said, and they both looked outside, fearing where this conversation was taking them. 'Your world lacks *educated* moral conviction. Few people believe knowledge and a feeling for art lead to a superior life any more.'

The landscape had given way to row after row of cheaply built housing blocks, fronted on the ground floor by public places. Dingy chrome signs seemed to have been handwritten in molten metal above the ground-level establishments. One place with net curtains and a closed door said 'Restaurant'. Another sign, red majuscules painted vertically on cream, said BREAD. In front of the shops the bus stops along the edge of the broad stone pavements were no longer deserted, but crowded with men and women weighed down by string shopping bags.

The silence persuaded Stikh he had gone too far. He remembered Marina and his old problem returned. As the bus approached the centre of town he said, 'Well, I have to get off now. It was nice talking to you.'

'Wait! Where do you teach, Dr Stikh? Here?' Diana Burke leaned out of her seat and felt she might run after her interlocutor.

'At the Politeknikum, as I said. Well, I would invite you for dinner, but I know this is not possible. Have a happy stay.'

The driver let him out at the lights and he walked back to the hostel.

He showered along the corridor in the trickle of water the dry summer left to flow, put on a track suit and lay down on the divan in his room.

★

Diana Burke watched him to the last moment when the bus moved away from the lights.

'Are you going to see him again, Diana?'

'Don't be stupid, Alan, this is Bezzakonia.'

'He's probably a spy.'

'That's all the same to me.'

'I shall write a thriller with your new beau in it as the chief spy. I shall escape the academic grind. Maybe you'll come with me, maybe not. Meanwhile here we are, back at the jolly old Sputnik hotel.'

'Do shut up, Alan.'

Beside the flat façade the colour of dirty sand, the disembarking clientele looked like a flock of exotic butterflies. They brought passing life to the driver's home town. He pulled away in a cloud of exhaust.

In the foyer a plywood table and cupboard had been rigged together to make what was called a kiosk.

'Do you have a map of the town?'

It seemed an effort for the saleswoman, aged about forty, to move her lips and say no.

'I see. Well, thank you anyway.'

'No! Not thank you!'

The woman was tormented because foreigners always said please and thank you, even though shopping in this country was impossible. Diana shrugged and went up to her room on foot. The lifts were out of order. Two hours later, Alan Smithers was smoking a cigarette on the steps of the colourless hotel, gazing out over the polluted road. All along the wide boulevard the trees and the walls of the buildings were thick with carbon monoxide dust.

'Want me to come with you, Diana? Seriously, I mean. Careful the militsia don't get you.'

'No. Thanks for your concern, Alan. I'm just going for a walk after all those hours sitting down.'

She headed down the boulevard for Bezum Square. It was almost dark, but there were still people going about with shopping bags.

54

An odd thing about Bezzakonian streets was you couldn't hear conversations, or ever smell food.

'Politeknikum?' she asked a man with his shirt open at the neck, who looked a bit like her quarry.

'I don't know,' said the anxious citizen, hurrying along.

But at the lights just before the square an old woman in a black and floral headscarf stopped Diana. She wanted the bus station, which was five minutes' drive in a straight line from the Sputnik Hotel. They had passed it each day on their excursions. 'Yes. I can tell you, citizen.' Perhaps the old woman was partially deaf and blind and couldn't tell Diana was foreign. Whatever the reason, calculating, Diana got in her question before she gave her answer, and found the way.

Stikh wanted her to come for his own good. He wanted to play out the tragic part to the end and be done with it, like his country had done. So he sat in a café opposite the entrance to the Politeknikum and waited. He anchored back the net curtain at the window table with a box of quartered napkins. The woman in the café noticed his waiting. Indeed, everywhere he looked half-familiar faces cried in chorus, as if looking down on him in a dungeon or a cradle, 'Live like the rest of us, young man! There's no point in struggling. After all, it's not that bad nowadays.' But he was determined to go through with the confrontation, if it happened.

Time passed. He couldn't in his anxiety measure it. A half-eaten plate of meat and potatoes, an empty ice-cream dish and a tea glass with a tin spoon filled the table. He looked out of the window. The far side, apart from the Politeknikum entrance, was one long concrete wall. If she wanted to find him she must come this way, for it was a small town, almost without side roads, according to the national ground plan. Suddenly he saw her upright foreign figure turning the corner. He got up, walked outside and crossed the street.

'Thanks for coming. I wanted the chance to ask you some things about England.'

'Thanks for asking me. I was painting too black a picture. You can make a good life.'

'In Bezzakonia we love books. What do you read?'

'What a strange question! People read what they want to: classics, poetry, thrillers, bestsellers. Anything and everything you imagine.'

'Nothing is banned?'

'Not really.'

'So why do you bother with this country? Because it is the enemy?'

'Good God, no! Because of whatever it is makes millions of you love books, Dr Stikh. It seems like a miracle.'

'So that's why you come, because you have a taste for miracles.'

'Sad, isn't it? When you put it like that I feel I ought to be ashamed.'

Two militiamen lingered on the corner, but Stikh pressed on. He was more hostile and more agitated than he had been in the bus, when he had been holding back.

'Indeed. You cannot know what it is like for us to be cut off from the world, Diana. You cannot know what *we* do not have and what we long for. Can you imagine longing to hear Mahler and not being allowed to? That was the fate of our most famous composer when he was young. Only later he realized the truth of what he had missed. Now he is dying. Like so many other Bezzakonian creative geniuses who do not die of drink or in a camp, he is dying of disappointment.'

'You could leave, Dr Stikh. I know it's hard but it's not impossible. I would, under conditions we could agree, be willing to marry you.'

Later Diana Burke would come to think, with justice, that she had never experienced such an unselfish and pure sentiment in her life as she felt towards Dr Stikh.

But he burst out laughing.

'I understand, dear lady. You want finally in your life to be useful. Well, you have been useful to me in ways you cannot know.' He shook her hand and turned away. What mattered now was to get back to Muzeb. He knew exactly how to please the Peasants, only till now he had lacked the will. He would begin two articles that night, one on the poverty of contemporary English literature and the other on the bourgeois notion of the writer as lost soul. And the Peasants would rejoice.

'Is that it?'

'Yes.'

'You bastard.'

He turned and shouted for the benefit of the police, 'Now leave me alone, shameless mees. You are trying to tempt me, but I won't leave. This is where I belong. You think you are a valuable person because you are an outsider. You are trying to tell me I am an outsider too, like you. But this is not true. This is my country. This is where I belong. Don't you have a country of your own? You should be ashamed.'

Diana walked away and didn't look back. It was for her the same experience of loss which had overwhelmed her in the Great Bezum Library, and it only made everything in her life more difficult.

5

COLD WAR

Roy Owedean, a senior Western reporter in Muzeb, had been travelling to the provincial city of Pskuria. The news period was quiet and as a good correspondent he used it to explore an unusual dateline. The train journey lasted overnight and his secretary, Nadia, debited the required two dollars' hard currency from the office account. In the event, the city of Pskuria, with a medieval fortress, an unmodernized pre-war hotel and a glut of bread and veal but no vegetables was only sad and dull, and he almost had to invent his story, but the journey on a Bezzakonian train was everything.

On that great iron harbinger of a better age, tea without milk tasted ambrosian. But the pleasure was not just sensual. Such a pleasing orderliness exuded from railway stations that either doubled as or once had been Manichaean cathedrals that you could feel you were queuing for heaven when you queued for a train. The female attendant, who delivered the tea from an urn with a tap, and provided and collected bedlinen, was like a hostess of the Manichaean religion. Thus while the train, making a sound like skis whispering through old tracks, whispered back through a life which for Roy Owedean every minute was becoming less substantial, announcing infinite loss, this woman confirmed, if ever so faintly, the possibility of hope.

'Hi, sweetheart. How was the trip?' Roy took off his overcoat and left his bag standing in the hall. Their apartment, comfortable, colourful, subtly lit and full of contemporary pine furniture and cool plain porcelain imported from Arcadia could have been anywhere Western in the world, and in that familiarity at least a kind of home. But Roy had become so preoccupied in Muzeb it hurt him to be anywhere except in transit, and she was hurt he had become so strange. She felt their marriage would fall apart if the effort did not come from her.

They exchanged the kind of routine kiss which reminds the outside world two people are connected, but does nothing for that relationship's inhabitants.

'Well, it was curious.' He sat down, tugging on the red scarf he so often retained indoors now, and tried to tell the story of the peasant woman. But the hour and the light were odd for relaxing on the sofa, eleven in the morning.

'Coffee?'

'No, tea.'

The flat was quiet. Tom and Meg were both now at the international school and the maid, Dusya, was shopping. Roy felt as if he and his family lived in different countries, or, if it was only one, that in that case he inhabited the war zone whereas his wife and children were roped-off spectators.

She brought him tea with milk, in a mug. He gave a low wail. 'I hate this apartheid we live under.' But now he was talking about losing his human substance by virtue of being a foreigner in Muzeb. Bezzakonians and Westerners were kept apart as if this were the chief goal of the Manichaean religion, to isolate light from dark, for purity's sake.

'Did something happen in the train, darling?'

59

'Just a mistake. There was a peasant woman with her child in my carriage all the way to Pskuria and I couldn't get her to even look at me. I mean, she just lay there, curled up, as if we were two hostile animals.'

'I expect it was just a mistake. It could even be encouraging that *they* didn't make a fuss. I mean, you're the threat to them, not the other way round.'

'But it's no way to live. Do you know, Pat, I wanted to tell her not to stick neat sugar in her baby's mouth. You get these batons of sugar on the train and she was using one as a dummy. There's a lifetime's visits to the dentist guaranteed!'

The bulky Bezzakonian child had lain swathed in a hat and leggings, in the curve of the mother's body, and thus protected from Roy. On another moral time-scale, where we would all be responsible for one another from minute to minute, he would have been bound to say something enlightening. As it was, he did nothing, except, before he left the carriage, he handed over his own sugar as a present. Now he despised himself for his inertia.

'Roy –' She walked across the room. 'Do you suppose people like us worry more about our lives here? I mean, there seems to be some pressure to sort ourselves out.'

'Yes.' He stood up. 'I think a lot about my childhood.'

Roy's mother had left him when he was twelve. Pat moved towards a chance to be close, but he broke off abruptly. 'Now I must go down to the office.'

Half-crying, half-swearing, she resolved upon a long walk.

Walking into the office, he smelt cabbage. Nadia was making an early lunch on the electric ring in the corridor. He sat back in the typing chair and surveyed what he mockingly called his 'little empire'. Yet it wasn't really self-mockery, because Roy did see himself as a hero, writing the story his world needed to know. He knew that Bezzakonia tried to destroy its expatriate observers with gossip and scandal and discomfort, to reduce the chance of anyone surviving long enough really to understand, and he was determined to hang on.

The office was situated in an old bourgeois apartment block

with high ceilings and parquet floors. If you were of a suspicious turn of mind, you might imagine Westerners had been placed there to be the inevitable victims of painful sensations. For set between the Bezzakonian and the Prebezzakonian world, neither of which they could quite grasp, they experienced haunting memories of what they called 'freedom' and 'happiness'. Torment inclined them to give up their rational tasks to read instead the symbols that lay all around. Bezum, the new broom who swept dirty; the besom who rendered all floors dull. Still recumbent in the typing chair, Roy found himself thinking of how these Prebezzakonian parquet floors once shone, and how they reflected human life, whereas now, despite looking up to huge windows which opened on to Bezzakonia and cast down bold light, they reflected nothing. Heaven forbid that in the dullness of these old floors there might be some deliberate plan, or counter-plan. The converse of one of Bezum's slogans came to mind: SUFFERING MAY BE THE PATH TO A SUPERIOR LIFE, COMRADE PEERS, BUT YOU MAY NOT BE ABLE TO TAKE IT. YOU MAY DECIDE TO STOP REFLECTING.

Life in Bezzakonia had gone beyond some limit. People couldn't take it much longer. He had to do something.

'Nadia? I'm just going to move the furniture a bit. I've got an idea.'

He pulled out their desks from the glass-panelled French doors that separated them and pushed the partition back against the side wall.

'There, that's much better. More light, more contact.' His and Nadia's desks now faced each other in a continuous expanse.

Nadia was an intelligent woman of about forty, quite attractive and rather puzzling in so far as she seemed content to be a scribe of the unreflecting system.

She joked, 'You don't trust me, Roy, is that it?'

'No, no, quite the opposite. I want to work *with* you.'

Nadia didn't grin. A grin is an open, childlike gesture, whereas this woman smiled sceptically as out of a dark-windowed car, like those driven by the Bezzakonian élite; she smiled out of a realm to which certainly no foreigner had access.

'I've got you that pasta, by the way.'

'Wonderful. They make the best pasta in all Bezzakonia in Pskuria.'

She turned his personal favour into praise of her country and shut him out again. They must learn behaviour like that in school. Nadia the mystery creature in the turquoise mohair jumper and the white rabbit-skin hat. The system she represented resembled just the whites of human eyes; whites without pupils.

'I thought we'd have some people round on Friday. We owe Harry and Maria, and there are a couple of new people in the English camp.'

Pat so longed for that larger world where her husband came and went. Muzeb wives lived in the wings of the world stage, around 1979, when other women were already leading independent lives in the centre. Any sensitive man would have understood the frustration.

'I may have to *work*.'

'Everyone understands that, Roy. We've been here three years now. But we have to live. And you have a family!'

Muzeb was using him up, wasting him, and wasting them. Sometimes she imagined he was having an affair and the suspicion stripped the flat of comfort, like some tool of warfare which did for the stuffing and the texture of all things, reducing them to bare bones. The stations of communal living, the places they sat to eat and talk, were wretched.

'I hardly need reminding.' He defected from the conversation cruelly.

She burst into tears watching the great Bezzakonian enamel kettle boil after he had gone. Then, because it was Wednesday, their half-day, the children came home for lunch.

Later, Leonid was polishing the office car and, tightly wrapped against the cold, Tom and Meg went down to help him. What an extraordinary figure he was! He stood six foot three tall in jeans and fancy padded boots, under the kind of navy cashmere winter coat popular with Western businessmen. He lavished care on the official Cadillac the office had inherited from an American correspondent, while a tape of Simon and Garfunkel played through the open door. Pat's children more waved than applied dusters. She came out to show them how.

'Greetings, Leonid!' she called over in Bezzakonian, watching her breath steam in the air.

Tom scowled. 'You always interfere. What have you come down for?' he muttered.

But they had another spectator. Fascinated by the car, a Bezzakonian boy watched from a distance. He was so small the militiaman at the yard entrance hadn't noticed him. Or, out of kindness, the guard just let this boy from his own kind creep to the very border. The boy called out to his mother, 'Look, look!' The mother slapped down the boy's arm and marched him off. Pat shook her head.

'Don't worry about the little blighter, *gospozha*. Curiosity killed the cat. Well-known Bezzakonian saying.'

'I prefer the one about cats having nine lives. What would you do with nine lives, Leonid?'

'Waste one in order to know the feeling, then enjoy the other eight.'

'You already have one more than the rest of us.' She was speaking without thinking. She wasn't counting *that* other life, in which he was paid to spy on her. 'I mean one as a chauffeur, another as a philosopher.'

His little bead eyes sparkled out from behind small round glasses. The frames were a present from Roy. 'Well, yes, perhaps I am lucky.'

Pat laughed and lingered until her own curiosity made her feel awkward. Then she ushered a loving daughter but a very irritated son upstairs.

For the Friday-evening gathering Roy sat at everyone's head, opposite his wife, at the Arcadian dinner table, with Harry and Maria on his left and the newcomers, Antonia and Eamon, opposite them, on his right.

Antonia immediately detected something quixotic about Roy. That red scarf, for God's sake, and the sproutings of a beard suddenly chosen in mid-life. She asked him if he had ever looked for the bugging devices in the office and in this flat, and whether he really didn't mind Bezum's lieutenants regarding his intimate life as open-plan. She put the same question to Harry about the embassy.

'It's not a laughing matter, Eamon. We have no privacy!'

Eamon thought, you've only come back because you like complaining, and reorganizing everyone. You've got a proper little housewife's mentality dressed up as politics, Aunty Tony. The former university students had arrived in Muzeb separately and weren't overwhelmed to see each other again. 'What do you want privacy *for*?' he teased.

'It's essential to the health of the individual.'

'Well, they don't care about that here.'

'Our safeguard is that we can always get out,' said Harry's wife. 'So even if the worst happens here, we can see it as if it were happening in a play that can be curtained off.'

Roy said, 'You can't get away from the spying. You just have to live with it! Have sensitive conversations outside.'

'Real cloak and dagger stuff, eh?' said Eamon, while Pat observed that it was difficult enough to find time to talk, without having to go out into the snow.

'Yes. Except I don't know why this Cold War I'm caught up in has to be fought at all.'

Antonia affected to choke on her wine. 'You don't know why, Roy? I do. This is an evil place. Bezum's lot will take over the whole world. If they thought they could get away with it without destroying themselves they'd press the nuclear button.'

Pat collected plates. 'That's the problem with all hostilities, isn't it? The degree to which you will get hurt if you join in. Only there aren't degrees of nuclear devastation.'

'So that's a case for avoiding Antonia's kind of extremism,' Roy said.

'But not a case for not standing firm,' she hit back. 'Muzeb seems to make people *sentimental* for peace and harmony. You're not succumbing to that, are you, Roy?'

Eamon grinned. 'What Antonia means is some people believe we should all just give up our quibbling and take Bezzakonian lovers. That would end the Cold War. I wouldn't mind.'

'All you need is love,' sang Pat. 'And a home to come back to.'

In the sudden fever that gripped the table, Eamon found himself admiring Pat's breasts. Pat decided not to invite Antonia again.

Maria diverted them all into a gentler conversation about decor by pointing up to the cornices that ended abruptly where the old room had been divided. 'You can see it everywhere you go here. They have ruined so many beautiful interiors.'

'Look!' Roy, exasperated, banged the table with his fist. 'This is a unique place. We'll never live in another country where everyone has what he needs, and has a job, and where our wives can walk out without fear.'

Maria asked, 'Do you, Pat? Walk without fear? I find the whole place intimidating.'

Harry supported his wife. 'Exactly, Maria. There may be a lack of petty crime, but what about the one whacking great crime this place is?'

'Meaning?' asked Roy.

'Meaning people can't leave, for God's sake. Brute force holds this place together.'

'That may be so. But there's also a spiritual bond among people here, and with their country.'

Eamon said, 'They've invented the spirituality because the reality's too painful. That's all.'

'Exactly,' added Harry. 'First World science, Third World lives. How do you account for that master plan, Owedean? Is it what Bezum had in mind when he plastered his cities with: SUFFERING IS THE PATH TO THE SUPERIOR LIFE, CITIZEN PEERS?'

Roy glared at his watch, tossed his napkin beside a half-finished plate of pork in sour cream, with rice, and sprang up. 'I must check something in the office.'

They heard the front door close and the clank of the lift.
'The office?' Antonia was puzzled.
'It's just downstairs.'

He sat in the office with a single light on, listening to the judder
and whine of the world-news printers. He was alone except for
the pathetic chantings of electronic intelligence. Shall I spell it
out? Bezzakonian lives are richer because they rely on their own
resources. This is a superpower in political and scientific might,
but in day-to-day living it is a poor Third World country. Money
doesn't cross borders. It's difficult to move about. Good
neighbourliness matters. He took a deep breath and was about to
go back upstairs. Instead he went out, without a coat.

He passed the park where *The Bezzakonian Truth* was pasted up
on reading boards. After the light went, around six in February, a
few citizens continued to read by the light of torches, or candles,
or North Korean cigarette lighters. All that effort to absorb what
was untrue! And yet the effort was good; he admired it. He walked
to a small café he knew. Unlike in most such places, the
manageress cleared the grey Formica table-tops regularly and the
clientele, mainly women, desisted from throwing leftovers on the
floor.

'Good evening!'

The manageress stared. He ordered tea at the counter, paid and
sat, tugging at the slight beard he had been growing since the train
journey to Pskuria. Different forces had been moving him about
like a miniature doll on a battleground since that day, while in
himself, like a secret agent waiting to be contacted by one side or
the other, he watched for signs. Two teenagers were eating cakes,
a woman about thirty was quietly reading a fat journal, and a
tieless man fed hungrily off a plate of meat and porridge. Thick-
fleshed and purplish, the male of the Bezzakonian species seemed
to belong to the living dead. Roy played with the near-weightless
tin teaspoon. No one spoke to him. No one would speak to him.
He was getting used to it.

Back outside he realized it was too late or too soon to go back, so he got on a tram and rode towards the Electricity Tower, supposed to be a monument to Bezzakonia's joy at entering the modern world, under Bezum. Lit by its power, back across the river the towering Italian-built Fortress, surrounded by its Manichaean churches, gleamed all the brighter over the impoverished life strewn below.

He wanted to understand. There was a song . . . He stood and sang it out loud: 'Anything you can do I can do better. I can do anything better than you . . . ' Thus the futile war of his worlds. The Cold War anthem.

Roy, knowing the worlds could not be measured one against the other, loved Muzeb for its self-abasement. Humility was the positive word. By day the waste from combustion engines consuming cheap, gassy low-octane fuel coated the whole city in mouse-brown dust, so that from up here, in his mind's eye, it resembled a prostrate monk at prayer. He loved the gloomy, half-empty shops and the repair counters and the queues for invisible essentials, or was it rewards? Cigars, toilet paper, books. He toyed with the glory of loss.

He had suffered so many setbacks recently. He went to a bakery to talk to the peasants about how they still made real bread and found they had changed their entire output to look 'Western' for his visit, so he had no story about authenticity to tell. He reckoned the whole establishment had been scrubbed and swept to banish traces of those raw and natural ingredients only Bezzakonia preserved in use and which he had wanted to praise. Someone did not want the West to discover Roy's new, appealing and necessary Bezzakonia; he thought afterwards it could only have been his own 'side'. So it was a token of not the whole battle being lost when he emerged from that bakery with a smear of flour on his red scarf, a token of his secret solidarity which another unknown hand had daubed on him.

The tram returned him to the old circus, from where he could walk. Not far from the stop he almost tripped over a massive man comatose on the pavement. Then a woman in a headscarf appeared from inside somewhere and kicked the sleeping soul to see if its human shell was still alive. Back home you couldn't easily pass a body in the street. But for a man to retreat for an hour into unconsciousness spread-eagled on cold stone or the dead earth of the park was almost normal here.

Retreat! Roy imagined himself retreating. And as the image formed in his mind he saw in a great blaze of light that the sense of all things in this country was provided by Bezzakonian women, who allowed the descent away from consciousness and watched over it. Mother Bezzakonia.

'Excuse me, foreigner, you dropped this.'

A young woman proffered a leaky Bezzakonian Bic. She was blonde, wearing a grey coat and stout leather boots, still carrying the thick journal she had been reading earlier in the café.

'It isn't mine. I mainly write with this.' He took from his inside jacket pocket a slim fountain pen sheathed in stainless steel. 'But thank you for your concern. Citizen. Peer.' He groped for his linguistic courage.

'May I see? It's beautiful. We don't have anything as beautiful to write with in Bezzakonia. I see you are a man who appreciates beautiful things.'

'Keep it, then. I'd like you to have it.' He pressed her hands around the pen, watched in surprise by a pair of clear blue eyes.

'Your hands are very cold, foreigner.'

'I came out in a hurry.'

She ran a finger along the smooth sheath, then unscrewed the cap and dabbed her fingertip with a full point of ink. 'But I cannot take such a present. You must have something in exchange. Please, I invite you to my house. My husband and I collect many interesting objects. I will write my address. Come on Saturday evening.'

He tore a page from his notebook, then, clutching the paper from 'Ksenia B.' in his pocket, watched her disappear into the Metro.

Pat coddled her children through those cold days of later winter. She fussed so much that Tom, at ten, shouted for the first time in his life: 'Leave me alone!' He ran and stood with his head to the wall of their building, leaving her shocked and motionless beside the car.

'It will pass, *gospozha*. I know about children.'

'Is that another piece of Bezzakonian philosophy? I should like to become a Bezzakonian philosopher.'

'I will teach you, *gospozha*. Now Tom and I will go for a drive. Are you ready, Tom?'

'Oh, can we?'

Pat smiled and turned indoors. She would like to have gone for the drive without her son. Nadia reported that Pat, with the carelessness that sometimes befell Westerners, even though they knew they were watched, was interested in Leonid.

Roy, clutching the warm paper in his pocket, turned left after the rank of blue metal mail boxes and rang. There was no name on the buzzer.

'You found us!' Ksenia B. was in thick trousers and a petrol-green pullover, and wore her hair up. 'Help yourself to slippers.'

He unlaced his boots, like a warrior removing his sword, he thought. The face of a girl about nine peeped round a door on the right, while Ksenia led Roy into a very large room on the left.

'This is old, from Prebezzakonia, this is from the time of Bezum II, and over here is contemporary art, including work by my husband. He is very modest.'

'I can see.'

The husband, Aleksei, having shaken Roy's hand, stood awkwardly by.

'You're collectors?'

'I am an historian, but yes, as you see, we indulge our interest.'

'I was lucky to meet you.'

Ksenia B. passed him objects to inspect: old tins, menus, a fan, a revolutionary plate. Inside an open wardrobe he spotted a Prebezzakonian Singer sewing machine.

'I sew for the girls on it!'

'Was that your daughter I saw in the hall?'

'I have two. They can't help being curious.'

'I'd like to meet them. They look about the same age as my children.'

'You will. They're laying the table!'

Ksenia led Roy to the kitchen and Aleksei followed, silent except for his slippers slopping on the parquet. The girls, both with blonde plaits, the younger with two front teeth missing, had put out plates and glasses for five. A fat-necked buttermilk bottle in the middle of the plastic-coated table held carnations, and an old icon looked down from above.

'Is it the real thing?' Beauty made Roy nervous.

'That depends what you mean. It's a very good eighteenth-century copy of the Mother of God Our Lady of K.'

Roy didn't know what he meant so he just stared. The icon's long endurance in a candlelit church had smoked the colours into the limewood tablet and something of that stored-up warmth in yellow and brown ochres played back into a kitchen Roy associated with his own childhood: the painted wooden cupboards, the cumbersome round-cornered refrigerator, the enamelled gas cooker on legs and the stick-legged utility furniture of the immediate post-war.

He found the story of his train ride to Pskuria easy to tell. 'Well, *I* was in the right bunk. I wondered of course what was behind it all.'

'She would have thought you were a spy.'

Aleksei looked on the point of speaking, but didn't. He refused alcohol.

'I didn't pretend, Ksenia. I said I was from the West, I asked her how far she was going and how old the baby was, but she kept her eyes low. It's awful that we should be so threatening. Why can't we all live as one human family?'

The girls received permission to get down. Roy's children never asked. When they had gone, Ksenia whispered, 'We know you're risking something seeing us like this, Roy. So are we. We are breaking the law —'

He dismissed the law passionately.

'But at least we can give you a present. A souvenir of old Bezzakonia that will one day return. A token of the real country that remains in our hearts.'

She reached over and took down the icon of the Mother of God. Then they stood on the nameless threshhold and she waved goodbye as he left the block. She called, 'Is it raining? Put it under your jacket, close to your heart,' and he went out into a night which filled his lungs with joy. Anything you can do . . . he sang. Absurd! What a waste of a good tune!

The icon he placed in the sitting room, in front of the books on the top shelf of the pine bookcase, where it might cast its good spell over future social gatherings in the Owedean household. When he got into bed Pat felt the thrill of lying with a passionate stranger who told her he had made contact with the other side.

The contact calmed her. For otherwise she had been plotting to leave, plotting to sleep with Leonid in the back of the Cadillac, plotting to set up in competition with Roy. She had got Nadia to show her how to work the telex; she had actually sent a story about Muzeb shopping to the *Guardian*, because if you had a derelict husband, or when he became derelict, and sooner or later most husbands did, or they left you for a younger woman, you had to be independent, and you were bound to take long walks and ask yourself questions and plot.

What are you going to become, Pat? What are you beginning, as you approach forty, with pretty legs and the loveliest breasts in Muzeb? Why are you so afraid of competition? It's no solution, just to keep walking. You have to run somewhere, and leap.

But Bezzakonian life kept intruding on her plans, because it looked so peculiarly needy. Not so much that it lacked something, but as if it wasn't concentrated on the target. There were shops selling ballbearings and bathroom mirrors, and dry groceries, and a second-hand shop where foreigners trawled in vain for pre-revolutionary souvenirs. Shops cropped up on the ground floors of massive apartment buildings and every sign indicating them seemed to be a kind of joke, for no establishment necessarily existed, or necessarily occurred in this place rather than any other. Everything in Bezzakonia seemed accidental, and the only necessity was that the consequences were bad for human life. The dirty buildings, the run-down buses and trams, and the burdened people in ill-matched clothes all looked starved of resources and bound to make do.

Pat paused to cross a two-lane highway and became caught in a tight bunch of other pedestrians, mainly women, mainly bulky figures, here two in leather coats, there one in a brown wool coat, and all with stout boots and fur hats, but none like Pat in a long sheepskin coat. They stared at her and tried not to show it. How could she have thought she wouldn't stand out? But truly she had forgotten. So it was curious. You began with thoughts about yourself and you ended up compelled to put them on one side and think instead of Bezzakonia. And then you found it had something for you.

She took the *Pocket Bezzakonian Course* with her into the bath. She put it by the bedside while she fell asleep in the afternoons. She raced through two lessons a day before the complexity of the later chapters reduced her to one. She taped her reading of new vocabulary and played it back in the kitchen or the bedroom, and the stations of a marriage became transformed into learning stations. Dusya caught her repeating the sound of her own inaccurate voice and took over the recording of new words. *Bez* was . . . and *um* . . . Good God!

'You could bring me up some newspapers, Roy, please. I need to practise reading.'

'*Bezzakonian Truth* all right for you?' he said sarcastically, but it was Dusya who intervened, telling him exactly what to fetch, namely the evening and local papers and those with magazine sections, to give the *gospozha* a taste of ordinary life. The fifty-year-old maid, who looked older, became expansive, beaming and exposing her gold tooth to the light as she listed, with the back of one hand repeatedly striking her palm, the recipes, knitting patterns, crime stories and jokes that lay ahead.

'Jokes,' muttered Roy, trundling back down to the office, hungry for dinner .

Two particular Bezzakonian words lodged in Pat's mind. Repairs. Productivity. Repairs. Everyone knew it. It was displayed outside shops and on the doors of all manner of establishments being refitted. You could, in the vicinity of the ghetto, get your baskets rewoven, your watch cleaned and your shoes soled and heeled; you could get a tear in your clothes restitched, and metal fittings and cutlery resoldered.

Pat took her black leather boots with the cuban heel to have new zips. She had been on the point of slinging them out, though most people in Muzeb gave unwanted clothes and consumer goods to their maids, or put them outside where they could be easily retrieved by a wider catchment of foreigners' staff. The boots had a sentimental value, having lasted since university.

Leonid saw her in the yard.

'I'll go, *gospozha*.'

'No, I'd like to go myself.' Her eyes said, 'Go on, admire me, even if I am the boss's wife,' and his seemed to say, 'Here's to you then.'

The little room, which predictably smelt of rubber and boot black, and where every surface seemed smudged, reminded her of something old at home, something stereotyped in her mind as old-fashioned, though possibly she had never experienced it.

She was going to say good morning, but thought better of it.

'How much?'

The cobbler barked out a price and she paid the tiny sum next day with great embarrassment. The new zips and the stitching were stout enough to last a lifetime.

The newspaper carried an announcement: CITIZENS! TOMATOES WILL BE ON SALE TOMORROW AT GASTRONOM NO. 273. The queue was fifty yards long by the time she arrived at ten a.m., in what mentally she called active sympathy. She stood for an hour, banging her feet and hands. Word passed down the snake of needy, silent humans that maybe the tomatoes would run out. But she took out a plastic shopping bag, which bore the name of a British supermarket chain, and secured her two kilos.

'Spy! Anti-Egalitarian spy!' shouted an old-looking woman in a headscarf. Silent men stared. One young woman stared so much that Pat said suddenly, 'You take them, then, and the bag. I don't need them. I'm just being selfish.'

'We don't need your gifts!'

'Well, give them to someone who does.'

'Spy! Anti-Egalitarian spy! Why are you meddling in our life? The Zionist–CIA conspiracy is paying you.'

'For God's sake!'

She walked home to try to shed the experience of hostility. By the time she arrived she knew she would write about it for a newspaper. But that was also the day the story about Roy was in the morning edition of *The Bezzakonian Truth*.

Roy spoke to head office on the telex before settling in to the morning's chores.

'These for me?'

Nadia's hair, revealed for the first time in months, had grown greyer during the indoor hat season.

'Yes. The one on top is most important.'

'I would have thought it some Bezzakonian peculiarity if you'd put it on the bottom.' He grinned.

She shook her bared head. 'Difficult language they use, Rr-oy.'

'When they want to criticize?'

'Exactly.'

He had to fetch a dictionary. The tortured syntax necessitated several re-readings of some sentences. It seemed that the *Truth* didn't know what to call the sin it had in mind, so it used a Bezzakonian no one spoke, full of foreign borrowings, ugly neo-logisms, absurd acronyms and concertinaed proper nouns. The article spread across two columns. He sat back in the chair and let the realization sink in. 'You mean this garbage is about me?'

By early afternoon the telephone was ringing incessantly. The most alarming came from a senior TV correspondent.

'Roy? Thorstein Meyerssen here. You really must call a press conference, for your own sake.'

'My job is to go to them.'

'Come on, pal. This is no time for fancy footwork. They've accused you of receiving stolen goods. You've been set up. You may find yourself in court. You need as much exposure in the media at home as you can get.'

Roy tugged at the useless beard. 'All right, four o'clock in this office. Spread the word.'

By a quarter to four Roy was sitting under the hot TV spotlights Thorstein's crew had rigged up to circle his desk. Nadia took herself discreetly off to the vicinity of the electric ring. Roy hadn't realized Thorstein wore make-up for broadcasting: matt foundation, lip-liner, eye-liner. But of course television news, all news, was essentially theatrical. The arrival of Roy's colleagues from every Western nation crowded out further reflections. The room was quickly full and it occurred to him how difficult it would have been to accommodate them had he not recently removed that partition. Their noise hushed.

'How do I feel about possibly ending up in a Bezzakonian gaol? Outraged. I thought I was on their side.'

'On *their* side? Were you thinking of defecting, or maybe spying for them?'

'For God's sake! All I wanted was to break down barriers.'

'But their whole life is barriers, Roy.'

'I don't see why mine should be.'

'So they're right to accuse you of being selfish?'

'Mr Owedean, the people here are not free to leave. They're locked in! It's your job to tell the world that certainly. But you can't dismantle the barriers single-handed.'

'I can make a start.'

Roy was visibly sweating under the lights. Television created unfair conditions, Pat thought, feeling for him from the first row of the standing audience.

'What comment from your office?'

'They're standing by me.'

In fact the office were preparing to send out what they called a fireman to rescue the situation. Then who knew what Roy's future would be. Pat heard a few people laugh at the question.

Another speaker said, '*The Truth* article mentioned a bakery trip you made to write a story. It said you wanted to portray Bezzakonians as simple people, the sort of people we should all imitate, and this was a lie. You were trying to destabilize the world balance by making them look small. But they spotted what you were up to.'

'They certainly spoilt the piece.'

Antonia joined in the attack. 'We heard you encouraged the Bezzakonians to put their prices up in the foreigners' gift shops, so they could take more money off your stupid colleagues and their even more stupid wives. Why do you hate everyone on your own side?'

'Why do you neglect your wife and children?' cried another voice.

'Everyone admires them. What is it you want from Bezzakonia for which you are prepared to make such sacrifices?'

Under fire, Roy lost track. He became a Bezzakonian being tortured by Bezumian extremists. He twisted on his typing chair, set under the television spotlights. The highly sprung chair wouldn't keep still. No, wait, it was his own community attacking, turning on him like a sick member who threatened their well-being, whom they would have to cut off, whom they disapproved of because of where he had been roaming .

'But it seemed right! Everything else about being here seems wrong. We are the ones who are foolish, for what we don't recognize, don't explore, don't understand –'

'Wait everyone! I have some real news!' Harry rushed in. 'Stop press! Apparently the daughter of some Bezzakonian high-up in London's been caught shoplifting, which Muzeb wanted hushed up, so we've agreed a swap. The Antinomian pilferer for the Melancholian receiver, as *The Bezzakonian Truth* would say.' He turned sideways and held out his hand. 'Congratulations, Roy. You're a free man.'

Pat burst into tears. Thorstein Meyerssen put his arm round her.

Roy shouted, 'No, wait!' He stood up perilously on his swivel chair to try to make himself heard over the noise of the dispersing conference, sticking out his arms for balance. 'I don't want to be swapped for a criminal. That's outrageous.'

He got down again and Nadia patted his shoulder. Roy felt he was twelve years old again, being comforted by his father's girl-friend, and it wasn't what he wanted.

Back upstairs, Harry, Pat and the children clustered in the kitchen. Pat announced her tomatoes story would appear in the *Guardian*. There was good news about Tom too: he had come top at school. And Meg? What about Meg? She had a new tooth coming!

Roy returned from wandering about. 'Where's the icon?'

'But that was what you stole! You can't expect to keep what you stole *and* go free.'

'Fuck off, you lying turd. You know I didn't steal anything. They gave it to me.'

Tom gaped at his father.

'You're very lucky to come out of this so easily, Roy. Only because your country and your friends think so highly of you.'

'Two men came, Roy, and took it away in a plastic bag. The children and I were frightened.'

Tom and Meg stood in full agreement beside Pat.

'I see. Right.' So they took away Our Lady of K, the Virgin and her Child, in a plastic bag. He thought, I'm back where I started. Except now I've had this warning. From both sides. Keep your wants to yourself. Be professional.

He had a cause and it refused to be defended. He had a fate and it was stolen out of his hands. This was what it felt like to be caught up in such a giant conspiracy that he, the little man, could not begin to measure it. He shaved off his beard and took long baths, and woke in the night thinking of his mother. For a month he went on sick leave, into retreat.

'I thought you might like to come with me out into the country. I have to do an Easter story.'

'I'd like that.'

'You can translate for me.'

'I'd like that too.'

It was a bright cold late-April day. The Outer Ring Road was a miserable, muddy circus of lorries in empty surroundings neither town nor country, but once they turned off on to a smaller road something like real countryside came into view. Roy said the Bezumian leaders' summer homes nestled behind the high hedges and fences. Here and there they saw a tiny post box and once, a militia car.

The church, with its typical golden domes, flaking masonry paint and rusty wire netting at a broken upper window, stood neglected but still active on the Muzeb river bank, and would have been a fine spectacle seen from the far side.

'I'm glad we're up close, to see it warts and all.'

She took his arm and they walked through a mêlée of stooped old women in black. Inside the cold body of the church, at a plain table, a bearded priest was saying words of blessing over Easter cakes being presented to him.

Responding to the sunshine, Pat had put on just cotton trousers and a shirt under a light jacket, but the temperature was barely above freezing.

'It's all so tangible and yet so alien,' she whispered.

'It's astonishingly backward.' Roy put his arm round her to keep her warm.

'You mean we shouldn't risk using the facilities.'

They knew it wasn't right to be laughing in the church.

'Are you Jewish?' asked one hunched younger woman, packing her cake back in a nylon shopping bag. Her legs were swathed in beige woollen stockings and her stout body encased in a blue and white spotted dress, over which she wore a beige cardigan.

Roy shook his head and found the question woeful.

'I'd like our children to grow up capable of humility, Roy. But I'm glad our lives don't include a church like this.'

'It's a savage place,' he replied. 'Come on. I wish I'd said I was a militant atheist. Or Antichrist.'

78

He put the car heater on high. 'It'll warm up in a minute. Just wait till the engine gets going.'

'Tom is so arrogant at the moment. I don't know what's got into him.'

'He's just asserting himself.'

'Will he ever stop?'

'We all go through phases.'

Roy drove through the desecrated, secret countryside with his hand on his wife's knee until re-entry to the main traffic artery forced him to concentrate .

Three days later a sweltering heat overtook Muzeb. Dusya rushed about unsealing the windows, stripping off the tape and wrenching them open, with a fair flaking of paint, to invite in the new air. Spring happened overnight and provided a fabulous blue backdrop to the May parade. Roy wrote engagingly about the pagan theatricality, the schooliness and the peasant bragging on a massive scale which gave this event a robust community-minded Greekness and a pathetically Evangelical tinge as well as a menacing military character. The office sent a herogram which pleased him so much he took a day off. Pat packed a picnic and they made for the river opposite the church. It looked magnificent, its cupolas highlighted by the strong sun into tokens of the highest earthly beauty. Here was melancholy confirmation that the human mind finds all things at a distance romantic. Except some favoured human beings find someone they love close up too.

There didn't seem to be anyone about. The heat was so intense they moved under a tree. She got bruises on her back and he felt like a brute, only she assured him, as her lips swarmed over his face, that he was wanted.

So it was that after three outwardly successful years abroad followed by an inner crisis, Pat and Roy found a new self-confidence that summer. For one thing, strange Bezzakonia, with its indoor goings-on so tightly monitored and its open spaces so unpatrolled, invited them into the temple of bodily abandon. For a whole week, when the children were back in England, they camped in the open and made love beside the river. But Pat also lost some fundamental dependence on her husband, which meant he had to wake up to her individuality or lose her.

Expatriate Muzeb was curious like that in that it acted as a magnet for all the most important forces for change current in the world, and even exaggerated them. You could get everything mended in Bezzakonia, and it somehow suggested that in a good world, with the right emotional economy, you could repair your marriage too and your soul. But for productivity to ensue, in that new experimental economy, many things would have to change. And that was the case with Pat and Roy's marriage. It had undergone a revolution and, even while Pat loved her husband, and understood his weaknesses, the propaganda of the Cold War had pasted itself up indelibly in her head. 'I can do anything better than you.'

6

THE DUSHEINOV CLUB

Thorstein Meyerssen replaced the plastic receiver of the Bezzakonian telephone, thinking as always how shoddily light it felt in his hand. Its red colour was ugly too. 'We can't go to the Bezum Hills, my love. I have to go to a press conference.'

He followed his voice into the kitchen, where Jean-Anne told the breakfast washing-up, 'Atheists have no respect for Sunday. You're just as bad as they are.'

'It's important. That was Piperov.'

She removed her gloves and turned, smiling, from the sink. 'In that case I'd like to come. All right? I'll be ready in ten minutes.'

Thorstein respected his wife. She was a pillar of the Muzeb Wives' Circle and her interest in Prebezzakonian art and culture was infectious. After she had recently led the wives on an excursion to the sole still half-functioning Manichaean monastery, many of the husbands were envious of a professional opportunity missed. Jean-Anne seemed even to herself to be a benign spirit promoting humane knowledge of Bezzakonia, and in her self-chosen role seemed happy, all of which contributed to their marriage.

They made the half-hour journey to north Muzeb in congenial silence. It was late August and autumn scrawled its heartless signature across the sky. For all her vivacity, Jean-Anne found this time of the year depressing. The too short summer was too soon over, and long winter was already hinting at its merciless diktat: *human* beings should either hibernate now or die of dullness.

'The rowans are already losing their leaves,' she said, as they parked in a roughly-made side road behind Piperov's block. There was a debris of yellowing leaf sprigs underfoot which reminded her of palms.

'Maybe we can get out for that walk midweek.'

He took her arm.

A pleasant smell of onions and garlic and dill frying wafted down the stairwell. Confronted by an 'under repair' sign on the lift, they went up on foot.

'The Bezzakonian authorities like to teach people to go without.'

'So their captive citizens will dream more vividly of heaven and forget about their real condition.'

'England was like that in medieval times.'

'That's a terrible comparison.'

'Another thing I call them is the unchosen people.'

'There may be more truth in that.' She stood and caught her breath. 'At least this exercise is good for us.'

'Keeping all the lifts out of order has made the Bezzakonian health service is the most cost-efficient in the world. You can see the logic.'

Husband and wife chuckled in noisy, un-Bezzakonian fashion, happy in each other's company.

On the fifth floor the Piperovs' door was open, and about twenty people were crammed into the sitting room. The Meyerssens entered a slightly foreign world. To a Western eye the apartment had no style, though it was obviously the home of serious and educated people, with its packed bookcases and a grand piano for which there was no space.

'Who's the very old lady at the piano?'

'Piperov's mother.'

'We'll have to stand.'

'Lean against the piano.'

'It's a Bechstein. How on earth?'

'Shshsh.'

There was a call for silence, and everyone looked towards Piperov, who was tall and kindly-looking, but had an already elderly manner for a man of Jean-Anne's age. He was wearing a greenish cardigan inside out, showing the foreign label 'Marks & Spencer'. Here was a man of such distinction that the foreign community brought him presents.

Piperov banged a tin teaspoon against a thick tumbler. 'Ladies and gentlemen, our first case is that of Dr Shaginyan, sent two years ago this week to a Snowland labour camp for his work as an underground priest. An open letter has been sent to the Pope and to the President of the United States, James Carter, appealing for their intervention. Yet again, ladies and gentlemen of the press, Franz Kafka has been outdone in his portrayal of man's injustice to man.'

Piperov looked unaffectedly sad at the moral shoddiness of the world, while a young aide-de-camp began passing out carbon copies of the letter. The paper, thin as onion skins, rustled like leaves in the draught of passing bodies. Later the correspondents would try dutifully to decipher the smudged typescript with corrections by hand, and a few lines would appear in the newspapers.

'Our second item concerns my friend here, Mikhail Marlinsky –' Piperov gestured towards the helper – 'who went to the Shaginyan prayer meetings and organized a similar group in his home town.'

Marlinsky, dark, with long hair and jeans reminiscent of Western fashion, gave a little bow. In profile his slightly ruddy face, with its small bright eyes, revealed a long straight nose, perfectly aligned with a high forehead. Because of the similarity in age he reminded Jean-Anne of her son.

Marlinsky read from a paper in halting English: 'Our aim was to rediscover the importance of caring for our individual souls. Without that knowledge and experience, how else could we throw off this barbaric yoke and return to the good life? Our government tells us the psychological realm is a hell every human being carries within himself, and that the only delivery is to hand over the soul to the Party. You may have seen the slogan in the streets, THE PARTY IS THE MIND, THE HONOUR AND THE CONSCIENCE OF OUR EPOCH.' Marlinsky looked up and grinned, but his face showed the same sadness as Piperov's, so that in the end his expression was grotesque. He went on reading: 'But many of *us* have read the great Prebezzakonian philosopher Dusheinov, from whom we understand that the secrets of the soul are to be *cherished*, not hated or feared, if we are to become masters of ourselves. So this is the work for which I am persecuted.'

'Can you spell that please?'

'*Wie schreibt man das?*'

The name Dusheinov was inscribed in a dozen notebooks, followed by a question mark. Jean-Anne turned to her husband. 'Their Freud,' he said. 'Something like that.'

Someone asked: 'I'd like to know what you mean by persecuted.'

'My parents have both lost their jobs. In the end, but who knows how soon, I shall be arrested.'

Jean-Anne thought of her son again. Marlinsky was twenty-five. It wasn't right that a young life should be destroyed.

'Bezzakonia has appropriated the soul for the Party because the soul is unruly, and Bezzakonia needs rules.'

This remark was funnier to Marlinsky and Piperov than it was to anyone else present, because in their language 'Bezzakonia' meant, roughly, 'land without rules'.

Marlinsky went on: 'We invite you foreigners to take a good look at our well-ruled world! It is like life on stage, is it not? People you meet seem to be bad actors or puppets, watched by professional applaudists. It's true, sometimes we dance and sing and feast in bright costumes to show we can enjoy ourselves, but everything we do is *formal*, because our masters are afraid of what is instinctive. That subterranean realm where there are no rules, in each man and woman's heart, even the real Bezzakonia, they cannot bear; because they cannot control it.'

Jean-Anne, unable to follow all that was said, noticed the old lady at the piano nodding, with her eyes closed. She hoped she wouldn't fall forwards.

'In sum, our masters have no room for personal authenticity. It is therefore the best weapon we have against them.'

The small audience clapped.

'We have some groups like yours in the West, Mr Marlinsky, and they do help people,' said Thorstein.

'Your groups are not punished and suppressed,' cried the young man, implying there could be no comparison; suffering was the test. 'So please, write about us, tell the free world we exist. That way we shall last a little longer.'

Jean-Anne, restored to concentration by her husband's voice, felt tears come into her eyes.

'We can't help him, of course,' said Thorstein once they were back in the car. 'He's like one of those suicide bombers in the Middle East. He's just destroying himself with his Bezzakonian T-group.'

'Surely you can do a feature?'

'He'd have to publish the novel of the century or win the Nobel Prize for it to make any difference.'

'Then it would make a difference? If he turned out to be someone special?'

'The Bezzakonians care abut their reputation. So they have to take note of other people's rules on genius. It's an inconsistency. Geniuses get a *choice*: abroad *or* Snowland.'

'He's only the age Sam was!'

Thorstein felt a lump in his throat. He didn't want to talk about their son now. He put a hand on his wife's knee.

His wife said, 'I know people think I'm old-fashioned. But my faith helps me here.'

Drops of rain hit the windscreen. Retrieving his hand, Thorstein turned on the wipers. Jean-Anne's faith was strong, though not of the kind that locates an angry God in a grey sky.

'Torry, what was the name of that district?'

'Bezumovo.'

'Bezumovo. It's all Bez something round here.'

A few weeks later Thorstein noticed that an unusual languor had come over Jean-Anne. They had dinner with Harry and Maria Blanchflower but the conversation foundered and they left early and once home retired straight to bed.

'I don't want to listen to Maria telling us we mustn't fall into that mood again. I don't want to hear you say this is an evil place either. We must *do* something.' From applying night cream in the mirror, she turned to speak to him directly.

'Life *is* hard for all of us here, Jean.' He put a paperback on the bedside table. He often didn't sleep well here.

'Because *we* are not saints, right? We can't live up to what this place demands of us.' She picked up his Le Carré, *Smiley's People*, and put it back down.

'I'm not sure going too deep into Bezzakonia is wise.'

'In that case I don't know what is.'

After she kissed him goodnight, she curled herself into a tight ball, like a creature in hibernation.

Then the languor disappeared and Jean-Anne's movements about the flat became not just as brisk as they always were, but unsettlingly purposeful. He was aware how well they had done to be married for thirty-five years and survive Sam's death. Sam died on the ski slopes of Colorado only a year after he qualified as a doctor. Sometimes when Thorstein woke in the night it was because of fear that he could no longer see his son's face.

Then the rumour that Jean-Anne was having an affair with a Bezzakonian reached Thorstein's ears. It came to him, in his best interest, from the lips of his Bezzakonian translator. Her colleagues among the block domestic staff were talking, she said. He ought to know. Jean-Anne's kitchen maid, Katya, looked at the floor in embarrassment every time she saw Thorstein, to make sure he got the message. 'Oh, surely not!' he told himself. 'We're way beyond that.' But he wasn't sure, knowing the way he responded to young women, though he never actually did anything about it. He exchanged sleep now for a nightly vigil.

Sometimes she went out before breakfast, sometimes in the early evening. She wore an old brown coat he didn't recognize, her old boots and a fur hat, and carried with her a nylon shopping bag. His wife so resembled a Bezzakonian in the crowd that the first time he followed her, on the Metro, he lost her. He lost her on another occasion in a department store that resembled to his eye a vast charity shop. But the third time she only walked to the top end of the triangular Antinomian Army park. In its apex there was a boathouse and, for the old men, a chess pavilion and a reading room. A male figure was leaning against the back wall of the boathouse. He and Jean-Anne walked together to a bench beside the water. There were no boats, for it was long past the season. Only the floes of ice from the first freeze and thaw scarred what might have been a mirror surface. Presumably the young man spoke English, for the couple talked, and at one point Jean-Anne took off her glove and squeezed his hand. Thorstein stared, and when he recognized Marlinsky he felt awe, mingled with fear.

The awe turned to self-consciousness as he walked back to his office. Had he really come to Muzeb, espionage capital of the world, to spy on his own wife? He felt hurt and had to help himself by getting things clear. But beyond that, what could he do? He decided to do nothing. Thorstein had left news management to return to the real world because he wanted to live in places that mattered and experience the world raw. He was afraid for his wife, but perhaps she also felt, as had their son, that there was something wrong with living too safely.

It was the Bezzakonian disguise Jean-Anne affected that first alerted Katya. Envious of her mistress's foreign grooming, she took it as a personal affront. When Jean-Anne missed two Wives' Circle meetings in a row it was clear something was afoot. Then there was the spring in her step, and the concentrated expression on her face. Katya divined a secret and got it officially minuted. Nadia, Roy Owedean's secretary, took then to strolling through the Antinomian park as part of her journey home every evening; and Leonid, the Owedean chauffeur, jogged and worked out there in spare hours of the day. Occasionally he took the Cadillac or even the little Brumairich for a run round the perimeter.

Young Katya giggled into his ear, 'I think our *gospozha* wants to give this handsome young man some Western consolation!'

'My personal view, to which I know I am not entitled, is that foreigners are entitled to their privacy.' Katya was a silly little trollop. Leonid hated her.

The minutes were read and re-read until eventually half a dozen Bezzakonians gathered round a green-baize table laid with beer and soft drinks. The rest, two young, two middle-aged and the ageing chairman, were dolts, but Leather Jacket was a clever man. He looked ageless, though he was, in 1979, about thirty-five. The chairman began rocking very slightly back and forth with pursed lips, like something thinking whatever thoughts are possessed by a clock. When the others became aware of the ticking, as they were meant to, he stood up, hands flat on the baize table, and peered at them. Then he reached down as if looking for a hidden microphone –

'I assure you, comrade peer, the room has been scrupulously vetted –'

Wump! Wump! Wump! The chairman, now standing in one sock, banged the table angrily with his shoe.

That's why they have baize, to muffle the blows, thought one young man, attending such a meeting for the first time, but he was afraid to whisper it to his colleague.

'I want something done!' shrieked the chairman. 'Teach this cow a lesson. Don't twit us.' The stiff fuzz of what was left of his hair looked like a plume of brown smoke.

'Don't upset yourself, comrade peer. These Westerners think it's humanity in themselves which Muzeb brings out. I can fix that.'

'Why can't these dames just screw their own men?'

'Voracious appetites the idle have, comrade peer. They don't work hard enough in their world, that's the trouble.'

'It's disgusting. Quite disgusting,' said the old man, putting back his shoe. The two young men either side of him exchanged glances. They had been thinking the same of the state of the chairman's sock.

'Whatcha gonna do? Screw 'er yourself?'

'I've got something up my sleeve, comrade peer chairman, not down my trousers.'

The meeting tittered and the chairman poured himself a glass of beer to calm his indignation.

Jean-Anne was shopping in the Bezzakonian market for bread, the good bread that everyone admired except Western children, brought up on sliced pap. A thin old woman sat against the wall, leaning forwards with her hand cupped. 'Money,' she croaked, as the foreigner passed. Jean-Anne put a finger to her lips, mindful of the danger of incriminating another helpless Bezzakonian, and fished in her bag for a handful of notes. The old woman grabbed her other hand and peered at her palm. 'I see a great reward for goodness.' Two passing Bezzakonian women made eyes at the sky, but this Jean-Anne read as official disapproval for the fortune-teller, and a sign that she herself should believe her, for her whole soul had become, through knowing Marlinsky, part of a struggle between what was real and hidden, and what only posed as real, on the official surface. Good spirits were contacting her; leading her on.

When she got back to the flat, unusually Katya was sitting reading in the kitchen. She looked embarrassed when the mistress arrived back, as if she had been caught shirking, though everything was spotless as usual.

'No, no, if you've finished early. Don't put it away. What are you reading?'

The maid put a finger to her lips. The gesture was catching, as if this whole country were a sort of tragicomedy, with liberal doses of overacting and whispering. Just as Marlinsky said. Jean-Anne followed Katya out down the back stairs, which functioned as the fire escape and also led to the rubbish chute. It was a door she never opened, beside the kitchen, for the rubbish chute didn't work. The smell of incineration and decay was overpowering. The maid held out the volume bound in purple leatherette.

'Dusheinov. He is a banned writer. You understand? This volume contains an essay about the attraction of opposites, you know, *gospozha*, how one half of the world longs for the other. Dusheinov developed a cosmic theory of the psyche.'

'Are there many Dusheinovs in Prebezzakonian literature?' When Katya introduced him he didn't sound quite the same.

'Only the one.'

'And lots of people are reading him, do you think, secretly, or just you?'

'I think all *young* people, *gospozha*. He gives us hope.'

'I wish I could read Bezzakonian.'

'You can. You can read him in English in the Great Bezum Library. If you want to understand us.'

'I didn't know that. Thank you, Katya.' She held a finger to her own lips.

Now what Jean-Anne felt for Marlinsky was so powerful it caused her torment at night. Not his youth alone, and nothing about the way he looked, or his character, because in fact his English was almost non-existent, apart from the ability to read declarations out loud. No, it was his presence; his real existence in the world. She slept in the foetal position because it was the only position in which her body did not silently offer itself to him. Curling herself up in self-preservation and waiting patiently for sleep, she found, was a way of temporarily diminishing her hunger. But the torture of his absence overrode all her previous notions of what was decent and seemly in a woman, and in a woman of her age, now desperately and suddenly aware again of her own nakedness. She had forgotten until a few months ago that she was still a woman, except in that way which involved doing her face in the mirror, and putting on jewellery, and enjoying wearing colours which flattered her face. But now nature seemed to have gone into reverse, filling her with a blind desire for sexual contact. She found herself enjoying the usual suggestive Wives' Circle gossip. It was shameful to her old self, but her new self tried to rationalize the shame. After all, it wasn't gossip, it was a fact, wasn't it, that because living conditions were so cramped and poor in Muzeb, young Bezzakonians took first-class return tickets on overnight trains to make love. One of the wives had seen a couple on a park bench. 'Of course she was underneath!' That they seemed to be talking about unjust social conditions only increased the excitement and the rather too vital sympathy. Moreover, after the shareable gossip, the tormenting solitude returned. The torment was worse because Jean-Anne was married, and she ought to have been able to conceal its origins and share it as simple joy with her husband, whom she did love. She felt embarrassment and shame.

She took the Metro and walked along the long exit passageway to the library. She mounted the granite steps which led to the main entrance. The steps rolled down like shallow waves. The library was in the massive, square-cut, classical style favoured by Bezum, from the years when Bezzakonia hoped to found a new civilization. In the frieze, inscribed in stone, were the words she had heard decried by Marlinsky: THE PARTY IS THE MIND, THE HONOUR AND THE CONSCIENCE OF OUR EPOCH.

'Are you maybe lost, *gospozha*?'

'That depends who you are.'

Jean-Anne had passed through the marble hall, walked up the red-carpeted stairs and was hovering around the wooden filing-box catalogues, wondering if there was an information desk. Her interlocutor was dressed all in black, with a leather jacket.

'I work here with foreigners because I speak many languages. *Hablo espagnol. Parlo italiano. Mowię po polsku.* You see?'

'If you speak English you can make yourself useful.' She instantly distrusted him. But she needed help. She showed him a piece of squared paper on which Katya had written the name Dusheinov in Bezzakonian.

He nodded. 'This way.'

They passed the glass-door entrances to the various graded and censored reading rooms. She hesitated.

'No. Come, come!' He pressed her shoulder.

They finally descended some broad wooden back stairs, which existed like an answering gesture to the red-carpeted flight out front, and found themselves in the library back basement. There was no decoration. The walls and wooden floor seemed steeped in urine, so acrid was the air from wherever the conveniences were, if there were any. The smart man seemed all the more suspect. His smartness could signal his genuine interest in the fashionable West, or he was an informer.

'You haven't told me yet. Who are you?' She looked round at the various individuals drinking from thermos flasks, eating sandwiches from plastic boxes, drinking syrup water from filthy five-copeck green dispensers. This was where library users descended to carry out the necessary functions of the body.

'I'm a friend of the wise. It's true I keep an eye on foreigners. But you needn't be suspicious.'

'Will I find the work of Dusheinov here?'

He grinned, exposing yellow teeth. 'Indeed you will, a form of it. Come.'

In the malodorous basement, a small door led into a large dark room. There was a crackly version of Western 1960s pop music playing, which reminded her of Sam's childhood: the Beatles singing 'All You Need is Love', and a curiously thin, unblended and innocent sound from even earlier, a song about 'Walking Back to Happiness'. The age of blue jeans and free love came too late for us, she and Thorstein used to joke, to Sam's embarrassment. They caught the tail end of liberation through their son.

'Where did you get the music? I thought it was forbidden.'

The record player was a vinyl suitcase box with a gilded built-in speaker. Beside it, on the only table in the room, rested a tape recorder with spools the size of saucers.

'Some records from friends in the West. Mostly we tape it off the BBC and VOA. Anyway, how do you like it, *gospozha*, real underground Bezzakonia?' There was something both sad and insinuating in his voice.

'That's not what I want! I came here to read Dusheinov.'

'And we wanted to show you that we understand your desires. We have them too. You see them all around you. But our rules forbid us to carry these desires into the open.'

Now that she could see better in the half-light, it seemed that about twenty people were sitting on the floor. Jean-Anne recognized some of the au pairs. The Swedish redhead was dancing close, while the pale, slender girl from Yorkshire was lying full-length next to another Bezzakonian man. Naked, they were gazing at each other, and stroking each other's hair.

'Sit down.'

Leather sat beside her on the floor of the dry, dark meadow. The music changed. She recognized something by the Rolling Stones: 'Some girls are so pure, others so corrupt . . .' Leather sat beside her, his beautiful white hands laced across his knees. He had taken his jacket off and pushed up his sleeves, to reveal forearms which seemed more muscular than the rest of his body, and which were streaked with dark hair. She felt giddy and careless. The sexual pounding of that kind of music had never sounded so lascivious to her ears, and perhaps she leaned towards him, because Leather Jacket's lips touched her neck.

He whispered, 'Where East and West love each other. Where pressures are shed. We call it the Dusheinov Club. We can bring your young man here for you, if you like.'

She slapped him. 'This is a vile place you've brought me to.'

'No more than what is in your own mind. Many true things about the psyche are vile.'

A young girl caught sight of Leather and he returned her languid wave.

'Your "club" is not in my mind.'

'Are you sure? Don't you remember what you felt, when Sam's friends came to stay and you saw them half-naked, coming back from the swimming –'

Leather received a second blow to his face. 'We don't have a swimming pool. You're just making all this up.'

'What am I making up? You're exploiting that boy. You believe he is "the underground movement". But *this* is the only underground movement there is in Bezzakonia.'

'Marlinsky has nothing to do with a place like this.'

The Blanchflowers' au pair girl, Sinistra, came over, nodded as if she didn't really recognize Jean-Anne and accepted a glass of Bezzakonian champagne. She leaned on Leather Jacket's shoulder. 'I don't know what I'm doing.'

He stroked her hair. 'But you're enjoying it.'

Jean-Anne exclaimed, 'That girl's coming home with me.'

But Leather Jacket continued to stroke the foreign girl like a child. 'I'll look after her. Trust me. She's abandoned herself here, and she accepts it.'

Jean-Anne re-examined the dark cavern in which they sat on the floor. The place tricked their senses into supposing they existed entirely in the night-time of life: a time for relaxing, lying low, sleeping. Another kind of hibernation, if that was possible. Even in love and death it seemed, Bezzakonia showed, there was a choice of path, though the ways had the same names.

'You see, *gospozha*, what Dusheinov showed is how ingenious the human capacity is to distil sexual pleasure from strife, from frustration, from twisted longing, as if, one might say, this is the condition for the human race to survive, that its libido is stirred as much, I think indeed much more, by misery, by absence, by pain, than by simple "beauty" and "happiness". Across the divide between your world and ours – like the discovery of the opposite sex – you – and our Sinistra Luck here – have discovered the attraction of the other *because* it is other, not because it is good.'

'I want to leave.'

She clung to her good choice. But Leather cast Sinistra aside and pulled Jean-Anne up and held her so tightly that she became afraid; afraid that she would respond to him and lose her grip on what she cared for.

'You are rather like your young friend Marlinsky, *gospozha*. You are both proud, so we have to teach you this lesson. You see, as long as there are two worlds which do not directly and openly interact, both sides will wreak these great deceptions, which lead to passionate adulation by the one for the other. It is the pride of the mind suddenly entering the body's realm, or the pride of the body feeling it has at last a *decent* inspiration,' he scoffed. 'You *straddle* this divide, *gospozha*, this stimulating gap between Bezzakonia and the West, between mind and body, and, well, can you picture it, picture yourself, enjoying it as pleasure? You can, can't you? *That's all it is. He fancies your world and you fancy his.*'

He set her down on a springless sofa with stainless-steel arms and threadbare brown-velvet cushions as if he were going to come over her, then he stepped back. She was lying on cast-off furniture from some fashionable foreign apartment.

'It's like a rubbish dump in here.'

'We're talking about your feelings, don't forget. Drink?'

'No.'

Jean-Anne lay instinctively in the foetal curve. 'So this is where you Bezzakonians have feelings you daren't express in public.'

'Our world would collapse if we did express them. Our country is called Bezzakonia, as you know. That means "without rules". It's a sort of reminder of how we would be without our rulers imposing order. A serious joke. Everywhere would be like this.'

'It would be primitive. It is primitive. You're like savages.'

'We show you your soul. That is our job in the world, quite possibly.'

'You haven't the faintest idea of the life of the soul.'

'Come now! I have read great writers too, *madame*.'

Suddenly Leather sprang up, stamped on the dull, scuffed parquet floor and spat three times over his left shoulder.

'Cockroach.'

'Why the left shoulder?'

'To ward off bad luck.'

'You people are not only primitive but *stupid*,' she burst out laughing, and the laughter culminated in a trickle of tears.

He shrugged. 'It's just another way of letting the psyche

breathe.' He took her hand and this time pulled her up like an old friend. 'All right, Mrs Meyerssen. We are very basic. If you don't think you are like us, what more can I do? I have tried.' He switched on a lamp beside the old couch and the music stopped.

'You've tried to make me hate myself.'

'I have a friend upstairs who will drive you home.'

'You tell your driver to fuck his mother, Mr whoeveryouare.' She took a deep breath. 'I shall of course be making a complaint to the authorities.'

'Quite so.' He saw her back up the urine-soaked staircase into the main building of the Great Bezum Library. 'They will make a complaint about you too, *gospozha*, for pursuing anti-Bezzakonian causes. I only wanted to help you understand where your love for our rebels might lead you.'

She shouted something back at him from the top of the red staircase, over the heads of the thronged researchers at the catalogue boxes.

'Where my love for your rebels might lead me?' She pulled on the brown coat and hat in a fury and took the third Metro line to the final station. There was snow on the ground, which gave the patch of scrubland between the road and the river a certain glamour.

Marlinsky liked to meet near water. 'Something to do with being born under the sign of Aquarius.'

'You're not superstitious too, are you?'

He nodded. 'In some ways I belong to my people. Don't be disappointed in me. I've brought you a present.' There was an actor's deliberateness in his tone, as if he knew they were being watched, and it reminded her she knew nothing about him as a person, only of the impression he made as a visitor in her world. He unwrapped a paper parcel and spread out a beautiful garment on the bench. 'It's a jacket in the style of one of our folk costumes. Perhaps you will wear it sometimes and think of me.'

She ran her fingers over the embroidery. 'It's magnificent.'

'Some "primitive" things about us are good.'

'Oh yes,' she replied hastily.

He smiled vaguely.

'I know what Western people think. Won't you put it on, under your coat? That way you won't lose it.' '

'Oh yes, I see.'

He helped her into the stiff, heavy ceremonial garment which only a loose Bezzakonian coat could have covered, and whispered something in her ear.

The Wives organized a shopping trip to Arcadia in the first week of December. A department store in the capital had become so wise to the needs of the expatriate community in Bezzakonia that it offered special facilities on its administrative floor, which included at this time of year the packing and posting of Christmas presents. To mail anything from Muzeb was too uncertain; many things were stolen.

The Wives took two neighbouring train compartments and crammed into one to enjoy a champagne picnic on the journey out. They made lists and retired to their bunks in high spirits, full of thoughts of friends and family across the world, and the kind of relief which always descended at the prospect of crossing the border.

When the guards boarded before dawn everyone woke with the noise of voices. Jean-Anne heard a dog's claws scratching against the corridor walls. Knocks on all the doors sounded down the carriage. The door slid back and two men in uniform stood, one demanding passports. The other signalled 'Out of the way!' and shoved his hand down the back of the lower seats. He pulled back the still-warm sheets. 'Open the bags!' The dog arrived with his handler, but their compartment disappointed him. No raw meat. The more zealous of the two guards took a copy of *Lolita* out of Jean-Anne's bag. Eventually he said, handing it back, 'This is pornography. Please do not bring it back into Bezzakonia.'

'I'd be happy to argue it through with you.'

He waved a hand. '*Thenkyou*, ladies.'

Jean-Anne said to her friends, 'They're so prudish in this country!'

They smiled uneasily, aware she had a secret, jealous of it. The train jolted forwards a few hundred yards. Then the Arcadians came to see the passports, and their men, in splendid white peaked caps, saluted.

Thorstein laughed with so much relief, the tears ran down his face. They had Christmas dinner alone: a roast chicken with tinned vegetables and imported Arcadian crackers, and People's champagne.

'What do you mean? Torry, you didn't think, at my age ... what would a young man want? Oh, sweetheart!' She was lying and telling the truth at one and the same time.

'You were so driven by something.'

I was, she thought, by love, but not really love of a boy, or not only.

She switched to miming, but he couldn't follow. So she wrote it on a piece of paper. 'I took out Marlinsky's manuscript. I had to keep it secret from you. With your job, you're so vulnerable. I kept thinking of Roy Owedean.'

He made a question with his arms.

'Onion skins sewn into the jacket. I sent it to Christine with instructions what to do. There are publishing houses in London always interested in this kind of thing.'

He shook his head in wonderment and reached for the People's champagne. 'Here's to you and my sister! The women in my life.'

Jean-Anne drank with one hand and held the paper in the candleflame in the other.

'The Bezzakonians will know in the end.'

'They know a great deal. But they don't know how to act on it. They just speculate.'

'You don't say!'

The Meyerssens were both rather drunk, in the end, courtesy of the Bezzakonian people. Praying the phone would not ring with work, they intended to spend the rest of Christmas Day lying on the sofa.

7

K FOR CORRESPONDENT

Eamon Cole heard the long tones of a Bezzakonian telephone. It was evening, around nine. No secretary manned the ill-lit IFN office and the other four workstations with their unoccupied typewriters slept in ugly silence. The diagonal crack in the yellowed ceiling seemed to be growing.

'International Figures and News,' he began in English, then, '*Agentsvo EEeffenna. Kak vam pomoch?*'

The other voice was muffled and the line across the city poor. The call might have been coming from Snowland. Eamon, who had been in Bezzakonia a few weeks, deciphered Piperov. What? He stalled for time to tune in his ear. Then he began writing with one of the pencils Lyuba sharpened before she went home every day. Lyuba was their Bezzakonian secretary.

Muzeb, 1 Feb. IFN – Nobel Peace Laureate Peter Piperov has appealed to the Bezzakonian leader, Bezum III, to reopen proceedings against three Christians executed early this year for a bomb attack on the Muzeb Metro in January 1977. Piperov accused Bezzakonian authorities of a travesty of justice over the executions of the men, who, he said, were not in Muzeb during the bombing.

In a separate statement Piperov, who has been harassed by security police for his monitoring of Christian rights, also accused Fortress Muzeb of persecuting Jews wanting to return to their homeland.

In Muzeb history stood over your shoulder like a schoolmaster. You were writing in the book of life every time you drew up a typewriter or lifted a pen. But Eamon had already put in a letter home to his parents that he was getting used to things. The teleprinter, as he clumsily tapped the keys, produced a stream of white paper tape punched with tiny holes. This news line he fed by computer to London.

'Holding the fort, I see.'

Gerald Pike leaned over the printer to read the recently dispatched report. He was dressed in a new-looking sweatshirt and he smelt of roast chicken. Relaxed by wine, he tried to relinquish his authority, but he sounded patronizing.

'Just a couple of stories.' Eamon felt he wasn't quite trusted to apply himself alone.

'Bedtime stories are all I've told this evening. Still, that's family life for you.'

Eamon wondered if he was supposed openly to envy Pike family life, for Pike did this every evening, strolled from his apartment to see how the unmarried junior was coping. He called over to Pike's back. 'I'm working on an in-depther about Bezzakonian justice, trying to pull a few threads together. That American who was framed for smuggling samovars, for instance. Even Roy Owedean's case. And these Christians. The Bezzakonians don't care who they sacrifice.'

'See what you come up with then.' Pike turned. 'But there's no need to be brilliant here, Cole. Both high-flyers and also-rans can do well in Muzeb. Understood? Your car's ready, by the way. We can pick it tomorrow, if nothing comes up.'

'That would be great.'

Eamon hungered for that little independence available to foreigners, to drive his own car, but he was perplexed, because he felt Pike treated its provision as a favour, and wanted something unspecified in return.

'Around ten then.'

'Thanks again.'

Pike, strolling back home across the yard, felt pleased with himself. Like his family, the office ran so smoothly under his guidance that the whole world, which shared one sky and one humanity, seemed peaceful.

They scanned the overnight news files, but nothing demanded immediate action. Pike liked it that way. He liked peace. The office driver dropped them in IFN's yellow Riva at the factory delivery yard on Bezpamyatny Chausée. Hundreds of new cars waited like shackled creatures with their tongues cut out.

'What colour would you like, sir, mustard or mustard?'

Eamon grinned. The sturdy Brumairich was a bargain at two thousand pounds, with payment over twelve months deducted from his London salary. Pike, using his seniority, had set up an interest-free deal and Eamon reckoned, since he didn't pay tax in expatriate Bezzakonia, he would hardly miss the money. Eamon watched as Pike signed some papers in the transparent booth of a man in overalls. He paid in local cash from the office account.

'It's great to be behind a wheel again.'

'I need my correspondents to function, Cole. That doesn't contradict what I said last night. A steady input keeps London happy.'

What was it about Pike, Eamon wondered. He didn't obviously take exception to Bezzakonia, the way others did, and yet he wasn't for it either. He seemed almost without personal views.

The day, dry and dull, was ideal for a test run. As Eamon pulled away, he noticed faces peering over the fence around the pound. Getting used to the gear shift in his right hand, he let the new

101

saloon, with its blank smell of plastic and the rubber mats underfoot, bounce over the exit ramp into a metalled side street. He fumbled for the indicator on the wrong side. This time he definitely saw two youngish Bezzakonian men in anoraks and woolly hats with their eyes to the pound fence.

'It's only normal. There's a five-year waiting list here for a Brumairich, unless you know someone. Even then it's not easy to get all those *senti* together. Poor buggers. Shall we take her out of town? Better get some petrol first. The Bezzakonians make their petrol tanks small, and there aren't enough garages.'

Eamon laughed. 'Alice-in-Wonderland planning.'

'Just that. No one knows why. They've more than their share of geniuses. Take a right here.'

The filling station displayed no signs or prices.

'You really know Muzeb.'

'I ought to. I've been here almost a quarter of my life.'

'No regrets? We hated it as students. It didn't seem like a good place to have fun.'

'But now you can see it's all one world.'

'I can see it's a privilege.' Eamon took two foreigners' blue petrol coupons from his wallet. A Bezzakonian motorist and a couple of women passing stared at his numberplate: K-603 MUZ.

'K for correspondent. You're someone here, my friend. A target for attention. That's why they're looking.'

'Mostly I feel less than someone,' said Eamon.

'I thought you just said it was a privilege.'

'I didn't mean it like that.' Eamon meant Romantic privilege, something only madmen and poets would be thankful for, but he didn't feel he could tell Pike that.

They headed for the Outer Ring Road, where there was no other leisure traffic and only a few lorries. The trainee with the jet-black hair of youth, following his boss's instructions, accelerated along the empty white road.

'Heavy but she goes well.'

'They start well in the cold. The Brumairich is one of the best things Bezzakonia makes.'

The car was smooth and quiet. Eamon tried the radio. The Beacon station played lightened versions of classical orchestral music and gave regular announcements of Muzeb time. American Forces Network broadcast a noisy, self-congratulatory rival service.

'Where were you before?'

'Madrid. Nice cushy posting, you know? Great food. Then South America.'

'And you really prefer Muzeb?'

'I took a decision, Cole. Right or wrong, it's in the past. It's like being married to the wrong woman. You've no choice but to get to know her.'

Pike probably wasn't talking about his own marriage. The Pikes were famous for being a family. On the other hand, just as the arable state of these fields around them was unclear, and the edges of the road were unmarked, so perhaps was the Pike marriage.

Suddenly a man on the verge sprang into Eamon's rear-view mirror, waving his arms frantically. Eamon reversed before Pike had a chance to intervene and wound down the stiff window.

'Your wheel's falling off,' the Bezzakonian voice rasped in a tone half-merry, half-grumbling at the shoddiness of the world. The face peering out of a red woollen hat was bearded, and what skin was visible was grey.

'What?'

'I said your wheel's falling off. You'd better be careful.'

'Thanks, citizen peer, all the best to you.' Pike added a few phrases in his impressively colloquial Bezzakonian and waved the creature away. 'Don't listen, Cole. They always try stunts like that. They like to test what power they have over foreigners. What would you expect, though? They've been living here even longer than I have.'

The demonic figure in Eamon's mirror walked on, seemingly from nowhere to nowhere, since no villages were in sight.

'You mean they're all bonkers?'

'I think so,' laughed Pike. 'That's why people like you and me have to keep checking our sanity. To make sure we haven't caught the germ.'

'How do we do that?'

'Remember this is just a job. Don't get involved.'

Eamon drove slowly just in case the wheel was loose. He couldn't imagine not being involved.

Central Muzeb's Revolution Square was an unnerving experience to negotiate on the way back. It was huge and empty, with room enough for two thousand soldiers, maybe more, and no motorist could see far enough to make his turn with certainty. Eamon was behind five other cars when his filter light turned green, and by the time he got across the other stream of traffic had started to move against him. He parked outside the militia box which kept Bezzakonians from entering the ghetto. The guard in grey waved.

'Is he worth tipping to keep an eye on things?'

'No. He'll steal your windscreen wipers as soon as the next man. Take them with you if you don't want to be ordering new ones from Arcadia every week.'

'Thanks, Gerald, thanks for everything.'

'Don't mention it. Glad to help.'

Eamon got as far as the office, then remembered he had forgotten the wipers.

He often went driving after that morning. The heavy car was short on kinetic thrills, but it made him feel under way, and the importance of being K-603 MUZ took the edge off his loneliness for a few hours on Saturday afternoon. Petrol, though not cheap for Bezzakonians, was a bargain for foreigners. It was the first thing Eamon as a reporter remembered knowing certainly about Bezzakonia. When he picked up a news report on a space rocket delivering fuel to an orbiting station, he commented that things were not so efficient on Bezzakonian earth, unless a person had special contacts, and Pike said that was good. That was the softly, softly way to do it.

The Brumairich was stationary at traffic lights at the Bezum Square intersection of Bezum Street and Bezpamyatny Chaussée.

Eamon was close to home. Suddenly a tall figure loomed over the front windscreen and was pressing the handle of the passenger door. 'What the hell . . . what the blazes do you think you're doing?' he cried. He was afraid and didn't know whether to accelerate and save himself, but risk injuring the attacker, or freeze like a cornered cat. He thought this highway robber must be on drugs.

'*Khigh.*' The figure who climbed in took off its fur hat and plumped its hair. It turned to him in the dark and uttered that greeting, which had an unfamiliar gutteral charm in Bezzakonian, and sounded more like a password. '*Khigh.*'

His heart was banging. It was a woman. She had thick dull blonde hair, the kind that seems contained in a halo of static, loosely fastened at the nape. She had a young face.

Cars were hooting behind him. 'God in heaven, what do you think you're doing?' He made the left turn homewards involuntarily.

'Don't you need a friend?'

He pulled over by the market. 'Not at the cost of being hijacked.'

She was pale, with blue eyeshadow and a frosted pink on her lips. The lips crinkled into a smile. She was about twenty.

'We could go for a coffee,' he said.

'We could go to bed. Are you not a man?'

The initial shock dissipated. Desire, desire for any woman, began to plait itself into threads inside him. They tangled and knotted when he remembered the militiaman, but perhaps this woman existed to smooth out his life.

'You do need a friend. Muzeb is a lonely place for an Englishman.'

'I'm from Northern Ireland. From Belfast. You know?'

'It's the same for me.' She put a hand on his knee.

'But how will I get you past the *miliman*?'

'Don't worry.'

They parked and as they walked past, the man slouching under the stiff grey coat winked.

'You must know people.'

'Many.'

He shrugged. He would go with his fate.

Eamon would remember that night for the rest of his life. He was in the kitchen pouring two whiskeys as Asya seemed to sway towards him, down the long corridor from the bathroom, her bare feet soundless on the dull parquet. She had long legs, small breasts, boyish hips. His clothes must be rough against her bare skin, he thought, as she hung on to his neck and sucked at his lips like the female of another species. Her white body had already yielded to him like a shot swan thrown over his shoulder, and he worried absurdly about treading on her toes, trying half to lead and half to carry her into the small bedroom with the unappealing turquoise velvet curtains. She smelt of artificial sweetness and her armpits were acrid. She dug her fingernails into him, bit his neck. It was all a bit of a feline performance, which left him with battle scars, and a feeling of deep peace. She was still beside him in the morning.

'Asya,' he said, as if checking he remembered her name.

She threw off the sheet and blankets to examine his body. There were stretch marks between his waist and buttocks, where she ran her curious fingers.

'I have a tendency to put on weight. Journalism's not a healthy profession to have chosen.'

She breathed an aspirate commiseration through her pretty, small nose. She didn't talk much. She coaxed him as if he were wet clay being moulded into a pot, and squeezed so much feeling out of him he wanted to cry.

'You're beautiful. Can you put up with me? Say you'll come back tonight.'

'Yes, Ay-mon.'

After that he worked with such a will, because he had to proclaim Asya to the whole world. His job was to understand every curve and fold of her body, which was indivisible from the mystery of Bezzakonia. Caress by caress, he would learn how it was possible to be happy here.

He wrote two or three 'soft' stories, which just happened to be the jargon, every day. They lacked the sharpness of superpower confrontation and contained no diplomatic intricacies, but he was sure that was what he should report. The thin, densely packed Bezzakonian newspapers, without the visual leaven of advertising, described how people led their overcrowded, poorly housed lives. He learned to interpret them. There was a shortage of foods and medicines, love was a game of chance and life was cheap. Asya told him about thick, unreliable condoms and no contraceptive pills. (Except in her case. How did you get them, then? I know someone.) All women had abortions. (And you? Already? Yes, once.) 'This is the way for Bezzakonian women. They must destroy themselves.' He felt hurt for her. (You sure you're on the pill? Yes.) He held her tight, as he held her tight in his stories, and felt he was in love.

He reported that Bezzakonians compensated for their drab subjection to necessity by wildly celebrating birthdays and namedays. Muzeb was the most convivial city in the world behind closed doors. Bezzakonians devoted all their spare time, a joke that, he thought, but still, let's say, all their spare time, to acquiring foreign jeans and sexy tights and classy leather boots, and secretly listening to the BBC, though presently, with Cold War tension high, it was jammed silent. Musical life suffered. From his window, Eamon watched the music exchange in the Antinomian Army park on Saturday mornings, where bootleg tapes of John Travolta's *Saturday Night Fever* and the new *Some Girls* album by the Rolling Stones changed pockets.

Muzeb, 10 Feb. IFN – The most radical political country in our time has Victorian values when it comes to love. The Bezzakonian media talk about 'intimate nearness' and 'romantic love' to address a growing problem of sexual promiscuity. There is a high demand for abortions, and a soaring divorce rate.

Western observers say the opposite is true to the picture painted in the conservative media.

Sex is widely regarded as a diversion in a country which has little entertainment to offer.

Living conditions are overcrowded, with often three generations coexisting in a two-bedroom apartment. Young Bezzakonians say that's why the cheap weekend sleeper trains between Muzeb and Bezumgrad are oversubscribed. The 20-hour round trip is a rare chance to enjoy 'intimate nearness' in privacy.

In this atheist country there is no morality advocating sexual restraint, although Bezum II quickly threw out the early Bezumian advocacy of free love as unworkable.

'Good,' Pike reacted to the story on the printer. But his next words sounded rehearsed. 'Eamon, I heard on the grapevine you had a Bezzakonian girlfriend and Marion wondered if you'd both like to come over for a meal. What about Tuesday?'

'I'll have to check. Sorry, it sounds almost as if I'm married, Pike. I'm not used to speaking for two.'

'Just let us know by the weekend.'

He asked her that evening, but Asya refused. You've met him before? How can you have met Pike before? But of course the militiaman knew her. Perhaps she'd had an affair with Cole's own predecessor and had known this flat before he did. He decided not to ask. He only longed to see her again.

'He was furious when I told him.'

'Sure. He is furious because he can't manipulate you. Like this.'

Eamon groaned and sprawled flat on the bed. Asya was amused.

'He's jealous. He's afraid you'll find out he's second-rate. There. Now don't spoil it by lying crooked. Lie flat. Look up at me.'

Eamon turned and felt he was lying on air and pulled her down to him. 'I don't suppose he has work in mind. Any man would be jealous over you.'

'I think so.'

The bedroom was so small in the junior flat that the double bed touched the window-ledge. Asya, who had the Bezzakonian gift for making even clutter useful, introduced the wooden sill into their lovemaking. She held it tight, so that her knuckles were white and her flat belly and her hard breasts rose and fell in one movement like a swingboat; like a white swan. Afterwards she changed her mortal substance to velvet sand and engulfed him.

'This is good,' she said calmly. Like history stood over his news reports Asya stood over his life. Never with so much force had he wanted to exist.

'Ay-mon, I want to tell you something about your boss. But you must pay me. You must pay me for the things we talk about. My love is free, but not what I know. The things I tell you use in stories, I know that. That's OK, but I have to live too. You get paid for your reporting. I think when you are in bed with me you never stop being a little bit the foreign correspondent. Right?'

'How much do you want?'

'One hundred *senti* a night.'

The cost of three tanks of petrol! He would have paid it for her sanity alone. 'My wallet's in the other room.'

'Now listen.'

A solitary evening loomed. He begged her not to leave. In the hall she fixed him with her fearless gaze. The brown coat was the same one she wore when she was a hijacker. He stroked the sleeve.

'Your eyes are not English.'

'I told you, I'm from Ulster.'

'Ulster.' She made his birthplace sound like the name Alistair. He imagined for himself an exotic new ancestor. It was part of the distraction she sprayed in his eyes, the confusion she wreaked on his senses. Before he was fully himself again she was out of the door. The pain of growing up at twenty-eight hurt. It hurt so much he couldn't stay in. He grabbed his sheepskin and his Fir Tree Stores fur hat and his gloves and dashed out into the night, to walk for walking's sake against the homeward-bound crowd.

Impoverished Bezzakonia was the sober core of a universe intoxicated by wealth. When you dug down to the centre of the earth, you came to Bezzakonia. Any decent man would want to defend this realm, even if he despised its political origins. The whole centrifugal force of the globe had been harnessed to crush human ambition and destroy life's joy, but something lived on, resurrected. Soon Eamon was sweating inside the sheepskin. The weather had turned milder. The black sky sprinkled a soft paste of snow and rain over the anonymous army of Muzeb pedestrians, in whose ranks he mingled, grateful for a hiding place.

An eye filled the squint-hole. Pat opened the door.

'Hi, Eamon, this is . . .'

'I know, I should have phoned. Is Roy in?'

Roy emerged in stockinged feet, sleeves rolled up. The jeans, the blue shirt over the white T-shirt, made him just as he wanted readers of the *Mail* to imagine him, Eamon thought.

Eamon jerked his head back towards the door. 'Come for a walk? It's a great evening.'

Pat felt something for Eamon. He had a purpose. She fetched her husband's padded coat. Roy knelt and laced his boots.

They took a stroll round the block, past the ironmonger's shop, and the chemist's. A small crowd at the bus stop identified them as anti-Egalitarian spies and pretended to have seen nothing.

'But what do you want me to do about it? Your boss is not guilty under any legal code because none applies here. Expats are pretty much immune, like diplomats. The most you can do is denounce him to your company. That's a gamble. If he has friends in high places, you can probably kiss goodbye to your career with IFN. I don't like your boss, never have liked him, but I don't see what can be done.'

Roy merely set out the problem, but Eamon felt relieved, now that his burden was an object in the world.

'Thanks for listening.'

'Won't you come up?'

'I need to be alone. Thanks all the same.'

He counted cars on Bezum Street for a while, then took the Metro home. The President of Bezzakonia, Bezum III, famous for his collection of foreign limousines, had the wisdom, or the low cunning, not to drive about in them, in case of arousing uncontrollable envy. What are we talking about here, Asya? Not about envy, but about bloody injustice.

The flat smelt of the heavy, old-fashioned French perfume he had given Asya. Neither recipient nor donor knew that olefactory fashions had moved beyond the Chanels of Eamon's mother's generation. He nursed an Irish whiskey and played Elton John. The choice of music was wrong. The modern, pacifist tone sounded not charming but weak and fey. He flipped through his student collection. The sound of an old record of Beethoven's Fifth Symphony when he put it on the turntable might have come out of a tin can. Yet it was regal. He banged his head against the soft sofa-back in time with the victory march. Four scatter cushions from Arcadia he threw one by one across the room.

He was waiting for the office to close. After the eight o'clock news programme, unless there was a new story, whoever was on duty would send a closedown message to London, check the overnight printers had paper and leave. The windows were visible from the yard. At quarter to nine they were dark. Eamon, minus his outdoor jacket, but with a black rubber torch he kept for the car protruding from his pocket, advanced in giant, dream-like strides. With his staff key he let himself in. The repetitive clatter of Bezzakonia's and IFN's uninterrupted world news service assaulted his ears but assuaged his heart: the printers pulsated like warm bodies in the depopulated wilderness.

Pike's desk drawers weren't locked. Eamon found, under a picture of twenty-four poses of two pairs of entwined feet, responding with various pressures to the act of love, a recent report on his work. Mr Cole unfortunately shows signs of persistent immaturity in his attitude to the job, and possibly for some personal reason, unsuitable for a newsman, shies away from the hard news on which success here depends. The report reminded Eamon of a changed will. He crept back home and slept badly on another whiskey.

'Gerald, I'd like to see you in private if you've got a moment.'

111

'I have to be at the Foreign Ministry at two-thirty. Can it be quick?' Pike was wearing a suit to pull rank. It was a small device he seemed to have learned from the Bezzakonian fondness for the visual pecking order.

Eamon stood ten yards from where he had read his professional obituary the night before. No one else was visibly in earshot. He revealed what Asya had told him.

'This car business. I can't believe it. I would never have accepted to be part of it, had I known.'

'Why? Who's losing? When you sell your car at the end of your stint you'll be glad of a wodge of hard currency to take home.'

'Five times more than I paid for it? I'm not used to making a profit on old cars. I thought that was just a joke.'

'Grow up, Cole. This is a rotten place, as you know. You might as well gain something at the Fortress's expense. After all the misery they put us through.' He glanced at the grey window. The mild weather had reverted to snow, which was knocking like grapeshot at the outside glass.

Pike pressed his hands together. Eamon thought of the feet in the drawer, and of the kind of sluggish human embrace he, Eamon Cole, beloved of Asya, would never again accept.

'What is crime when this whole system is a crime? If you think about it you'll surely see that any means to the end of our survival here as reporters is a good one. There must be some diversion, and some reward, otherwise who would choose to live for years in hell, when heaven is only an air ticket away?'

'We're stealing.'

'So are thousands of banks and governments and institutions across the world. The Bezzakonians steal people's lives. At the same time life ticks over for most of us. It's all you can hope for.'

'All I can hope for?'

'If you want to maintain your place in the real world.'

'My job?'

'That's what most people mean by it.'

Pike got up. Eamon turned away, into the main office.

The driver came in to take Pike to the wedding-cake

skyscraper on the Ring in the yellow Riva. Pike rammed on his fur hat in response to the snow.

Eamon could at least bury himself in work while he still had it. Two young men from the T— region had expressed a belief in the Christian God. This God, they said, forbade them to inform on their fellow men. This God decreed it was wrong to promote human suffering, and He declared that to profit from evil was evil, whatever its worldly name. So, early in 1979 the young men were taken before psychiatrists, who diagnosed religious conscience as an illness threatening sanity. The things people suddenly knew more about in Muzeb were sex and madness, thought Eamon. It was true of him. So why not for Roy and Pat, and even Pike? The struggle for sanity over the darker forces of human nature was reported in the centre pages of *The Bezzakonian Truth*. It *was* true.

The back page, meanwhile, reported a huge air crash. It came in a single paragraph, ringed in red biro by the translator, who served two masters.

'Why can't they face up to it? In the West this would be headline news.'

Lyuba had chin–length dark hair and plump cheeks. No other Western office in Muzeb was favoured with such a young and pretty secretary. Eamon was supposed to let her get away with saying, 'I don't know,' because those were the terms on which she was employed. But he persisted.

'It's inhuman. They'd do anything to persuade the world this is paradise. They don't care how many lives they destroy in the process. Agree with me Lyuba. You must.'

She avoided his eyes. He was breaching office etiquette. They all had to rub along together. Otherwise there would be no foreign correspondents in Muzeb. No news would get out at all.

'I have seen many correspondents here, Eamon. I have been working for IFN for ten years. You are the most naïve.' One breach of etiquette deserved another.

He subsided, but his thoughts blazed. Air crashes were messy things, the sort of things well-mannered people didn't talk about in public. It wasn't cultured to mix up with public celebrations of

113

heroic achievements, and cheery optimism about the betterment of society, talk of twisted limbs and burnt corpses, severed torsos and ownerless belongings scattered over the unconcerned tundra. No, none of this could be decently spoken of in a land which didn't believe in the immortal soul. Yet see it from their point of view. To talk openly of disasters in Bezzakonia was like staring with death in mind at a cripple's withered leg, or a stroke victim's disjointed face, instead of focusing on their sound parts and inviting them to hail the future. Thus, if there was no God, there was the Bezzakonian spirit. But if there was neither, this world was humanity on the scrap heap, a pile of human debris. Or, from their point of view, if Bezzakonia was not perfect, no life was entitled to be.

With trembling legs Eamon typed his stories, containing none of this. Yet the experts who read them, who knew the truth of Bezzakonian psychiatry and Bezzakonian aviation, and the view of cheap, manipulable human life they shared, would know and add it to the great dossier of incrimination.

Lyuba. He looked at her intelligent, sensual face. An Egalitarian intellectual of low rank. Educated, middle-class functionary. The higher people rose, the greater must become the competing Faustian pressures inside.

'Any queries from London, I'll be back in a couple of hours.' He grabbed his coat and patted the pocket for his car keys.

No soothsayer hailed him from the verge this time as he drove out to the village of Mnogoderev to visit a woman called Belinda, who had given him her card at the embassy New Year do. Outside the two-storey wooden villa stood a shaggy brown bear all of eight feet tall. A dumb waiter from another age of entertainment. Belinda lived in some style, unlike Bezzakonians who were not Bezum III and his closest advisers.

'You got my message?'

'Yes.' Belinda, though plump around the hips and visibly wearing three layers of woollens, was still an English rose, marooned at forty-five in the insanitary suburb it had been the tradition since Bezum II to reserve as a treat for writers of the right persuasion.

'I knew you'd do things differently.'

'We have a bit of scope out here. Scope for large pieces of furniture that is. We're not so cooped up as in the town. I hoped Gyorgy would be here.'

He followed her through the baronial hall into the dark kitchen. A country table and a rectangular white sink made it seem undesigned, pre-war, and rustic, like a feeding place for common beasts with straw underfoot. But there was a warm stove.

'But he's away on business.'

'It's you I wanted to talk to. You may think it's impertinent –'

Something about Belinda's age, not far off his mother's, made him defer to her, even in this wretched situation of every man, woman and child for himself.

'I wanted to know what makes it possible for you to live like this. The double life. Your husband writes for London newspapers and works for the Fortress. Everyone out here knows that. Yet no one says so. How? What makes it possible? And even supposing the two intelligence services are in agreement, how can you do it, Mrs Belinda Byam-Pring, with your two sons at Eton?'

'Won't you call me Bela Viktorovich? I've grown to prefer it. I've just made a batch of scones for the ambassador. Would you like one? The kettle's nearly boiled. Here, take a seat. Maybe afterwards you would like to look at Gyorgy's library.'

Three bunches of dried roses hung from the ceiling. On the worktop beyond the wooden draining board stood a jar of Chiver's marmalade and a large box of Kellogg's cornflakes. He bit into the buttered scone.

'Can you bear the tea without milk? Bezzakonian milk just doesn't taste the same.'

'Do you often cook for the ambassador?'

'It gives me a role, Mr Cole.' Belinda Byam-Pring fixed him in her sights. He felt a stab of longing for Asya. 'In any case, I find the best Bezzakonian things go very well with the best of England. This butter, for instance, the best butter the *senti* can buy, and this blackcurrant jam made by my neighbours. We live out here all year round, but not many people do. That's why it gets a little lonely, when Gyorgy is away. Do you have your story now?'

'It's not a story I came to write. I came to see you. How you live. I want to understand how people live in Bezzakonia. Believe me.'

Eamon groped towards the idea that just as married couples begin to sound and eventually look the same, so foreigners long resident in Bezzakonia grew into its ways, like Pike, whose IFN fort resembled the Fortress, and Belinda, on whose transposed English life a permanent Bezzakonian frost had settled, so that it only looked like nature in all its lovely activity, but in reality was frozen.

'I do believe you. Anything is possible here. It attracts all kinds of people, mostly interesting. I'll rephrase that. Either they become "interesting" like me, or they go home, or they die.'

He felt incapable of any satisfactory answer, being not 'interesting' himself, so he just shrugged.

Belinda abandoned her court shoes for boots and saw him back to the Brumairich. Mnogoderev was still snow-covered beyond the cleared roads. The snow melted more slowly in the countryside.

'Do you have a car? I mean, you must have, living out here.'

'You won't believe this, Mr Cole.'

'Eamon.'

'Eamon, but there's a Rolls-Royce in that shed.' She pointed back towards the two-storey wooden house.

The view from a slight distance was impressive. They might have been living in Prebezzakonia. But then he remembered the darkness inside, and what must have been stale cornflakes, and the ice-cold surface of that sink. When he went to relieve himself, the lavatory was a hole in the ground. The cold wind tunnelled up to whip your buttocks and freeze your private parts. He smiled at how he would tell that story, just as he smiled at the idea of Lady Belinda Byam-Pring sweeping into Muzeb, past the traffic cops and the green BREAD vans and the blue petrol tankers with only one headlight, in a Rolls-Royce with a proud pennant pointing

116

the way ahead like a lodestar. Everything here was not impressive so much as 'interesting'. Interesting in some simple sense too, because he liked Belinda.

'It hasn't worked for years. No one out here can fix it.'

'I bet the ambassador could.'

'That might be taking collaboration too far.'

Eamon grinned. 'If you'd like me to look at it some time, I'd be happy to. I mean, I've got some skills under the bonnet.'

'I think you have, Eamon. Safe drive home, and do come and see me again.'

I remind her of her sons, he thought, and wondered why they couldn't fix the Rolls. But perhaps she liked the sight of it stranded far from home. Out of service, at least nothing worse could happen to it than gently to rot away, part of the 'interesting' scenery.

On the way back he found Harry in the so-called English pub. A pretty, but to Eamon sexless, woman in a tweed skirt and with well-groomed shoulder-length hair served Watney's draught bitter in thick Bezzakonian tumblers, and Eamon paid. The pub was the diplomats' social club, where journalists were tolerated as guests, but only on the understanding that they paid more for their beer, for someone apart from the Crown had to subsidize the place, which looked like a church hall rigged up to be a pub in an amateur dramatics production.

'Cheers. We haven't seen you for a while. Did someone say you had a ravishing Bezzakonian girlfriend?'

Eamon fixed Harry in his bloodshot eyes. He was learning something from the women he studied in Muzeb. 'Harry, what's the embassy's attitude to all the Brits who live double lives here? I don't mean that spy from the 1950s. But the ones who do a job like mine and yet take money from the Bezzakonians? Do they get an invitation to the Queen's birthday party?'

'Whom did you have in mind?'

'You know who I mean. You can tell them from their pretty Bezzakonian secretaries.'

'They're possible conduits. The important thing here is to keep the dialogue open.'

'Peace by any means.'

'Look, old man, you're not threatening some kind of Muzebgate, are you? Her Majesty's government has worked pretty hard at some kind of *modus vivendi*. IFN, *Ballet Times, Sunday Times*, we're all part of it, all part of the family.'

'Family values, eh? I say, Harry, would you buy a used car from Pike? Apparently black men here do, black men from sympathetic governments, and brown men from Borowola. They pay for them over the odds with soft money. They've got so many *senti* stashed away in their wardrobes they're only too happy to get rid of them. Pike then uses the soft stuff to run the office, and pays himself with the hard stuff in Switzerland.'

Harry whistled. 'Everybody subsidizing everyone else.'

'I agree it's hard to work out who's losing. I've tried it on paper. Man A gets a car in exchange for money he can't otherwise spend. Bezzakonian government loses a bit of hard currency that might have been changed to cover local transactions, but hardly worth worrying about. Man B, running his office, makes a fortune just doing his job.'

'I wouldn't mind being in on that. We dips pay tax out here.'

'That's why you make us pay double for our beer. But there must be some advantages in having access to the diplomatic bag.'

'Works of art, precious stones, that sort of stuff? Hell, no! Eamon, what's got into you?'

'Just finding my feet, Harry. Everyone says it takes six months.' He glanced round the miserable hut, attached to no church or country or brewery. 'God, this is a dismal place. A sort of banal version of hell. When I go to hell, I demand to be surrounded by crashing pillars and roaring flames. Right. I'm off.' He stopped and turned back. 'You and Maria must come round. Asya's a great cook.'

Eamon in his present mood wouldn't be Maria's first choice, Harry thought.

Back in the office Lyuba was typing an official letter with three carbons on the Remington with a Bezzakonian keyboard. Pike's

118

door was closed. Eamon, not needed, was relieved to get back to the solitude of his own flat, but once there found himself restless. No drink, no music, no relaxed posture was more tempting than the active expectation of Asya.

He paced the corridor from kitchen to front door and back, past the bathroom, whence emerged her voluptuous ghost, and the bedroom, the least glimpse of which aroused him. She wasn't usually late. Fridays they always met at nine. Since Wednesday he had felt empowered, though now the powers were waning.

So much did he crave another dose of her that he vividly imagined the power of the drug ending. He had to find her he had to tell her he had to thank her and make love to her even if she had finished with him and returned to her beat on Bezum Street in search of another hapless foreign soul. Maybe she sometimes took on Bezzakonians too. Maybe, swaying down the middle of Bezum Street after dark, her real name was wisdom.

It happened in Revolution Square. The distance from one side to the other was so great no normal passenger vehicle could foresee all possible hazards. He had been waiting at lights, contemplating this hugeness which was so unkind; such a brutal form of control through disorientation. The traffic light was a glass eye in a black hood high up in a grey sky, and it trailed cables like an uncurtained puppet. In this terrible dimension which life in Bezzakonia had entered, a fast car from another direction could seem to arrive from nowhere, as this one did, a bureaucrat's black Chikchak with pseudo-American tail fins and blazing headlights. Cockroaches, the Bezzakonians called them, though they were more like sharks. The Cockroach bore down on the Brumairich, which was crossing the privileged middle lane of the highway at twenty miles an hour on an egalitarian green light. The Cockroaches, as was well known, didn't always obey egalitarian lights, when higher Bezumian causes intervened. This one catapulted the Brumairich against a traffic-police tower, from where it rebounded, landing upside-down.

Great black wings closed over Eamon: love's end, world not without end. The bureaucrat sat on the pavement in the dark, a

119

spectator of his own near-demise, listening to his heart thump and watching the trickle of fluids on the road. K-603 MUZ. Direct hit. Cars and vans occasionally passed.

The traffic police, intact inside their steel tower, called an ambulance and the militia. The militia called the embassy and IFN to say a wheel had come loose, slewing the Brumairich on to a collision path, nothing could have been done. By midnight the traffic police had loaded the smashed saloon on to a pick-up truck and replaced it in its usual parking lot, just under the militiaman's unfocused gaze. First the wipers, then the wing mirrors, then the bumpers, the radiator grille and God knew what else out of sight: passing Bezzakonians picked at the defunct vehicle, and Asya forced herself to watch them, a self-test which made her curse her existence.

8

WHO WHOM AND WHY

A Bezzakonian woman in a white overall watched and listened as the tyres of a foreign car crunched the loose stones on the forecourt. The green car, unknowable to the woman as a reliable German make, stopped square, and a tall foreigner who had been bending down to change her shoes finally got out. Her legs in beige jodhpurs and long boots gave the attractive impression of athleticism and youth. The man who emerged from the passenger seat was older. He wore generously cut blue jeans and, as his wrinkled, plump face would soon show, he was obviously middle-aged.

The lady gatekeeper turned from the window, on which stood three red carnations in a fat-mouthed green buttermilk bottle, and opened the ledger on the desk. Excited female voices jostled and speculated through the wall. She slid back the window. Their restlessness seemed to press against it like water against a dam. Urgently expressive hands and faces surged forwards from all angles to meet the stern face she had composed. The face was a kind of second, instinctive bulwark against popular demand.

'Arrow.' The first voice was loud and determined.

A second calmly asserted her rights. 'For me Boy.'

A third chanted, 'Bandana, Bandana, I want Bandana.'

Not everyone was happy. 'Last week you promised me Boy. You promised him to me,' complained a plump girl in a crimson nylon jacket and dark, thick Bezzakonian jeans. She kept her head down, not looking at the rider who had gazumped her.

The gatekeeper clapped. 'Girls, girls! One at a time. So. Boy. Arrow. Bandana. And for you, Anna Mikhailovna, Katyusha. Boy next time.' She picked up a biro and began writing tickets in a large, round hand.

The foreign couple lingered in the metal-rimmed doorway. It was an odd place, one-storey, made of concrete, with a plaque saying the People owned it via the Ministry of Sport. The plate-glass wall might have fronted any public building of no character, though a riding stables seemed least suited to the urban modernist touch. Still they were grateful to find such a place at all. When they left the Bezumgrad Prospect, where grime hung like grey cobwebs from dead twigs on the roadside, they found themselves, by virtue of one of those peculiar Bezzakonian transformations, immediately almost in the country. A rough path, flanked on one side by birch trees and on the other by a paddock, led into the space occupied by a single green lorry.

'It reminds me of yet another queue for groceries.' Frank Brisk was coming to the end of his second tour of duty in Muzeb, seven years in which he had seen many things.

'You have to struggle here for every single thing you want,' she sighed.

'You're too much of an idealist, Anna. Another way of seeing it is you just make a few phone calls. You give something to that sweet little old lady who was just staring at us through the window.' Old Frank Brisk was smiling.

'Bribes?'

'Why not?'

'But there *is* something special about this place.'

'You mean you like the idea that in Bezzakonia not everything can be bought. It is a lovely *idea*, I grant you.'

'And it may yet be the reality. Come on.'

At her best, Anastasia Morgan would say she was in Bezzakonia for the adventure; only the toughness of the place, and the enforced solitude for a single foreign woman, dragged her down.

The Bezzakonian girls with their tickets were already dashing off. The rider of Boy had tall shiny rubber boots which, when they struck the concrete floor, made hollow, watery drumbeats. A few riders waited for each other, reminding Frank of how his teenage daughters had clung to their friends in the crucial years when they didn't dare be different. But horses enraptured girls' hearts too. Perhaps at a later, critical age, an age of graduation, some were torn between the animal and the human and had to choose.

'Many adults go on preferring animals to people, because their pets don't criticize them.'

Curious about his younger colleague's solitude, he wondered whether she was like that, but before he could frame a tactful question she said, 'The pleasure is in the teamwork. Animals are very intelligent.' She leaned into the Alice-in-Wonderland window. 'Good afternoon. We're here for the first time. My office spoke to Mr Taranshchikov.'

The woman was dam-faced. 'Are you a Pole?' Poles were old rivals for Bezzakonian territory and since Prebezzakonia's greatest poet had felt free to attack Poles, so did his distant descendants.

Anastasia tensed. 'I have a British passport. I work here.'

'Who spoke to comrade peer Taranshchikov? I know nothing of it. What horse then?' asked the sullen woman.

'We need two.' Anastasia stepped back to let Frank Brisk become visible. 'Good ones. Nothing too quiet.'

He shook his head. 'Any old nag will do for me.' But next minute he found the lady gatekeeper stretching out a hand like the Lady of the Lake. She wanted to hand the tickets to the man. She thought foreign women were always putting their men down, not like in Bezzakonia, where men officially were more important.

He smiled. 'My colleague is in charge.'

The old woman ignored him. Finally she shouted, '*Tuda!*' before pulling back the arm-in-an-overall and slamming the window shut.

He shrugged. 'It's somehow exhausting when everything is political, like it is here. Don't you find?'

'The person who has talked most about politics so far is you.'

'Pax. Bear with an old man's questions before he finally leaves this place for good.'

'I feel sorry for her. She knows the money's peanuts for us. Ten *senti* each! It offends her that we should have things so easy.'

'Try giving her a tip and see if she smiles.'

'Stop it!'

'But I have to enlighten you! You still don't believe this country is driven by a scheme quite different from the visible one, do you? How long have you been working here? Bribery and corruption, my dear! It's everywhere. And I noticed even you used your office to get what you wanted, which means it's catching.'

'I've been here eighteen months,' Anastasia replied defiantly, 'and today I've taken the afternoon off. And don't call me "my dear".'

'You're already regretting letting an old man come along with you.'

'Oh, *come* on. The ride begins on the hour. The trouble with old men is they're slow.'

Frank grinned at his inefficient effort to move his own bulk forwards. He rather liked the innocent role he had chosen.

Down several corridors, through a space which appeared to be neither truly interior nor exterior, as if the architect didn't understand how a riding school differed from a human institution, they arrived at the stables, where the sweet smells of horse sweat and straw dust and well-soaped leather and dung engulfed them. The packed space hummed with enthusiasm and activity. There weren't many places in Bezzakonia of which you could say that, only some schools perhaps and sports meetings. The girls were preparing their mounts.

Anastasia whispered as if they had discovered a holy place. 'It's well organized. I'm impressed.'

'Me too. Let's hope the Bezzakonians are as good at nuclear safety as they are at equitation.'

The tall chestnut, Arrow, already wore his green felt cloth and saddle. His rider fished under his belly for the dangling girth. The rider of Boy was standing on tiptoe, forcing a set of yellow equine teeth to receive the metal bit which would stand out shiny against his black cheeks. Bandana gleamed under a fierce encouragement of natural oils to the surface of his coat.

'It looks as if we have to do our own tacking up. That's just what I want, to be part of something real here. Excuse me . . . '

But the rider of Arrow, so commanding in her own world, when faced with a foreigner froze like a cornered animal. Silently she pointed to the tack cupboard.

Anastasia whispered, 'She's afraid of us. That's terrible.'

Frank, clutching his bridle as if it were a heap of nautical rope, nodded. 'A great deal here comes down to fear.'

'Frank, let's ride, shall we? Your horse is called Mercury. I'm riding Wise Man.'

'A wise woman sits astride a wise man. That's another thing. Everything here is preordained.'

'Give it a rest.'

Wise Man, head over his stall, turned away as Anastasia advanced across his threshold. He shuffled his hindquarters provocatively. Like that poisonous old woman ignoring me, she thought. Like Muzeb telling me to give up and go home.

She looked around and wondered why she was so ill-prepared. Any normal human being has a stock of tricks to help her get by, as it were, in case a strange horse kicks out, or in case life plays hard to get. Brinkmanship. Bluff. Bread in this case.

'Excuse me, I wonder if I might . . . '

'Ah, welcome, Mees Morgan! I see you already know what to do.'

Ivan Taranshchikov strode into Wise Man's box and leant his weight against the flanks of the big bay. Anastasia slipped the reins

125

over. Frank watched. She likes that, the big boss on her side, he thought.

'Mr Taranshchikov?' Anastasia saw a swarthy man in his late forties, with long straight hair growing thin and vivacious eyes. Riding had preserved the life in him. 'I'm Anastasia Morgan of United Press.'

'I think you must be. Interesting name! Reminds me of something.'

'Yes, I suppose it would.'

Together they finished tacking up Wise Man and led him out.

'Now I must tell you that I grade my classes: beginners, lower intermediate, upper intermediate and advanced. Upper intermediate includes cantering and small jumps. Advanced is what it says. You must choose.'

'I could manage upper intermediate.'

'Me too. I'm with Anastasia. Frank Brisk.'

The men shook hands.

'Good! Then you will both ride with Anton Pavlovich today and I will watch.'

They led their horses out of the stables.

'What was your degree?'

'PPE.'

'Don't politics, philosophy and economics cancel each other out? Politics isn't very philosophical, and philosophy is bad for the economy.'

'Are you trying to chat me up?'

'You're a very attractive woman. Unfortunately I'm happily married and ancient.'

She smiled and put a finger to her lips as they lined up in the centre of the sawdust ring.

'Mount!'

The young Bezzakonian riders eased themselves gracefully into the saddle. The foreigners, much stared at and reduced to copying, because all the commands came in Bezzakonian, followed a few seconds behind. Anastasia rose in her stirrups and buckled the leathers down two notches. Frank looked relaxed astride Mercury, the way some non-riders instantly do.

Anton Pavlovich Makariev, in a military-camouflage pullover, semicircular breeches and tall black cavalry boots with spurs, began the inspection. 'There will be foreigners today, Anton Pavlovich.' The lady gatekeeper had sent word. He immediately bristled. So, what of it? Riders were riders. But as he slid the protruding end of Anastasia's throat lash into its keeper, he knew he would have raised his voice to a Bezzakonian girl. Still, so what, nothing to be done.

Anton Pavlovich stood back, admired his brigade and then said quietly, 'Team leader! If you please!'

They began a gracious and orderly circle round the ring. The lovely moment gave Anastasia pleasure, as it used to please her to drive smoothly from Oxford to the north Devon village where her parents had retired. Avoiding the motorway for the distinct pleasure of mechanical traffic, she respected traffic lights, negotiated roundabouts, gave way and waved gratitude to other drivers. To participate in the great machinery of disciplined traffic, knowing that a personal mistake would upset the whole order, was thrilling, as thrilling as it was to pull over for ambulances and fire engines, and see what seemed like the whole world also stop and bow down to the human emergency.

Frank thought only that it must be difficult for the Bezzakonians to have them as guests. But he was glad to have come. His wife had gone early back to England and he still had three months to go. He needed company and diversion.

The team leader here meant leader of the ride. He was about sixteen. Frank, stationed towards the rear of the cavalcade, could see across the school the face of a creature so proud that what showed was the pride of excessive humility. You could see that expression on the faces of the guards at Bezum's mausoleum.

'Trot!' came the order.

The leader gave his horse a little heel and they accelerated. Anastasia exulted in the controlled formation in which they moved. She felt a few tears welling. 'I'm pleased for Bezzakonia. So pleased to be here, and part of things.' Patting their mounts, they walked again.

'Stop, Arrow!'

The girl in high boots turned in. Without looking at her, the instructor bent her toes upwards and brought them closer to the horse's flank. 'Oh, thank you, Anton Pavlovich,' she whispered.

'Continue!' he barked.

'Wise Man!'

'Anastasia, that's you.'

She didn't react. The example of the expert girl on Arrow dipping her toes deliberately, wanting to be noticed, struck her in a way she couldn't fathom. From across the school, the team leader and his follower both glowered. 'Oh, sorry, that's me.'

'Yes. Turn in.'

The instructor held up his gnarled yellow cane before her foreign eyes and moved it between Wise Man's ears. Head straight! But all this happened without a word, as if he feared any speech would upset delicate communication between potential enemies. Like the girl on Arrow, Anastasia wanted passionately to please. However, in Bezzakonia things were arranged so that no one pleased anyone, or at least did not show it, while those still fresh with desire strove on, kept trying.

'Prepare to canter. And canter!'

They turned and rode side by side across the school, before resuming single file in the opposite direction, then one by one they turned out of the line and joined the back of the ride.

Anton Pavlovich shouted, 'Two hands on the reins, girl! This is an academy, not the Wild West.'

'Sorry! I was so happy,' cried his foreign pupil, so admiring of Bezzakonian order, and then wished she hadn't spoken.

The ride thundered round the ring, while in the middle stood Katyusha and her rider, who had not yet mounted.

In most positions Anastasia could see without turning her head. She saw that every time the girl put her left foot in the stirrup, Katyusha moved on; or lifted a foreleg. The girl kept regathering her reins, but that was just a signal to the mare to begin again. As the class thundered past, ignoring them, it seemed to enact some Bezzakonian rule that it was cruel to be kind. Only kindness would surely have been possible. Nor would the girl get the ride she paid for. On the other hand, she hadn't paid much, so perhaps she couldn't complain. An exchange of real money would have given her rights, whereas without money all people had left in Bezzakonia was to be strong and self-possessed and consumed by a sense of their own honour. And not everyone was or could be.

Then it happened. They had crossed their stirrups over the front of the saddle, to improve their knee grip, and were now rehearsing all the same movements they had first executed with the standard supports, to test what real skills they had. In front of Anastasia Boy, who sensed another canter was in the offing, began to dance with impatience and Wise Man got the idea. Anastasia had experience and skill, but without stirrups she was like a tobogganist already a few inches down from the top of the slope. Wise Man tucked his head down and threw his hind legs in the air. Mercury behind him jerked out of the way and stopped short. The rest of the ride concertinaed to a halt. But the bay wasn't finished. He returned to the ground furiously straight-legged. When Anastasia's weight slid sideways he knew he was winning. He bucked again, then tore off, reins and stirrups flying. She collided with the ground, where the team leader stared down at her in shame.

Taranshchikov vaulted down from the gallery and Anton Pavlovich caught the runaway, who stood panting, defiant eyes blazing at the clumsy stupidity of humans.

'God, Anna, are you all right?' called Frank.

Anastasia lay for a while, surprised, since she was better than him, that Frank was still in place. She felt sick and was shaking, though no part of her hurt.

Taranshchikov shouted angrily, 'You shouldn't have chosen a ride for which you were not sufficiently experienced.'

She wanted to say, 'I am experienced. It was just a mishap.' But what came out was, 'I'm sorry.'

The Bezzakonian riders circled the school, their faces turned one after the other towards her in disapproval, like a circular version of the gauntlet.

'I said I'm sorry.'

'Well, you must get back on.'

Frank turned in towards the scene of the disaster. 'Don't let him bully you, Anastasia Morgan.'

'Frank, I'll handle this. You go on. Please.' She almost shouted. 'Actually my shoulder hurts a bit. I must go and sit down. Wasn't there a seat, by the gatekeeper's window?'

'Want me to come?'

'No-o! Shut up! You make it worse.'

'OK, OK, so I'm an old woman. I've heard that before!' He shook his head and rejoined the ride. Bloody Bezzakonians! She'd only fallen off. It wasn't a moral crime.

She made to leave the school. But the circling horses wouldn't stop. The team leader hadn't received any order. That unlocked her tears. 'What is this, a prison?' she cried.

Frank, kicking his horse on, held out his arm like a policeman. They stopped and let her through.

The panicky Wise Man picked up his legs and arched his neck and went like a dressage competitor's dream when Anton Pavlovich mounted him. 'I'm being ridden by the master,' he said, and the Bezzakonian riders watched him say 'I'm being ridden by the Bezzakonian master.'

A furious Frank rode over and seized the bridle of the errant Katyusha. 'Now, get on,' he said in a mixture of tongues. 'I promise you I won't let this nag budge an inch.'

The girl shook her head. 'I must manage alone.'

'Oh, I see.' He sat for a moment. 'All right, ladies and gentlemen, I'll have no more part in this barbarity.' He swung a leg over Mercury's neck and slid off, thrusting the reins on Taranshchikov. It was a gesture guaranteed to give offence. The petrified ride parted and he strode out.

She was sitting staring out of the plate-glass window. He touched her good shoulder. 'Come on. I'll drive.' Then, remembering it was her car, and women were so touchy these days, added, 'Shall I?'

'I've made an awful mess of this, Frank.'

'Nonsense. It's not a sin to fall off a horse. Who do they think they are?' It was a supportive kiss he gave her, though the watching gatekeeper couldn't have known. Wicked rich people slaking their thirst for pleasure on innocent Bezzakonia!

She handed him the car key.

He adjusted the driving mirror. 'Look, that bitch in a white coat is watching us, from behind those flowers. Someone's always watching here. As for that Taranshchikov, he should run his riding school better. I'd like to punch him on the nose.'

'I'm glad you didn't. Ouch. It hurts a bit when I laugh.'

He smiled.

The tyres of the car crunched over the gravel and rediscovered the relative smoothness of the road.

She added, 'You're a good rider.'

'You must be joking! I didn't take my feet out of the stirrups. I would have been on the floor a lot sooner than you. And I wouldn't have got up so fast, at my age.'

'Why didn't I think of that?'

'Because you're proud. Like them. Proud of being able to do everything without help. The ideal liberated woman. You need a bang on the head. But perhaps a bang on the shoulder will do for a start.'

'You've got a cheek. I don't have to listen to you telling me these things.'

'No.'

'Why did you come today?'

'I told you. There you are, an attractive single woman in Muzeb, and I'm a lonely old soul condemned to spend a few more weeks here, one way and another. If you're willing to put up with me, then here I am. Harmless company. Good clean fun.'

She twisted her shoulder. 'I can hardly believe it's me saying this, but I see now. I imagine the Bezzakonian world is such a fine place that I'm not good enough to join in unless I make a superlative effort.'

He nodded. She went quiet.

After a while he said, 'Perhaps I do have other motives. None of us can ever be sure, can we? It's funny. I have this desire to see you on the right tracks, as if you were my own daughter. Or perhaps I worry about the future. For me the future of politics, at least at home, lies with women, and yet when I see you I worry.'

'You really have got a nerve. Ouch! It's far too corrupt a business for me.'

'All right. You remind me of my mother.'

'You're determined to make my day a happy one.'

'No, no, I mean what you have in common. My mother to a certain extent was the victim of her generation. She could have done more, been something more. But she thought you shouldn't have what you want in life, so she deliberately held herself back. She apologized for herself. She behaved as if everyone else was better than she was, and it wasn't true.' The car juddered as they restarted after traffic lights. 'You see, I still mind. She was like that. She refused to change into a higher gear and the engine of life resisted.'

'I fail to see how that is like me.'

'Dear girl, it's the problem of your generation. You've turned the old attitudes you had towards womanhood into a fearfully pure view of society. If you were in politics, in the naïve, freshly liberated state you are now, you'd make it a monastic institution, for which no one would be good enough, and then you wouldn't know how to punish anyone, because you expected too much in the first place. You're like the Bezzakonians in a way. They are young and inexperienced in politics too. You love order, and rules, and self-discipline, but you've no idea what to do about those who don't conform.' He turned off the main road and their foreigners' block came into sight. 'Beware the country that doesn't know how to punish! That's what I've learned in seven years here. And fifty-seven years of watching women, starting with my mother. I've seen how women like you, intelligent and demanding a lot of themselves, tend to idealize this place.'

He parked. The guard on duty outside the ghetto observed their arrival.

'So we've arrived,' he said in his few words of Bezzakonian. They stayed sitting.

'I'll think about what you said.'

'I talk too much when I'm alone.'

'Mary'll be missing you.'

'Not at all. She's got my welcome home to prepare.'

As they stayed talking, the guard looked in and grinned. She waved a cross hand at him, as if he were an insect. 'Insinuating brute!'

'Good. You're getting the idea.'

'Thanks, Frank.' She kissed his cheek. 'Maybe we could go to a Bezzakonian film next week.'

He observed what lovely long legs she had in those jodhpurs. He was old, and he felt all his energy now flowed into his mind, but that had its compensations.

Anastasia's life changed after that day. She became much bolder in her job. She gave up seeking the praise of head office, and found it showered upon her. A little over a year after the riding-school incident she married an Irish diplomat and gave up her job to accompany him on a posting to Rome. There, belatedly at thirty-three, she had her first child. Frank Brisk, meanwhile, went home and no sooner home retired. He and Mary took a world cruise to make sure they kept their broad horizons, and on the cruise Frank took up watercolour painting. When they got back he continued his leisure activities, including golf, and became a prison visitor. He never did write his projected book about women and politics, because he was led to believe that in the current political climate no one would publish it. But at least he knew he was well rid of Bezzakonia. What a warning for the human race! Which undoubtedly it wouldn't heed.

As for the lives of Taranshchikov and Makariev, it was hard to say whether the Anastasia incident changed them, when so many greater changes, known as *the reconstruction*, were in the offing.

In the tack room, Taranshchikov produced a bottle. Vodka had become scarce with the new Fortress plan to increase productivity and repair economically ailing Bezzakonia.

'I'm not a drinker, but that woman's given me a hangover.'

'At seven in the evening, Ivan Vassilievich? In that case you are very fortunate. A man who first feels his hangover in the evening has an easy solution ahead of him.'

Anton Pavlovich turned over a couple of buckets and cushioned them with newspapers. Ivan really wasn't a drinker, but as a Bezzakonian he coveted whatever was short, as if it were his own soul. 'This *reconstruction*,' he said, 'I sit on it. I don't burn it, or tear it up, but I sit on it. Cheers. Your health.' They drank from yoghurt jars, with the bottle perched on a third bucket.

Ivan, expecting a rocket from somewhere, probably a low level of the Foreign Ministry, rehearsed an unsuitable defence. 'They asked us to be more accommodating to foreigners, to let them see how things really are with us, without foreseeing the difficulties. The reconstruction's like everything here, all theory which won't work in practice. All my life, alas, I –'

'It was an accident, Ivan Vassilievich.' Anton Pavlovich looked meaningfully at the bottle as he poured himself another. 'If there's trouble you should write to our new leader, Antibezum I. Tell him how things really are out of the mouth of the people. What's that fashion he's got from the Americans?'

'Walkabout.'

'Vorrlkaboot. Yes. Among the people.'

'It's not us he cares for. He wants to show foreigners that we are orderly people capable of restraint.'

'Why should we care what foreigners think?'

'Because they'll blow us to pieces otherwise. The trouble is it's a competition we started. Who's the best rider in the world? Who's got the best horses?'

'We have.'

'Of course.'

Ivan drank a half-jarful. 'Except you and I, Anton Pavlovich, know it's not true any more. You know what today reminded me of? When Yura fell. He said something I'll never get out of my mind. You know, when your children say something true it hurts most. My son was lying in a dark room. His mother insisted this was the way to treat a fall on the head. I went in about ten in the evening. The horse had already been destroyed. My heart was heavy on that count alone. Yura screamed, "I don't want to compete. I don't want to be a good rider." He was hysterical and I blamed it on the fall. But it wasn't that. He wasn't hurt. A few days later he expressed himself quite lucidly. "That horse's death just shows you what's happened to this country, being ridden by those bastards for so long. They're no better at governing than I am at riding. They don't have the will to do it freely and fairly. They've driven it into the ground. In the end it's fit for nothing but death. Don't you see?" That shocked me, because I had always thought of our system as the horse, not the rider. The system was not at fault, but the user, the citizen, imperfectly using it. But bad riders make bad horses. How could we go on believing the horse remained good, Anton Pavlovich? In my defence, I just say I was an idealist and it was a beautiful idea. When I was young, Yura's age, I thought our country was full of beautiful ideas.' He shed a tear. Vodka never really agreed with him. 'It was a good way, a decent way. You didn't deserve a satisfying life if you didn't take responsibility for social failings. If you overestimated your abilities, you bore the consequences. That was the way I ran the academy too.'

The intermediate instructor was a quiet man who declined to think for himself. But he knew his last ten years here had been the best of his life. 'We've protected ourselves, Ivan Vassilievich, working here. We had our own order of things. Otherwise what would life have been, without our horses, without our independence? You wanted to protect Yura in your turn by passing on the business.'

Taranshchikov stood up and wiped his face on a cloth that had dried the horses' bits after rinsing. Like this drinking among the saddles, it was a sign that he liked to live closely with his animals. 'I did and I've failed, because he's not like me. Not an idealist. In the end, all we can do, Anton Pavlovich, is look after ourselves.

Our generation.' He held his palms to the roof, a superstitious way of telling. 'Weather's changed. That's nice. Won't you join me in raising our last glass to the change in the weather?' He sniffed the air. He believed his life could not go too far astray if he stayed close to nature. 'I think we should let the horses out in the paddock tonight. I can do it. You go home.'

'Sure?' Anton Pavlovich addressed a few words of disappointment to the empty bottle. 'In that case I will, though it won't please anyone but me.'

The horses' hoofs clattered in neat groups over the concrete. Knowing the privilege ahead, they pushed the master, Ivan Vassilievich, tried to walk ever faster, picking up their feet crisply like dancers. One by one, he unstrapped them and watched them run free. They moved skittishly, chased each other, threatened to bite, and Arrow rolled, his strong slender legs folded like cat's paws, to shed the saddlemarks of the day. Taranshchikov held the empty halters for a while, as if mourning the loss of their partnership, then he returned them to their hooks. When the last horse was turned out it was now pitch dark.

9

THE TRANSLATOR

The fiction was nearing its end. They were translating Bezzakonia back into Russia, re- or backnaming everything, showing that the self-referential Bezzakonian language had no self to refer to, so that Reg Bowman felt his work redoubled.

'You know how the Russians are – up all night drinking vodka, a bottle an hour, then at work at dawn, stoking furnaces, driving taxis, hunkering down in obscure institutes to dusty ideological tasks, making love on park benches, writing the only lyric poetry left in the world – you have to get in their shoes to understand. What else can a translator do? Especially now, as they are re-entering our world, we must make that effort and pass on what we know from within. From within the language. Through the very sensation of Russia, as it strikes us.'

The fire in Bowman's words, delivered to an undergraduate audience, contrasted with the dull clay of his overlarge face, his balding head and his gangly height in advanced middle age. He lectured gownless and the students sat in silence. The silence seemed to isolate the top floor of the arts block from the rest of humanity.

He began again. 'You have to feel what it is to be Russian. Feel a startlingly different world-view, created by a different language.'

He told the students they should reproduce that world-view faithfully: wholenesses generated by each man's use of language were sacred. *Um, umie, zakon, zakonie.* The region of mind, the existence of law. *Bez.* Without. A wholeness might also be what a people was not.

Through the window wet, massy, cumulonimbus clouds formed and re-formed shapes to accommodate Bowman's adventure into cosmology. The students sat hunched over the grey stacking tables. Thelma May, as yet in her life evoking no one's passion or antipathy, scrutinized an imaginary darkness, created by men.

'Wholenesses have a compelling power. They are also untouchable. Do not rearrange another man's sentences.'

'Or a woman's sentences. You're talking about rape, Reg.' Thelma put up her pale freckled hands to guard her face against intruders. Calling him Reg was a kind of intrusion into *his* privacy, he thought, though only he noticed.

'To put it dramatically, Thelma, yes. The opposite is love. Love of the text.' Bowman wrote and underlined, green on white, with a lot of squeaking: THE INTEGRITY OF THE TEXT.

'Love of the text? Give us a break, Reg!'

The class shifted uncomfortably. Someone squeaked a metal table leg against the rubber floor tiles. Vic Waddis had a pasty skin and wore a biker's leather jacket. Bowman did not care whether he was understood by this alien or not.

'I mention love, Vic, to help you understand that just as life is not as easy as it looks, nor is translation. You cannot translate word for word.'

Thelma wrote it down. Carina did not. She was more fascinated by how disgustingly rustic was their teacher's knitted waistcoat, burgundy with a bright pattern. For his part, Bowman had always labelled red-haired Carina the two-one girl, competent, organized and *basta*. A pretty visible ceiling.

'You're trying to make it sound difficult so you can feel good about telling us what to do.'

'I had wondered what I was doing, Mike.'

The lad with long legs sticking out in the aisle looked like a giant cherub. Bowman stared angrily out of the window. Wherever he fixed the shoreline, their minds ebbed away from him. A rule of the generations? Oh, probably, but that was no comfort. He flowed with a great tide away from youth. He sought meaning. Why should he feel guilty for that? No man without a metaphysical metaphor for his activity on earth could be happy. The translator had his dual role. He was a link in the Great Chain of Being and he was a watchman, ensuring that men and women across the world continued to understand each other. Synchronic and diachronic functions.

'Translation happens in spite of a God who has chosen to make linguistic communication, and communication across cultures, difficult.'

Piqued by their silent resistance, he almost shouted, 'For God's sake, this is a university.' But the bloody kids packed up their books and the first few even bolted for the door, as it was four o'clock.

He yelled with dignity, 'Richards, passage thirty-five, then, for next week. In my box by Wednesday at the latest.'

Doreen, admired by Mike, bent to dislodge the hem of her jeans from the top of her ankle boots. She had already promised herself to the real world, and Mike strove to present himself as part of it.

'You're not serious about becoming a translator?'

'If you charge by the number of English words, which he says come out more than Russian, I reckon I could make something of it. Anyway, it's better than being unemployed.'

Carina weighed up Bowman's television potential, as he belatedly marked his register. She whispered to Doreen, 'His image doesn't work for him.'

'You can say that again.'

139

Bowman moved to wiping the board. The latest economic cuts had targeted cleaners. Academic staff had to help out.

Vic hung on in. 'Did you say God made communication difficult, Reg? You don't seriously expect us to believe that crap?'

'It's just a metaphor, Vic. There's no need to be afraid.'

'I'm not afraid.' The young man was incensed. 'Except for your sanity.'

'Well, there we are, that's my problem.' Bowman wiped his hands and collected his papers. Only Thelma remained, in a sweatshirt with foreign words. He tried to be friendly. 'What's that written on your top, Thelma? "Ton sur Ton"? Music or colour?'

She backed away. 'It's just a slogan, Reg. It doesn't mean anything.'

'Everything means something, Thelma.'

'All right, it means you're staring at my breasts, then,' she shouted, and piled up the books to hide her vulnerable parts.

His face tightened. A recent staff memo stipulated they should never be alone with any student, for fear of misunderstandings. 'You don't really think . . . Baah! You wilfully misunderstand me. All of you.' He stormed out and hid behind the office door.

It took Thelma ten minutes to reach the coffee bar. A sprinter could have done it in one, but she was a slow girl physically. 'My students don't understand me,' she muttered. The older generation would try anything on. Sex arrived too late for them, that was their trouble.

Bowman stayed in hiding. No, no, Vice-Chancellor! Please, don't misunderstand me! It's just her breasts are enormous. The words are strung between peaks. What on everyone else is a hammock on Thelma is a taut canvas. Stretched out just waiting to be read. He giggled himself into hysteria. No, sorry, Vice-Chancellor, forget I ever asked to see you. The fact is I'm becoming like one of Dostoevsky's madmen. I see I can't win here, even though I am Baring Professor of Russian Language. With dangerously pounding heart, he snatched his briefcase and raincoat, said good night to no one and ran down the clattering stairs. The inside of his second-hand car was cold and damp, and failed to warm up in the ten minutes he took to drive home.

'If you go back to Russia again I'll divorce you.'

His marriage, never having been passionate, was now entirely undemonstrative. Perhaps if they had moved house once in twenty-eight years it might have shaken them up, made them more appreciative of each other. Now all they did together was eat, and even that eating didn't really happen. Reg put away unused cutlery with the same disappointment as Anne ended each day feeling uncared for.

'Do we have to eat this supermarket muck?'

Anne was large and blonde. Her appearance had never altered since he had known her.

'What's wrong with it? It's Marks & Spencer.'

On what was wrong, Bowman could have written an alpha-minus essay. Preformed cottage pie, like modern students, gave a man nothing to bite on, whereas he, Reg Bowman, Baring Professor of Russian Language, liked food that required a fork and a *knife*. And whatever was the equivalent in students. But how could he explain that to anyone? When he stood in the kitchen doorway the salt and pepper grinders, equal weights in his two hands, felt like weapons. She busied herself, stacking the dishwasher, flipping the kettle on.

'I suppose the food is better in Moscow.' She loathed him for his oversized clumsiness.

'Food? It's my work I want to go for. It's me.'

They squared up to each other.

'It doesn't matter what the reason is, Reg. I'm fed up with being neither married nor divorced.'

'I'm only talking about three months. They've offered me a sabbatical.'

As she made for the sitting room with two mugs of weak white coffee, he backed up. She thought he had got worse since he started translating political memoirs and getting himself in the news. Everyone wanted to know about Russia opening up and hard-working Reg Bowman had all the clues. She tucked up her stockinged feet on the sofa and zapped on the television.

'Another bloody sabbatical.'

'Anne, you could go on a course, or have a holiday, or join something. It's not another sabbatical anyway – 1989 was an exchange.'

'What was 1990?'

'A holiday. Anyway, a sabbatical looks enlightened. It shows the Vice-Chancellor reads the papers.'

She sat up and banged the sofa-arm. 'My God, Reg, you always have to snub someone.'

'Why shouldn't I? I'm fed up with the university.' He paused, astonished at his self-justifying tone. 'Now, shall we watch the news or talk through it?'

On the screen, locked in its ugly black box on a low pedestal above the nasty sage-green carpet, or so their co-owner felt tonight, a familiar figure enumerated the last Communist President's options. The young reporter stood in a sheepskin coat and fur hat under the high walls of the Kremlin, with flurries of snow pelting his head. He had abysmal pronunciation. The contorted Russian subliminally said to Bowman, 'Help, I'm a bloody foreigner. Get me out of here.' Bowman laughed out loud. His wife reflected that perestroika was driving him barmy.

The camera switched to Sakharov's widow, then to hardliners in the new parliament who opposed the liberation.

Bowman leapt to his feet. 'There, that chap is the one to watch. Stalin purged his father. He's trying to legitimit his father's death by hanging on to the Soviet Union. Real politics doesn't interest him. He doesn't care how many people he kills.'

Anne's hand had stuck to the zapper. Eventually she turned down the volume. 'Reg, I'm thinking of doing a degree. For the first time in twenty-eight years I have the time, and all you can do is say university is rubbish.'

Not for the first time that day, Reg Bowman's body turned stiff. Why did women keep reproaching him? A degree? How could he possibly be rubbishing her ambitions, when this was the first he had heard of them.

'What subject?'

'English literature.'

'Good. Excellent.' He sounded as if he was talking to a student. The story moved on to South Africa. A hardline government kept in place by fear of Communism had been left without a defence. It was a mirror image of what was happening in Russia. Hell, he didn't mean to sound condescending: 'You can do something with that. You'll probably write a book. We'll be a two-career family.' But just as he was trying to sound enthusiastic on her behalf, something drove him to go and dig out his passport. He returned waving the little red European thing at her. 'Look, everything is changing in Russia. I must go.'

Anne grabbed the toes of one foot. 'I want sex in my life again too.'

Sex? Women these days were always talking about sex.

'Is it a reason for getting divorced?'

'No, probably not.'

Anne wondered why she didn't want to cry, but then even desirable change, when it is unnaturally retarded many years, fails to pierce the thick shell of indifference grown in its absence. Perhaps they felt like that in Russia too. For so many people it was too late. Her voice sank into the kind of silence which descended over her husband's seminars.

The house watched them. The children, having successfully overcome the social disadvantage of bearing Russian Christian names, had married and left their parents with an uncomfortably large amount of space. There were two empty bedrooms, even if Anne and Reg slept separately. Indeed, the house now contained the facts of their twenty-eight years of married life like an attic contains empty boxes.

In an aeroplane bound for Moscow three months later, a round, sleepy, unsaintly face lent over Bowman. 'I see you read Russian.'

'I do.'

The garrulous Belorussian had moved a few months ago from Minsk to Seville. Bowman was so impressed he almost wanted to talk.

'You're surely better off living in Spain. I wouldn't pin my hopes on Yeltsin's Russia, any more than on Gorbachev's.'

The Belorussian slapped his knees. 'Of course! Of course! In Russia they don't understand capitalism. They don't understand money. And they don't know how to work.'

He must have been permanently angry once, thought Bowman, looking at the flabby face, and he must have drunk the anger away.

'I blame the Church,' the knee-slapper continued.

One of those conversations, feared Bowman. He tried to swing it round. 'Are you married? I bet your wife likes Seville.'

'Vladlena Andreevicha goes red in the sun. It is a great problem. She really hoped she would enjoy the sun without a problem. But she will never return to Minsk.'

The knee-slapper was probably having an affair with someone who tanned easily. His wife too, with someone who didn't mind about suntans. Like Anne and Thelma, Vladlena would be sitting at home thinking about sex. God! Bowman was tempted to slap his own knees.

'Don't you feel at all homesick? Isn't there a problem transporting the great Russian soul?'

Sasha's eyes shot up in his head. He dragged Bowman's first name out of him. 'Look, Reg, the best thing about leaving Russia is you no longer have to care for your damn soul.' His arm in a blue lumberjack shirt stretched up to the service button. 'Shall we have a drink? It's free.'

A smiling blonde appeared, a French two-one girl, thought Bowman. Moderate intellectual ceiling.

'*Dos whisky, por favor.*'

'*Est-ce que vous avez un whiskey irlandais?*'

Bowman felt a childish delight in being able to speak to the French airline in its own language. The French were currently running the cheapest flights to Moscow, so he might as well benefit from the ambience. Otherwise only disadvantages sprang to mind. Wedged between the window and his large neighbour, Bowman felt he was flying in an undersized coffin. Blame the

Orthodox Church for what you like, my Russian friends. But don't forget the Protestants. The Protestant Church encouraged competition and sanctioned pain. This is why even atheists like me will put up with physical misery to save a hundred pounds.'

Sasha wondered if Bowman was peculiar. Peculiar people were sort of mad people, only rather more deaf than peculiar. You had to say the same thing over and over to make them understand.

'I could put up with the weather in Russia, but I can't put up with a country where they don't understand capitalism.'

'Yes, you said.' Bowman found in the whiskey the confidence to bridge social gaps. 'Perhaps you can tell me *why* they don't understand when they had the best teacher. No one *understood* capitalism before Marx. They just did what came naturally. So you'd *think* the Russians more than anyone else would get it right. Capitalism, I mean.'

'I beg your pardon. I didn't realize. You are a professor. Am I right? One thing the Soviet Union taught us was to know human nature.'

Sasha's plastic beaker made the tiniest tapping sound against Bowman's. Bowman pulled down the plastic blind against the vivid sunset and considered a map.

'I'm going to the Urals. My mother lives in Nizhny Tagil. North of Sverdlovsk.'

'Sverdlovsk. Where the Romanovs were shot.'

'You know everything, professor. Look, this book is for my mother.' He delved into a new-looking leather bag protruding from under the seat. *Como comer alla indiana.* 'What do you think? You like it? I'll tell you the story. Now everything in Russia is *bartterre*, as you know. Well, the Indians send us food in exchange for books. You know Nizhny Tagil has a famous printing works. But nobody knows how to cook Indian food, which means if no one takes an Indian cookbook to Nizhny Tagil the town will starve.'

'So you're taking one in Spanish?'

'I live in Spain.'

Bowman liked to have his scepticism about the world confirmed. It sanctioned his retreat. He almost grinned.

'So you give them Dostoevsky in Hindi? And get chillies and poppadoms and tins of vindaloo sauce in return?'

'And Chekhov in Bengali.'

'Aah, Russia's a crazy place.'

'As you say, it's crazy.'

'And they don't understand capitalism.'

'No.'

'*Mesdames et messieurs, nous allons commencer notre descent. Veuillez extinguer vos cigarettes et attacher vos ceintures . . .*'

Bowman's heart leapt. He greeted their arrival in the crazy place with such joy, he felt he was a young man in love.

He stood tall in the crowded bus, where his soft, pink-cheeked complexion, weathered neither by vodka nor cold, made him conspicuous. Russians shot him furtive disapproving glances for suffering less than they did. He stared back at the public notices about the walls. Don't talk to the driver. Fares are going up. Give up seats to invalids and war veterans. The old terminology was disappearing. No more comrade this and that. Only citizen. No one spoke much. They mostly travelled in ones. It was already dark outside.

At River Station, where the Metro began, Bowman and half the soft- and ample-fleshed occupants of the bus shoved their way off. He minded less about the proximity of other people's bodies than he did in London. He took a stock of old dirty gold *dvushki* from his coin purse and phoned Ninel from the grey-tiled underpass. He wedged the laptop between his feet and spoke Russian. A gypsy woman tried to pin a rose to his padded nylon jacket while his hands were tied up. 'No. Oh, all right, yes.' He still felt odd until he had partaken of the three-station interchange under the bottom end of old Gorky Street. But that extraordinary informal convergence of tens of thousands of marching bodies finally confirmed his familiarity. With pleasure he sank into the anonymity of transit. When he resurfaced from the Metro, he was Russian.

Ninel's first sentences to him were in English. As a fellow translator she knew the language well. But he was Russian. He gave her the rose.

'These forced blooms don't always open, but you can always hope.'

'Free Russia is a forced bloom. But I shall hope. Hope itself is beautiful.' She put her rouged lips to his sagging reddish cheeks. Once, twice. Once again for love.

In Andryusha's crowded, neatened room the desk stood clear, ready to accommodate Reg Bowman's laptop. Ninel's son, forced to grow up with classic books in leatherette bindings from wall to wall, had fled to the army. Ninel slipped away, self-consciously discreet. Bowman set down his bags, put the laptop where it was meant to go and threw up his arms with contentment.

'You know how the Russian are, don't you, Anne? Up all night drinking vodka, a bottle an hour, then at work at dawn, stoking furnaces, driving taxis, hunkering down in obscure institutes to dusty ideological tasks, making love on park benches, writing the only lyric poetry left in the world – you have to get in their shoes to understand them. What else can a translator do?' His salute to happiness sent the overhead light flying and he steadied it again with affection.

Ninel had switched off the kitchen light. As he ducked under the door frame, she lit a candle and poured vodka into two tiny glasses. The round, childlike face touched him. He knew what his first supper would be: orange caviare on boiled eggs, and some slices of sausage because he wasn't keen on herring, then hot beef and potatoes. He loved every mouthful.

'Glasnost!' He raised his glass a second time. 'Russia has her voice back. And her real name.'

'Glasnost! And happiness!'

Ninel kept filling his glass. 'I like to cook for a man who is hungry.'

'You have a nice life here. I'm not surprised you came back.'

Her flat was on the Lenin Hills, not far from the university.

She put her head on one side. It had only been six months. 'I was so homesick in London, Reg. There's nowhere like Russia. As Tyutchev says, "Russia you can only believe in." I know now. I like to be among believers.'

She had filled out, even more than when he saw her last, but her face had matured well. She now ran a literary magazine.

'But I kept my British passport!' She waved it at him, then seemed to offer him her whole life in tribute. 'How I want to be like you, Reg! You work so hard, you understand so much. I think woman can learn a lot from men.'

'We had a prime minister not so long ago who said she learned everything from men. Unfortunately she didn't like universities very much, whoever was in them. She ruined my job.'

'The Iron Lady? I am not iron.'

'But you're strong, Ninel.'

'I don't want to be strong. It's not feminine.'

'The Iron Lady was strong *and* feminine. She throve on fighting back. Perhaps that was the trouble.'

He wished his hostess wouldn't keep pouting and putting her head on one side, but someone had told her — no, all Russian women — that it was feminine to be perverse. She tilted her head till it almost rested on her shoulder and looked up at him. The performance was absurd in a woman in her forties and yet he felt touched.

'I brought you some chocolates.' He got up and the vodka made him feel dizzy.

'I think you want to tempt me.'

She was like a child tearing off the wrapping. He sensed demands he couldn't deal with tonight.

'Did you say you wanted me to do some translations for the magazine?'

'I'd like you to meet someone tomorrow. We call him the Russian James Joyce.'

'I'll be honoured, as long as it's not a *Finnegans Wake* he wants translating.'

But it wasn't the sort of joke she would laugh at. There were barriers between peoples no translation could bridge. She patted his arm. 'Now you need sleep.' He took himself off, leaving her to relive several times that pleasant moment of contact with the arm of a strong man. Through the bedroom wall she heard the tap of his machine and admired him more than ever.

'They don't make coffee like this in England.' He fingered the long-handled *turka* pot.

'Your eyes look tired. Would you like an egg?'

'I don't know why I'm so hungry. Are my eyes red?' He went and peered in the bathroom mirror. 'I should have gone to the optician before I left. I need new glasses.'

'And a banana? I found some bananas.'

'All Russians love bananas.'

She blushed. 'A long-forbidden fruit.'

Then, in her Russian way, she suddenly switched to something quite different as they sat down at the small formica table. 'You should keep yourself for art, Reg. To do the memoirs of political people is a waste of your talent.'

'I need the money,' he said out of British habit. But she was right, he admitted. 'It's true. I most want to be part of what's happening. The next most extraordinary thing to being Russian is to be a spectator.'

Ninel studied him tenderly, with her head on one side. 'It's admirable but not sensible, Reg. You only have one life. Look, I'm going to get some shopping now. You can start work whenever you like. I will look after everything else.'

He produced twenty roubles from his trouser pocket.

'No! I'd be ashamed. You know where the phone is –' she cried, as she slammed the door. 'Use it! It's free everywhere in Moscow. Local calls are free. Phone the whole city if it's useful to you and your art.'

That was Russian too, he reflected. Russians suddenly upped and went. They did nothing gradually. If they tried to do things gradually they ended by not doing them at all. Russian deeds had to be immediate and complete in one move. Russians never finished things off neatly, not their novels, not their towns, not their conversations, if they took more than one creative thrust. Everything here was either inert or explosive; life was either frozen solid or running in torrents. And when it ran in torrents it ran right into your bones.

He took his second coffee back into Andryusha's room. Behind the sofa-bed, where he had already stowed the bedclothes, he opened the window and breathed the morning air. Oh, sweet work! So much to do, so much talent to reveal to the world, so many secrets to uncover. Better get on without delay!

Reg worked all day, as did Ninel when she got back from shopping with two string bags full of vegetables and fruit and meat wrapped in some of Russia's 101 new sensational newspapers. She and Bowman, mature people both, basked in each other's silent companionship from separate rooms. Then in the evening they went visiting.

The Russian Joyce was called Andrei Nikolaevich. Through the fug, as Ninel and Bowman entered the open door of the fifth-floor apartment, he barely nodded. He was small, slender, his hair receding, and there was no obvious kindness in his face. He worked with the radio on, drawing and jotting, just as if he had no visitors, or felt that since they had come to see an artist at work they already had all they needed. People came in and he didn't care, in his fug of artistic success, whether he knew them or not. Ninel thought the smoke filling the room was like the almond-shaped mandorla around the saint's head on an icon. Andrei Nikolaevich nodded like a man who, favoured by God, depended only on his own genius, his superior grasp of Russian politics, and the cutting edge of his voice, serrated by cheap cigarettes. In this way he would survive with glory.

'Andrei Nikolaevich, I wish to introduce you to a famous English translator. The most distinguished of all.'

The Slavic incarnation of a Dublin genius barked the obvious question.

'Solzhenitsyn of course, and Gorbachev, and most recently our very own Artyom Nikolaevich Nachalo,' Ninel said, but Andrei Nikolaevich didn't look at her. Verbally he only addressed males. Females were for touching.

'Nachalo is talentless man,' he spat. 'You waste your time, Meester. As for Aleksandr Ivanovich, he is reactionary who belongs to past.'

Andrei Nikolaevich railed against every author Bowman and Ninel mentioned, blowing smoke in the faces of absent authors and present guests, and waving his hands in the air. His humanity evidently all went into his writing. Yet he had this power of the Russian artist. His filthy shirt cuffs and hairy forearms brought Ninel a stab of sexual pleasure no foreigner could equal.

'So you get me published in America, Meester?'

Two sample chapters weighed in Bowman's hands, as if spirited there by the Devil's magic. Ninel produced one of her string shopping bags to contain them. Suddenly Bowman felt immensely sorry for her, being a Russian woman. She went and buried the manuscript bag under her coat. When she fought her way back to him he touched her shoulder and smoked for the first time in twenty-five years.

A slim pretty dark girl of a woman brought plates of open sandwiches, cucumbers, apples, tomatoes, pickled mushrooms and boiled eggs. The crush at Andrei Nikolaevich's half-cleared desk might have signalled a recent famine. It forced Ninel and Bowman to stand close together, her bosom slotted, together with her plate, under his chin.

'You are eating sausage? You know what they say about Russian sausage these days, Reg. They finally got the order to defrost the Gulag victims.' She giggled. 'You know if there is no Soviet God we eat our brothers.'

'If I eat a defrosted Russian poet I'm sure it will make me a better translator. By the way, Ninel, say God, not Gott. Gott's German. At least as a word he is.'

Bowman refound himself after so long. He liked the sound of what he was saying and, as if to keep his soul fuelled, he shovelled in food. So what if dead Russia was entering his body?

'Where's that Scotch we brought?' he shouted. 'I know they drink spirits here by the tumbler, but it's surely not all gone yet.'

Ninel stroked his arm, which, because of their difference in height, was close to her face, and tried to snuggle her way into a common state of mind. 'They are all drunk, like us, Reg. They don't care what they drink as long as they drink it all up.'

Bowman was still looking for his Scotch when he caught sight of their host. Freeloaders, admirers and friends, all drunk: all were trees in the Cyrillic wood through which this Russian would-be Irishman wandered, night after night. Moscow literary life was extraordinary, and Bowman was astonished human beings could survive it.

'Is his stuff likely to be any good?'

'His Russian is full of inventions. Quite new. Yes, I think so. We can work on it together.'

The room seemed cooler on the fringes. Bowman, resorting to pushing his way through hot, immovable bodies which did not respond to polite exhortations, examined the pictures on the wall. They were also Andrei Nikolaevich's work, and most extraordinary among them, in terrible violation of the very shape and dignity of nature, was a crucified horse.

The dark beauty who had served the food approached him. How such a lovely-looking young woman could have wedded herself to the dishevelled megalomaniac wanting Bowman as a stepping stone to world fame was beyond imagination.

'My husband is very talented, no?'

'He's certainly prolific. But why would he want to draw something monstrous like that?'

'Russia is a monstrous place.'

For a slender woman she had pronounced breasts, rounded by the neat cut of her floral dress. The cream and the green of the fabric highlighted her olive skin, or so it seemed in the occluded party light. Some kind of hybrid pop-cum-Russian folk music played in the background.

'Shall we be the first to dance?'

'Western people are not usually so bold.'

'I'm not feeling very Western tonight.'

The breasts lodged against his shirt. He perspired and his head was spinning. He fell against a small table by the door where coats were strewn and on which a mirror was propped. The dislodged mirror broke into a score of pieces.

'Sorry,' he said breathlessly, holding on to the young woman's arm. 'I'll be all right in a minute.'

'You're sure you want to go on dancing?'

'I wouldn't miss it for my life.'

The artist's whore doing her ugly little duty, muttered Ninel, fiercely jealous. When the mirror broke she joined the group of surrounding men and women who, having reviewed the facts, silently touched wood.

Andrei Nikolaevich considered standing on the table, but finally began declaiming from the floor from his antediluvian story *In Russian Paradise*. This was a chronicle, he explained, spanning two millennia. When the crisis came, when the Mongols arrived in the fourteenth century, the best Russian couples went into a secret ark on the Volga two by two. Once inside the ark, random coupledom was roundly encouraged. The lascivious text was peppered with biblical Slavonic. With the invented memory of a primeval national orgy in mind, the assembled party sang. Andrei Nikolaevich produced a guitar, although he had nothing by way of a voice. Now this country is free, we will change the literary map of the world. We will dazzle the world with Russian genius uncaged.

Bowman shouted, 'Russian Hamlets, Russian Shakespeares, Russian Venice, Russian Château d'Yquem. Russian Dickens. Russian Joyce. Yes, let's have more of them.'

Ninel whispered, 'You are being ironic, I think.'

'No, my lovely. I just want to be a mouthpiece.'

'I'm not your lovely.'

'Who told you that?'

'I think we should go now.'

When they got back, Bowman was still in party mood. Ninel sulked while he stood in her hall and cried, 'How can I convey this, this magnificent country? Aah, how . . . ' His upraised arms crashed into the light fitting and put out the bulb.

'Doesn't matter. We can still see the way to the bathroom if we leave the kitchen door open.'

He found himself looking towards the kitchen.

'Are you hungry?'

'Starving,' he raved. 'I feel as if I haven't eaten for years.'

She made him another supper from what she had in the fridge: some dark bread, and eggs and salami.

'Not too much coffee, Reg. You've already had two. You'll never sleep. So what do you think of our Joyce?'

'I'll read it tomorrow. I can't judge a writer on what he's like as a man.'

'And a woman? Will you only judge her on what she looks like?'

The vivid picture of Bowman pressing against that young wife's breasts wildly excited Ninel, which was cruel of nature. Well, the time would come. In a few nights she would kiss him at the table, after they had been drinking, and say, 'Reg, don't you want to sleep with me tonight?' He would say, 'Nineshka, I've always wanted you,' or, 'How can you want me? I'm so ordinary.' If he had any tact, he would take off his wedding ring before he touched her.

They said good night. It must have been quite late: after three. He couldn't fall asleep, perspiring, and with his stomach full, and when he woke suddenly he felt not only peculiar but that he had not slept at all. In his pyjamas he walked barefoot over the warm carpet to the lavatory, his way lit by the kitchen light. His cheeks looked feverish, and the eyes which had stared back pink at him in the morning now looked unusually white and fierce. Inside his room once more he saw his outdoor shoes and his jacket at rest. It was a strange moment before he got into bed again, when he seemed to be outside himself and to be hovering over his life. He saw himself shouting to Anne, over and over, 'The Russians, you know how they are – up all night drinking vodka, a bottle an hour, then at work at dawn, stoking furnaces, driving taxis, hunkering down in obscure institutes to dusty ideological tasks, making love on park benches, writing the only lyric poetry left in the world – you have to get in their shoes to understand them. What else can a translator do?'

This time she shouted back, 'You left me. You left me years ago.'

154

'Because you didn't love what was best in me. You tried to stifle it.'

His excuse tailed away. He poured himself a vodka from the bottle on the desk, knocked it back and lay down. An odd thought from his childhood almost immediately disturbed him. His mother used to clean her wedding ring in gin. Maybe he could clean his in vodka. He slipped off the plain gold band and covered it with an inch in the bottom of the tumbler. Afterwards sleep came easily.

'Breakfast, my nice one. Are you up?'

How lovely it was to look after a man again, even if she wasn't snuggling up close to him.

'You're naughty,' she called in English. 'You've been working into the small hours again.' She liked the word naughty and the phrase the small hours.

No sound. No sign. His outdoor coat hung on the hall peg. Tired, poor man. Exhausted. No longer young, though so enthusiastic. In the kitchen she sat half an hour, sipping tea. His coffee went cold. When she heard the lift clank she opened the front door.

'Neighbour, Mikhail Ivanovich, could you come please.' She put her head on one side, but, a mature man, he would have come anyway. He could see there were tears in her eyes. 'Thank you, Mikhail Ivanovich, I couldn't face this alone.'

Mikhail Ivanovich was still in a track suit after his morning exercises. He pressed down the door handle on Andryusha's room, entered, then stopped and hung his head. The atmosphere weighed on them like iron. He crossed himself.

'Don't touch anything,' he said.

'*Umer?*'

'*Umer. Da.*'

'*Bozhe.*' She wet herself.

'Is there a sheet, Ninel Petrovich?'

'Of course.'

Bowman's mouth was open, his face was mottled with purple,

where the soul had nevertheless not wanted to depart.

The doctor and the police coincided.

'Heart attack.'

The medical man peered at Andryusha's books, while waiting for the official documents to sign. The army would knock those books out of the kid's soul and no mistake. The doctor's skin was grey and his blue suit seemed destined to be the one in which he too would soon take up the horizontal position to meet his maker. The young policeman said it was the first time he had seen a dead foreigner.

'Lord,' exclaimed Ninel, putting her hands to her face. 'Tea, gentlemen?'

'Why tea when there's vodka on the table, lady?' The doctor had gone all through life believing he could charm people by insisting on his own way. Often it worked.

The policeman opened the laptop and tapped at the hollow-sounding keys on the unlive keyboard.

The doctor held up the glass in which rested Bowman's wedding ring. He sniffed. 'This foreigner was crazy too. When there's no vodka around, Mr Foreigner, we drink cleaning fluid, but not the other way round. Eh, young Mr Policeman. Your health.' Fishing the ring out, he drained the glass.

Ninel seized the ring. 'It must be returned to his wife.'

'She won't want to hear from you, ducks.'

The policeman blushed at the audacity of the older man and Ninel burst into tears.

'He was a translator, a great translator.' Responding with emotion, she almost entirely swallowed the first syllable of his profession.

'So now he's been translated. Everything is circular in the end.'

The policeman remembered he was on duty.

The doctor, already drunk, grabbed the sleeve of his grey uniform. 'Young man, this is a foreigner. Ask the lady to telephone his embassy. They'll want the body flown home. I'll call the morgue.'

'It's my first time with a foreigner, old man, I told you. Sorry, lady.'

'If that's all the formalities done with, I'd like to be left alone,' said Ninel, with dignity.

The doctor finished the bottle of vodka in two small glassfuls and they left.

She sat five minutes beside the body, hearing the lift arrive, the door clank and the cage descend. In the Orthodox tradition they kissed the lips, but a private taboo stopped her. What had not been enjoyed in life should not be snatched in death. She dialled the embassy. The phone plastic was still warm from the policeman's living human cheeks.

'Make an inventory. Then we'll collect the stuff.'

'What, everything?'

The British diplomats were always well spoken. 'Yep. We'll let his family know. They'll be in touch. Give us your number and your address.'

After the undertakers did their work, with surprising efficiency, she sat again, now in the empty room. A sense of responsibility and trepidation stopped her weeping. She opened Andryusha's cupboards to see Reg's clothes hanging on pegs, enough for two months. His underwear lay folded in the drawer below. Three pairs of shoes awaited pavement duty under the desk. The pair of worn blue Turkish slippers she'd lent him was still beside the sofa-bed. He hadn't been an obviously orderly person, not outwardly, but here was evidence of what, in the English phrase she liked, made him tick. Tick reminded her. She looked for his wristwatch. It had been a nice one with a silver-coloured expanding strap. Vanished! God in heaven! She snorted contempt. One of death's Russian attendants had pocketed it, leaving the diary, his fountain pen, a set of cheap biros in different colours and a sheaf of paper untouched beside the laptop. She felt for the gold ring in her pocket, took it out and kissed it.

The two open suitcases covered the entire available bedroom floor. To halt death in its tracks, she switched on the word processor. The last living function of Reg flashed, winked and beeped at her from the desk above. Come on then, get on with it, no more sadness! The ritual was soothing, taking each of Reg's possessions, folding it, packing it and then registering it in English and Russian on a double list. 'Singlet' was new to her. She found it in the dictionary. Thinking of other things, she misspelt 'waistcoat'.

On the third day Anne rang up. The lines to Moscow had improved since she last tried dialling direct. It was nine p.m. Moscow time.

'You must be Ninel. How awful for you.' She spoke nicely too. Until very recently it was only educated Britons who had contact with Russia, Ninel thought.

'For me? No, for you.'

There was a silence, while words were found. The spirit profits at the very moment it seems to be losing. The literature course, apparently almost a random choice for a dissatisfied older woman, would, Anne knew from its first hours, illuminate the life she had led with Reg, and what they had not done and said. Whatever inclined him to take Russia as his real partner, Anne never stood a chance.

'Reg died in the right place, Ninel. He was completely absorbed in Russia. I think he had a good death. What I mean is, he died in your house and you were his friend. You were part of his Russia. He will have taken something of you with him, and that must hurt.' The shock had unblocked something in Anne. She felt magnanimous again, joyful, happy to be in the world, not because she hated her husband, but undoubtedly because he was gone. Her imagination flared up like a torch, burning with the very oxygen he no longer needed. 'So I want you to give his things to someone in Moscow who needs them. I don't want them back.'

Ninel was wistful. 'Not even his wedding ring?'

'Don't Russians need precious little objects, on which to make promises?'

'I will keep it for myself then.'

'Please. And when you come and see me in England, you will bring with you a part of Reg.'

Ninel really thought she would. She even imagined making a

trip specially. 'Goodbye, my dear Anne. We will be in touch.'

Bowman's suits made Mikhail Ivanovich look like a scarecrow.
The shirts gaped so much at his neck they made him look ill.
  'Enter, please enter!'
  Ninel urged him to take a look in the long mirror in her
bedroom. He hadn't laughed so much since, heavens, since they
dropped the coffin at Brezhnev's funeral.
  'But I look ridiculous!'
  'I admit it! But I can't let you leave empty-handed.'
  Ninel stuffed her neighbour's arms full of handkerchieves and
socks, and kissed him on the cheek. Death made her energetic.
Then she visited a home for retired people down on their luck.
With permission, she looked about. In the communal lounge the
inmates were watching television and reading and playing chess.
  'I need you to stand up, gentlemen, please. There is a Party
competition to see who can touch the ceiling.'
  The joke worked. Indignation stirred even old age.
  'Party? Don't give me Party! The Party's over, as they say in
England. Ahah ahah ahah.'
  'You speak English?' Ninel said in Russian to the tall speaker.
  Thin grey hair, falling straight, failed to cover his shiny pate, but
he had thoughtful eyes behind his brown glasses, eyes that were
not afraid to fix on a stranger. His fawn pullover had a hole near
the bottom hem, and his shirt cuffs trailed threads, but then
everyone here wore old clothes. They were at home, after all.
  'Please, *madame*, we are educated men. Don't make sport with
us just because we are old.'
  'I'm in deadly earnest, gentlemen. I need to give someone here
a gift. But I see, sir, that you – ' the man in thick glasses had stood
up to defend their honour – 'may well fit the bill. You should be
about two metres tall.'
  'One ninety-seven.'
  'Would you follow me?'
  The assistant matron had offered Ninel use of her room. If the
clothes were unpacked in front of everyone, regardless of size,

there would be an unholy scramble to get something for nothing. The assistant matron was plump, smiling, with dark curly hair and well made-up. Almost a beauty, thought Ninel, working with old men. At least God gets some things right.

The recipient looked through the clothes lying on their brown paper with the string hanging down the side of the assistant matron's desk. His fingers were slender and the fingernails neatly manicured. A dark suit held his attention. His mouth worked in silent embarrassment.

'What a strange thing to happen to me,' he said finally.

'I would be honoured, and I think my dear departed English friend would too, if you would take them —'

'I accept, on condition I do not have to give you my name.' He held a finger up to his lips, looking towards the pretty matron.

'Done.' Ninel smiled.

'You really don't want to know anything about him?' asked the assistant matron, already looking in her file, when he had gone.

'No. But thank you. For everything.'

That was something else good about Russia, Ninel thought, as the assistant matron saw her to the main exit from the uninspired building. The women, above all the women, helped each other.

Ninel went back to work on her magazine. She commissioned translations, she found new writers and she hosted parties not unlike Andrei Nikolaevich's, only more than one man wore the halo of artistic identity. She felt that a great renaissance was due to Russia, that it would probably not come until the twenty-first century, when she herself would be dead, but at least she could pave the way. She began to circulate her magazine abroad. It was noticed in newspapers; people bought it in English and German editions. Within two years of a free Russia, she had a life so rich and busy.

But she never forgot Reg. It was at a concert given by the Odessa Philharmonic, revivified by the enthusiasm of its new American conductor, that she saw the one whom Leviathan had swallowed, whose body the changes had used up. From the far end of her row, he came walking up the red-carpeted Conservatoire aisle in the interval, jovial after hearing Shostakovich's Second Jazz Suite, wiping his glasses with mirth on a familiar handkerchief, completely absorbed into Russian life.

'No, you see, in the act of translation you really do bring another whole, autonomous mind into the world, by giving it existence in a language where it can acquire new companions. "Am I then God?" you may ask. It is tempting to have a hubristic pride in your work, to feel you are situated in the nameless beyond, deigning to visit chosen worlds by invitation, to bestow names. Indeed only the problems you will encounter acquiring the passport, which is your craft and art, eating into your life, I'm afraid, will keep you humble.'

In her magazine Ninel reprinted Reg's lectures one by one, from papers sent by Anne.

10

IN AN UNUSUAL KEY

The rain was falling so hard it slowed the traffic right across London. The clocks had only just reverted to winter time, so seven in the evening seemed especially dark. Across every white streetlamp, as trapped motorists let their attention roam, water fell like pale welding sparks. Every hundred yards drains clogged with autumn leaves sealed the plug on pools of muddy water, which promised a final disaster for those on foot, already struggling with umbrellas and no boots. But the frustrated cars could only proceed with a stately shshshsh on the delayed route home, or abroad.

Fergus Mallet, whose destination was a quiet dinner with friends in the riverside suburb of Barnes, envied the foot soldiers their exposure to the elements. He sighed as he turned into the Triples' quiet street, and had to circle twice till he found an end-of-pavement big enough to accommodate the Rover. Human London feared anything unpredictable, and was consequently overfull of cars. Its citizens had got used to moving from box to insulated box, and calling it living.

London, though, was rich in every kind of house and flat, of car and of person. Hal and Susan lived in a lovely block of mansion flats, with gracious staircases and broad landings. He leaned over the intercom to avoid the drip of water from the eaves.

'It's Fergus.' Upstairs, red-faced and round-shouldered, Hal stooped over the door to open it, then went to pour his old friend a large whisky. 'Still chucking it down? It must be time to build the ark.'

'The traffic was appalling. Thanks. Just as it comes.'

'God knows when Adrian will get here. He's coming by bus!' Hal sat down in his usual armchair by the door. 'His idea of meeting the people, you know, to do everything the uncomfortable way.'

Fergus, who thought he could see both sides, smiled faintly at this reminder of the human comedy. 'And you think I can help?'

'Unofficially.' Which meant psychoanalysis was expensive and Hal didn't want to pay, even though he could afford it. 'In any case, I'd be grateful for your advice.'

'You shall have it. My pleasure.'

Hal was a real bull of a successful man, Fergus thought, who included in his success bringing up a family and keeping his wife. So it was no bad sign that he could humble himself and acknowledge trouble in what deeply mattered to him. The psychoanalyst and the newspaper columnist resembled each other in more ways than just having gone through university and early, relentlessly ambitious professional life together. At sixty they both were immobilized in the established way of things, like men in a quicksand. But their heads were clear.

'How's business?'

Fergus took a seat opposite the grand piano, diagonally across from Hal, and stretched out his legs. 'Surviving reports of the death of the profession.'

'People mind about the money factor. There's something wrong with a society which puts such a high price on self-knowledge.'

'You mean analysts should be missionaries.'

'Hell, it takes too long!'

'Don't books take time and effort to write? It's rather like that, rewriting your life, page by page.'

'I can't wait five years to see my son on his feet again.'

'But it's not *your* choice, is it? Ah, Susan!' Fergus rose and kissed a petite woman with short, tapered grey hair.

'I'm interrupting.' She was the kind of woman who could never have meant that sincerely.

'I see *Aphra* has had wonderful reviews, Susan.'

'"All you need to know about the temptations of adultery and why you should resist them".'

'"The most erotic woman writer of her permissive day" was the tag I liked. She must have been very sure of herself to hold back so.'

'Self-possessed. It's not a term you hear much these days.'

'Men possess women and people possess things.'

'You're an old reactionary.'

'What do you expect, darling? I'm a newspaper columnist.'

After thirty years the Triples were clearly rather happy with each other. As Fergus saw it, Hal had chosen well. Capable, adult and elegant, Susan had her own work, which made her restful company. She was just the right companion for Hal's life as an intellectual odd-job man. She was restful because she lacked nothing. If that was possible. Well, Fergus wasn't about to psychoanalyse the mother. It seemed more likely Susan only gave nothing away. The life in her, so well moulded and so carefully managed, went into her books and her social life: precious liquid poured from one container to another without spilling a drop.

'You forget, you two, how vague the goal of life can be. Starting with the choice of a mate. Your son wants to decide who he is, I dare say.'

'Adrian chose what he couldn't be: a Russian, for heaven's sake.'

'I agree it's extraordinary, but no more so than a black African.'

'It is more extraordinary, because we don't share one world with Russians; with other races these days we do.'

Perhaps Hal wasn't so reactionary after all.

'But he does share one world,' said Susan. 'That's the problem.'

The wedding had taken place in Moscow and Susan had gone alone, for Hal remembered just in time that he had once signed the Official Secrets Act, which, alas, made such a trip impossible.

'That's right . . . ' He panicked a little now, as the tale was told.

The smell of a peculiarly acrid tobacco, sweet children's perfume, and some general cleaning fluid, equally sweet but not quite pleasant, still hung over in Susan's mind after two years. It clung to the navy suit she bought for the occasion, when she had looked painfully smart. People over there wore man-made fibres in crude colours, and mixed fabrics and patterns and styles as if their entire wardrobe came from a jumble sale. No, in fact the girl's mother had looked quite nice, in a grey-flannel pinafore dress with a scarf and brooch. She even spoke English. Still, they had allowed a great distance to remain between them, as if both had regrets for their children. The Palace of Weddings was a square-built, massive office, with marble on the floor and that Russian smell in the air, compounded by wet fur. For Susan there was the additional social loss of not seeing her only son marry in church.

Susan stayed with Adrian and his new wife, not relishing two nights alone in that monstrous hotel off Red Square where there had recently been a fatal fire. That meant fifteen minutes on the Metro to reach the centre of Moscow, which revealed more of life than Susan cared to see. Every hour she grew more horrified at the world into which she was losing her son: a world in which people lived crudely, in blocks of flats with ice-cold and reeking concrete stairways; with Utility furniture, machine-made carpets and ancient valve televisions, and no art visible in daily life. If people painted pictures, designed objects, wrote music, poetry and books, which Adrian said this family did, then they did it so far away from the grey surface of what Susan saw, or was willing to take in, that she derived no comfort. Least of all physical comfort. The flat was so small that she feared and feared her desire to overhear her son and his new wife in bed, though that last detail was one she did not disclose now to Fergus.

Adrian pressed the intercom. He had forgotten his key.

'Dear boy. Terrible weather. We were beginning to worry about you. But I daresay a veteran of the permafrost is used to worse.'

Nervous, Hal turned into a caricature of himself, circling in the middle of the room. Fergus, not getting up, raised a companionable glass to Adrian, as if commiserating for having such a father. Susan sought approval by not kissing him. The young man wore black cord jeans, a collarless white shirt and a beige pullover with holes at the elbows. Everyone noticed that he had not shaved.

'Didn't I say I was coming by bus? All these wretched cars get in the way.'

The truth which immediately struck Fergus was that, whether actively by meditation or passively by hurt, Adrian had removed himself from the immediate pressures of the world and become a sightseer. He put Fergus in mind of what he had read of World War I veterans, men who came back feeling half a hero, because they weren't dead. Adrian sat down on the piano stool.

The scene, which might have been photographed as a family group with a trusted friend, in a spacious London interior, was lit from a standard lamp behind Hal and a table-lamp from the grand piano. Fergus spoke of his children. His son was being overworked as a junior hospital doctor in Leeds. His daughter was a musical agent. She didn't get much time for her own singing these days. Music turned all their attention to the piano, like a guest so far excluded from the conversation. Adrian used to play, the cello too, and Susan played the piano a little.

Susan flexed her wrinkled, ring-bedecked fingers. 'My hands were too small for real achievement. That wasn't true of you, Adrian.'

'I preferred the cello, but after I heard Rostropovich I knew I'd never be good enough.'

'That strikes me as the first real step towards achievement in the world, to know one's *artistic* limitations.'

At Fergus's words a flicker of pain passed over Adrian's stubbly face. The parents felt it, and Susan moved everyone on.

In the kitchen, the harsh functional lines of which were softened by sole resort to under-cupboard lights and a candle, they sat down to hot ratatouille and garlic bread.

'The food of the smart tribe,' observed Adrian. 'I haven't eaten like this for ages.'

'What, darling?'

Fergus jumped in to save the mother. 'How was the food in Russia?'

'Plain.'

'There's just some grilled chicken after this. Adrian, you haven't gone vegetarian? I wish you'd told me.' Adrian shook his head, while his mother continued, 'I just don't know how they live without supermarkets over there. All we saw were queues, and people struggling with bags.'

'It's all political, of course.'

'What? No supermarkets?'

'Of course.' Hal became very assertive on home territory, and with a couple of drinks inside him. 'The deliberate waste of people's time and energy is (a) a way of seeing off excess manpower and (b) a means to stifle the energy of revolt.'

'Dad! That doesn't *explain* anything.'

'*I* was talking about women, Hal. Women are the real victims. There's no Women's Lib in Russia, that's for sure.'

'I read somewhere that the women mend the road while the men watch, and everyone ends up unhappy because the men feel powerless.'

'I am explaining the political *origins* of the situation, my boy. These are the political facts. Fergus here has supplied the sociology.'

Adrian revived a little with food and alcohol. He hadn't eaten since breakfast. 'I wouldn't call it a waste of people's time and energy anyway. They have time to observe what an odd thing it is to find oneself in the world, like a bird in a cage. It's why I like buses now. I like to put a nice fat windscreen between me and the outside world. Russians use their minds as windscreens.'

Susan was uncomfortable, as if drops of another world were being spilt on the tablecloth.

Hal laughed far too loudly to betray anything but a father's broken heart. 'If they can hang on to their minds, Adrian. I hear it's quite difficult not to get sent to Siberia if you're a thinking person. Anyway, your situation is quite different. No one's threatening to take your mind away. If you want to drop out you needn't expect a call from the police.'

The tension at the table was palpable. Adrian might have got up and left.

Fergus tried to keep the peace with an objective observation. 'The Russians have been expelled from the World Council of Psychiatry for their abuse of mental science. Just a few months ago in Vienna in fact.'

To which the young man replied, almost idly, 'Life goes on.' For a while they just ate. 'Mother, these chicken breasts are very dry.'

'Also very slimming.'

'It's what your mother and I like.'

Five years ago Adrian had been the sort of person no one minded. A student of English who played the cello, he was quiet but not insignificant. Odd-looking but not ugly. Unassertive but not without ambition. The God of High Achievements, the Goha, or Goer, as he preferred to write it, had welcomed him to Oxford at twenty-two. This had not been the case when he had applied for admission at nineteen. The Goer had not seen Adrian Triple as made in His image, far from it. So he graduated from a provincial university and then went to Oxford.

Adrian was an amiable sort and he went up to Oxford more in persistent puzzlement about the point of life than in a vengeful froth. He resembled a clergyman meekly wanting to know why he too should not acquire immortal wings, while at the same time wondering whether he did actually believe in God. That puzzlement kept him quiet.

But sooner or later he would have to seize life in his hands and almost certainly it was the arrival of the great cellist Mistislav Rostropovich in the West in 1974, and the concert he gave in Adrian's Oxford college, which was the turning point. The resolute C major chord which opens Bach's immortal Third Cello Suite seems to say, 'I will not be afraid, or deterred from my path.' With this magnificent sound in his head, Adrian sought the earliest possible trip to Soviet Russia, in Rostropovich's honour.

(Hal protested again, as some of this was being briefly retold: 'I *couldn't* go. I've never been. The Official Secrets Act. *Bloody* nuisance.')

The best way to go in those days, continued his son, unless you were an influential left-winger subsidized by the KGB, was to participate in an educational visit. So that was what Adrian did. A mixed group gathered for the Aeroflot charter from Gatwick airport. They included an art collector and his art historian wife, a retired banker, a Jewish professor from Hampstead and his cowed, spotty son, an elegantly dressed and handsome lady professor of German, an estate agent and two middle-aged engineers whose time working in the Middle East had broadened their world-view and excited their curiosity. A few uneasy jokes were exchanged as to who was the spy. The group leader, male, London-based and of Hungarian birth, was the obvious choice. You could see it in the stiffness of his amiability and of his anti-Soviet remarks. Both had the same theoretical tone. Then there was his jet-black hair in his late forties, which simply turned other people against him. He even looked false, though the design quite likely belonged to nature. Still, he was not a very important spy and since the London end of the arrangement paid his ticket, Moscow had only to provide a few perks: a girl in his bed if he wanted one, and plenty of caviare, vodka and champagne. (Hal expostulated that such things happened with Foreign Office blessing while the Labour government of '76 was in power. His column wouldn't allow people to forget that.) 'Give it a rest, Dad! Gyorgy came with us on factory tours and home visits, and to the theatre and to museums. He may have been a spy, but so what if he really believed in the place?' ('Why didn't he live there, then? These people, Adrian! I can't abide them. What is he now? A polytechnic teacher?')

'Let Adrian tell the story, Hal!'

'To answer your question, Fergus, I met my ex-wife on that trip.'

Oxana was a soprano with the Bolshoi who had already progressed from the chorus to minor solo parts. As a reward for receiving the English guests to tea in her apartment, the director gave her the part of Tatyana in Tchaikovsky's *Eugene Onegin*. Looking back later, she would see her career was made by that deal. The guests, meanwhile, were thrilled to meet a real Russian. This was what they had paid for, especially the Jewish professor, who was most anxious his son should wake up to life. The lady professor of German was more urbane and relaxed in her manner. Everyone she met over the age of forty wanted to know more about her. Only the art historians were stiff, and felt they were wasting their time in Russia, and it was a pity they came that afternoon really, because after everyone had piled in and sat down at two tables placed edge to edge the room became impossibly cramped.

'I still remember them. Prissy, impossible people. I can see them now. He was sharp and impatient in a red polka-dot bow tie, and she looked so smooth and cold in navy and white. But there you are. Even under their imposing foreign pressure, the existing furniture, a grand piano and a bed, simply refused to melt away. I remember there was an extra table requisitioned from neighbours, piled high with food. Well, there must have been because next time I went round the room seemed quite empty. We were crammed together in front of plates of open sandwiches, apples, and giant fairy cakes and a pyramid of wrapped sweets, wondering if anything interesting was going to happen, or just a series of formalities.'

Here Adrian looked bashful and wondered how he could phrase it. Oxana was squeezing past him with a score, on her way to the piano, at the same moment as he was examining his first-ever Russian bonbon. The surface was dark chocolate, overcast with white. In short it looked mouldy. She bent over and whispered, 'Don't worry! The white is soya. It's good for you.' Under the crowded conditions, he felt the incentive of her hard round belly against his spine rather more intensely than her verbal encouragement. Looking back and up, his eyes took a course between the twin peaks of her breasts in blue gauze and found a pale and sweet blonde female dressed for the stage staring down at his sparse curls. Tucking the score under her arm, she looked down, took his glasses off, examined his face and replaced them.

'Sorry it's such a squash.'

'I'm enjoying every second of it.'

After she moved on he resumed his exploration of the chocolate. A sweet, soft centre yielded to his cautious bite. It was, as was Russia, really quite unexpectedly nice.

That was it, really. The lady professor of German who witnessed the scene could have said as much straight off. Technically, Adrian entered Oxana in the first real sexual experience of his life. But as we all know, literal sexual metaphors are hopelessly inadequate to describe reality. The truth was, when he came back on a different visa and they got married in the Palace of Weddings, she entered him, turned him inside out, so that all he saw of the Russian outside world was her extravagant clothes, her shoes, her pale limbs, her large and powerful body, and all he scented was her sweat mixed with sweet perfume, and the vinous smell of musty apples from the summer dacha that permeated the Moscow flat. Besides love, he found too a role for the formal suit he never wore at home. He wore that suit to get married in, and to concerts.

He loved music and he loved Oxana's music especially. He grew to know all the Russian pieces then hardly heard in the West, especially the Rimsky operas and the less well-known Tchaikovsky pieces. In *The Tale of the Invisible City of Little Kitezh and of the Maiden Fevronia*, Oxana made a buxom, implausibly immobile Fevronia, but her singing was radiant. His other love came to be walking. Once they were married, he always seemed to be out walking in town, otherwise known as vaguely shopping.

'You understand, darling, I need the flat to practise.' She stroked his face, ran her fingers through his hair and, groaning, unbuttoned his shirt and nibbled his collar bone. There was never any question of a physical distance between them. Only such

171

delicious foreplay became increasingly the prelude to his being handed a shopping list. 'See what lovely things you can find us today.' She said it in such a way that, exploring the dismal shelves of Soviet grocery stores, he had the illusion of exploring her luxuriant body. Every high, slightly unpleasant smell from the dull counters of meat and fish his captivated senses transformed into those pungent odours of love which heighten our fantastic joys by reminding us these are real, ordinary bodies affording them. All the pushing and jostling of Soviet queues was bearable too, because mentally he was in constant happy collision with the naked loved one, she rolling over him, he locked tight in the cave of her mountain.

Sometimes, in a shop, his reverie would get the better of him and a woman behind would poke him. Someone else would say, dividing the potential crime of addressing a foreigner, 'Person, remember you've got to pay. Everyone here is waiting to pay, young person. Have you got your ticket from the cashier? This is the second queue, for paying.' Sometimes the system got the better of him, but since he had time he hardly cared.

After only three months in Moscow they moved to Riga to be closer to Oxana's family. Baltic Latvia then was a reluctant Soviet republic. They had a larger flat, though in order to practise in perfect freedom Oxana daily turned Adrian out there too. He became like a pet required to wander the streets because his owner had not time to look after him.

It was a cosmopolitan city which had been under dusty wraps since the war, but only a fool would have taken the dust for the substance. The German tongue, visible here and there in a street sign or a museum, and occasionally audible among educated older people, was not quite lost among the Russian, the Latvian and the Lithuanian babble. Had it not been for his now evident problem with his Russian wife, Adrian would have loved Riga. As it was, he became a connoisseur of the art nouveau architecture, and cafés which sometimes had tea or coffee, sometimes neither. He heard many concerts in the precincts where the young Wagner was Kapellmeister and wrote *Rienzi*. Oxana, meanwhile, became a principal soprano at the opera house. The stately pale red and yellow building sat on the edge of a small park, while the main street brought strollers and shoppers over a pretty nineteenth-century bridge and past the front entrance. The old part of town could have been a stage set, so few were the cars and modern buildings.

Oxana's father, Karl, a young sixty, was powerful, and Oxana admired his power. He had Baltic German baronial blood, one reason why he had gravitated westwards at the first professional opportunity and encouraged his grown-up children to follow him. The other reason was greater artistic and social freedom at a distance from Moscow. Karl's excellent wife agreed with him entirely. Marusia was an anglophile Russian, whose childhood an English nanny had embellished. Oxana was the last of Karl and Marusia's four children and the only daughter.

The family, like nearly all Russians this century, had had an eventful time. One of Karl's brothers died fighting against the Russians, the other fought with the Russians but because of a muddle over his identity, and the suspicion he was Jewish, since he came from a polyglot family with artistic talents, he was sent to Siberia after the war and disappeared. Presumably he died in a camp. By then nearly thirty years had passed since the Revolution and since the other great but muted drama in Oxana's family history, which began when nanny Betsie hid.

Marusia's father, who was a professor of fine art and a man of standing in St Petersburg, found her in the cellar, pale and thin and frightened, living off bread and water, a week after the family thought it had waved her goodbye on the Neva quay. 'Oh, please, *pozhalsta, gospodin*, let me stay.' She had no other home. She loved this family as her own and had grown to feel herself almost Russian. Marusia's father relented. So for the rest of his life and much of Marusia's, the whole family including nanny went underground in spirit, afraid to display its talented heritage, its traditions and its cohesiveness to the world. Nanny learned perfect Russian and stayed on as a friend and equal until she died.

The change came in the early 1960s, when Oxana was at

school. Khrushchev opened up the country a fraction after Stalin's death. The art world experienced a new freedom, especially on the Baltic fringes of the Empire. Karl, a Riga theatre director, was seduced on to the musical stage by a brilliant Estonian production of Shostakovich's *The Nose*. Meanwhile, his daughter's singing already promised success. Karl and Marusia saw Oxana as a symbol of that new breath which came into artistic life. She was a flower that had grown out of near-darkness. They had nurtured her, as they had nurtured her brother, Tari, who was a film director. There were grandchildren still too young to know they should grow up to find their place in this family which lived in its bones for talent and for art.

'So, how are you finding life in Russia, Adrian? It must be a shock!'

When Marusia spoke, the complete naturalness of her English shocked him, which is how he came to hear about nanny Betsie. They were driving from the parents' town apartment out towards the sandy Baltic coast, down a rare section of decent wide road, with Marusia and Oxana in the back of the 1965 Volvo, Karl at the wheel and Adrian beside him. It makes me feel bloody inadequate, he felt like saying, but instead he spoke of a wonderfully rich and diverse country he had not realized existed, and how he needed to work on his history. Karl found him a bit wet and Marusia thought he ought to grow up.

The family dacha was a two-and-half-storey wooden house deep in the pine forest on the edge of the sea. The roof was steep, with ornamental wooden eaves. The windows had a lovely large squareness. You thought of well-heeled nineteenth-century family life when you saw a house like that. Marusia gardened and designed textile patterns. Karl worked in his library. Tari and Oxana came and went. They spoke Latvian with Karl, Russian when Marusia was there, and English for Adrian. Karl also spoke German, and Tari French. Karl's library contained books in many languages.

Adrian didn't have much to do. He felt like a student come out for a holiday to learn a language. Or someone stationed in what he could only see as an idyll because he had no place in it. He borrowed a floppy straw hat against the sun and walked in the pinewoods before the dunes, and eventually to the shallow sea they said was dirty, though everyone local swam there. Out in the country it was difficult for him even to do the shopping. At Marusia's suggestion he painted a little and made slow progress reading in Russian a magnificent Chekhov story called 'The Kiss'. He and Oxana made love every night, but she was careful not to conceive a child.

So careful he asked her one day. She said she couldn't see them staying together for ever. The system had made her too ruthless, too selfish. She was beautiful and spoilt, he wanted to say, but that sounded too much like every other woman, woman as legend, and Oxana was spoilt only for art, so he concentrated less on thinking, on judging, than on being beside her in the rare hours they spent together. The family seemed to regard him rather as she did, like a charm on her bracelet, harmless enough, though not part of the essential business of life. He hadn't been through enough, neither personally nor by virtue of his national origins. English history had neither starved him nor forced him to speak one language here, another there, nor tried to get him to denounce his friends and loved ones because their blood origins were different, nor made him subordinate his life to the whims of dim peasants in Moscow who maintained a network of thugs and prisons across the lands they had usurped. And he had no idea what he could do about it.

Back in town in early autumn he heard a cellist play in the Petrikirche, which had been turned into a concert hall. Laaaaaaaaaa! Lalalalalalala. Straight down the scale. It was almost the last thing he remembered, and after a while it was the last thing, for the touch of Oxana's hands faded. The senses cannot hang on to things as long as the mind, which perhaps is merciful.

He realized that this noble family expected him to behave in the most elegant and forbearing and impersonal manner, though he should not betray himself, nor, in conquering the aggression of sadness in rejection, offer himself as essentially cold. He should be like nanny Betsie but also the opposite of nanny Betsie and go without a murmur.

'Just tell me what you ever saw in me.'

'I think it was the language, Adrian. Hearing you speak to me in English then, it was like hearing a beautiful melody in an unusual key. There was something in me which loved all Englishmen with beautiful voices, but yours was the best.'

'Then I began to speak Russian.'

'Yes, then I knew we were quite different.'

'She's still a singer. A very good one.'

'Beautiful too, in a Russian way,' said Susan.

There was a silence after Adrian's story. Fergus perceived a young man caught in contradictions he enjoyed, because they were the only certainty he had. He said, 'Well, Adrian, it's good to see you after so long and I look forward to hearing of your next conquests in life.' Susan pressed Adrian to stay the night but he insisted on taking a night bus back to his room. He felt drained and dissatisfied.

Hal rang up Fergus next day. 'You're saying we're out of touch.'

'In my view your son is traumatized by the suffering of his wife's family and his inability to help. The point is he can't help. He must do something else. He needs a good job with responsibility to help him get over it.'

'I'll get him to apply to the BBC. It is still a respected place to work for people of talent. He might even be able to use his Russian.'

'Keep me informed. And thanks again to Susan.'

Adrian sat downstairs on the Number 50, contemplating the layers of protection which enveloped the life he came from. Material layers of course, and also spiritual layers. Such layers defined Conservatism, Hal once said, which is why, smiled Adrian to himself, Conservative philosophy can only work if everyone has a home and stays in it. It won't work on the London buses, whose draughty rear end reinforces the unsewn-up life, where the only charm is what is unpredictable. Which is not to say I am a Socialist, like my father was at my age, hard as that is to believe now! My politics, my view of the world, have been neutralized by the spectacle of Russia. All I can do is stare in wonderment at the extent of human works, and the scope for error and pain and misery. Man's inhumanity to man, or, in Lenin's version, '*Chelovek cheloveku volp*'. Man preys upon man.

'Oi! These yours? Don't leave 'em on my bus!'

More than once Adrian's shopping, forgotten in his metropolitan reveries, came unpredictably flying towards him on the pavement.

He had little money and a basic shopping list which he wrote out in Russian and used over and over again: herring, cheese, bread and cucumbers. He carried a Russian string just-in-case bag for the moment when he found, from the bus window or from his pedestrian wanderings, the right kind of shop.

syr
khleb
luk
moloko (semi-skimmed)
yabloko
red kapusta
kartoshka
myaso (pork?)
pivo

His money comprised the last year of a grant for his long-since-stranded thesis on Conrad's *Under Western Eyes*, and a top-up from Hal. After he had paid for his shopping he was left with sixty pence for the weekend. Clearly life was funnelling him into applying for a job. He never doubted he would get a job, even in those difficult years, because he was well connected and his father would help and we cannot be critical about all aspects of our heritage. It seemed even to him that wandering about London doing his Russian shopping, as he had done his and Oxana's shopping in Moscow and Riga, was rather more of a luxury over here. Life taunted him with that truth by allowing him to stumble on just the right kind of shop, a new establishment owned by Russian exiles, in Moriarty Street on his way to Broadcasting House. He saw Cyrillic labels in the window, stopped, filled up the string bag and arrived with a minute to spare.

At the BBC the hemispherical foyer in marble reminded him of the Palace of Weddings. The neat female with a clipboard had to say twice 'Mr Triple?' before she mobilized him to follow her downstairs. The board of interviewers included one evidently wearing a toupé, the blackness of which recalled old Hungarian Gyorgy. Wonder how he's getting on. Another was unnaturally tanned for February.

'So you're interested in Russia, Mr Triple?' said a dull-looking functionary whose attempt at sarcasm came out as expression-lessness. 'That sounds like an easy option to me. Russia's been in the news a lot. The story can be followed from the papers. What we'd like to hear is what *you* would do to give us the edge over the opposition, to make viewers – and listeners of course – realize we care . . . '

Care? Crikey. Under pressure Adrian proposed a new version of the Grand Tour to take in that neglected part of the world and broaden the Eurocentric narrowness of most of us today. He explained why he would be a good person to make this programme, nay series, and even present it. He finished up then, not knowing quite why he said it, 'My ex-wife was Russian, actually.'

It was a bombshell. Adrian heard silence whereas they heard something like Beethoven's *Fidelio*. A man who is one of us and yet knows the Cold War *intimately*. They heard the background music to the emergence of human beings into freedom and light. Defence of the realm, of human decency, the continuation of the war in other terms, a focus for human aspiration: the interview minted new coins in the banks of their conventional minds. The suntanned one came round the desk and shook Adrian's hand.

Adrian apologized for the Russian shopping beside the chair. Possibly the herrings were leaking. Russian shopping? Russian shopping bag? What was that exactly? God, how pitifully ignorant we are in this country. 'Chance for little feature on that shop, John,' said the man in the toupé to the expressionless one. 'Do you have a really *good* recipe for borshch?' begged Suntan. Adrian left with a producer's job in the bag, as it were. What had the BBC done to have such a stricken conscience? He must ask his father.

Lin picked him up in the canteen. She knew him at Oxford, she said, though he probably wouldn't remember. Lin with her smart clothes and nippy little red Peugeot car, because he was a success, picked him up like a stray dog and carried him home to Fulham. On the far side of daily traffic jams which she blotted from her consciousness with an in-car stereo she lived in a trendy flat with a mezzanine bedroom floor open above the living room. Mentally he called it after Chekhov's story '*Dom s mezzaninom*'. The spiral metal staircase he found difficult to negotiate after a few drinks but once she got him up there she found he wasn't bad in bed, by the sheer accident of being so slow to know his own needs.

So, after the necessary formalities, he got married again. Susan arranged a big wedding with a marquee in the garden of their house in Wiltshire. Hordes of people turned up he didn't remember having met before and Lin didn't know either. Her father was a wine merchant who looked the part, but who was Hal to complain, said Susan, strained and irritated by the big day. Fergus's son was dragooned into being best man. In his speech he said the most recent chapter of Adrian's exciting life had included escaping the clutches of a Russian bear and finding happiness with a beautiful English maiden. Adrian really enjoyed the day, as he enjoyed the first six months of his job and the first year of his marriage, for when you have been outside the door for a long time it is a relief to be invited in. Even if in the end you do not care to stay inside; because they are not playing your tune.

It had never been the case with Oxana, because of the awe-inspiring difference between them, even as they lay so physically close and tried to love each other. But Adrian guessed now, from his to Lin, that most marriages are like simple harmonic music. They are music, they can be astonishingly beautiful, yet beneath it all they move only back and forth from the home key to the dominant. Like the marriage of Dolly and Dmitry Oblonsky in *Anna Karenina*. No wonder people got bored. Only his Russian marriage had taken him into a very remote key where he felt the strength of the unprotected life. He heard his Russian marriage over and over in the unsupported line from Bach.

He and Lin bought a house in Shepherd's Bush to be near Television Centre. Lin had their baby, a son they called Justin. They got a Swedish au pair with red hair and black clothes called Anna-Lena. They had dinner parties on the pine table Susan bought them from Heals as a wedding present.

Adrian took up paragliding. And once he saw from the sky that this world was secure all around him, tucked in by hedgerows, and roads with neat verges, and sturdy houses with domestic staff, he left it and went to teach English in the Falkland Islands. That was after the war, of course, in 1983. Neither analysis nor the therapy of time always leads to a cure. And anyway, if you have that line from Bach in your heart, why let it go?

11

THE REVOLUTION

Four old men, having acquired a building from the state, ran a museum. The lovely building was an early-nineteenth-century villa once owned by a merchant, in a pleasant suburb where even now little traffic passed the door and larch trees still flourished. The thick brick walls were stuffed with straw to hug air against the winter cold. Light poured in from tall windows, and those too were double-layered against the cold. It really was a snug place where the four proprietors could preserve their memories and inspire their visitors with a vision of the good life.

Each in the not so distant past had been involved in feeding The People. Ivan, a jolly man with spectacles and whose face was still middle-aged, had helped to feed Writers at their Union restaurant. Prokovy, former catering manager to State banquets, still answered to the title 'Chief Cook to the City'. Bushy-haired Andrei had worked a notch down, in hotels, and had a line of medals to show for it. Menzel made up the team. He had trained as an icon painter, but switched to restaurant interiors to please a woman.

The museum of the consumable was closed every day except Thursday. The four men needed Tuesday to meet and plan strategy and the gentle pace of their lives claimed the other days for research. The visitors, therefore, as to any museum open only on Thursdays, were mainly teachers and schoolchildren. The curious parties left their outdoor clothes and bags in the cloakroom and waited in the vestibule until the small brown-suited figure of Prokovy appeared with a reel of tickets printed at two roubles, but charged at three.

'Welcome, my friends, to this unique display of the history of how and what we consume. I hardly need tell you young people who have grown strong on its nourishment how wonderfully tasty our People's food is.' He thought how very young the children were and how buxom. Children in his day were skinny after the famine. 'Our consumption is the finest in the world. Our industry has increased yields fifty-fold. Production has tripled in the last twenty years. We pickle more cucumbers than any other country in the world. The skills of our cooks are known worldwide.'

The children, aged about thirteen, wrote down the statistics, leaning on each other or on the wall, which was less fun.

'What is pizza, please? Do we make pizza?' The question came from a girl with shiny black short hair and dimples.

Prokovy pretended he hadn't heard.

One of the teachers raised a finger to her lips and said, 'We can do anything better than they can.'

'This is the case,' said Prokovy, whereupon a boy with an already manly face, at once sweet and rugged, like a young film star, shook his head, though only for the benefit of his friends.

Andrei, with his bush of grey hair, waited on the first floor. He thought privately that his country's restaurants were not what they used to be, and his corner of the museum, with its display of odd pieces of silverware and some photographs of pre-war restaurant crowds, seemed designed to say so. He thought restaurants ought to make people feel special and happy, as once they had done.

As the children approached, he put on a crackly record. The voice of a famous singer from the red jazz age crooned a song about smugglers. The tune had a lilt and a swing. 'Da da dada.' He held out his arms, miming an imaginary performance. It was the American tune 'My Blue Heaven', though not even Andrei knew that.

O time! reflected the older teacher, Galina, sadly, as the orchestra bodied forth round, fluid shapes like the ballgowns of dancing women, and the figures in the photographs sprang to life, flirting with each other and the unkind times they lived through. Andrei watched her, and the expression on his face suggested he had earned his strip of medals for kindness to his fellow human beings. But the children were relieved to shuffle on.

'What did these old codgers get their medals for? Stuffing their faces?' The girl with the shiny hair and dimples made a boy in short trousers laugh.

Galina touched her colleague's arm. 'Look, Masha, green cheese! Do you remember?'

Like Andrei's, Ivan's section, which exhibited a recipe book from the 1950s and tins and packets of foodstuffs, also worked better with adults. The teachers felt pure nostalgia for foods which had suddenly appeared and just as suddenly disappeared.

'That year I made everything *au gratin!*'

'What's that, mademoiselle?' Ivan was rather deaf and short-sighted, despite his middle-aged face.

'I said my husband got fed up eating leftovers with a fancy name!'

'Exactly so. The menfolk complained to the Central Committee. That's why they took green cheese out of production. In 1976.'

'You don't say!'

Ivan beamed, still proud of being a man.

Galina was left reflecting. She had always thought an order must have come from *somewhere* requiring green cheese no longer to exist. Or the world ran out of the stuff.

Prokovy reappeared with a long pointer, wielding it like a

military cane. A tattered poster with a picture of a spacerocket declared 'Food in space! The food of the future!'

'Imagine, children,' said Galina, anxious to fill the silence. 'This spacecraft has just blasted off. Look at the trail of smoke and flame! Imagine inside that rocket are hungry cosmonauts!'

'Do you suppose they're leaving here because it's better to live somewhere else?'

'No!' Prokovy tapped at the poster.

The embarrassed teacher saw the rocket excreting fire on the world it had just abandoned, and thought hope might indeed be part of the equation.

'So why are they going?' the boy in short trousers persisted.

'For the honour, Maxim Andreyevich.'

'What are they going to eat, then? What do honourable people eat?' asked the pizza fan.

'They eat the membrane from the sturgeon's womb, a most nourishing substance left over after the caviare has been removed and sent to our shops.'

'Ugh!' cried several voices.

Prokovy made an exaggerated face, pleased at last to be dealing with normal children. If you ran a museum it was important to be a good actor, to bring the place alive.

But the teachers were whispering now, about that caviare. 'Sent to our leaders, more likely,' grumbled Masha.

'Comrades, when you're ready.' Prokovy tapped the cane irritatedly.

His final duty towards the visitors on the first floor was to recall publicly how he had created National cola. He stood there beaming at the bottle, arms outstretched, like the father of the prodigal son.

The boy who looked like a budding film star finally found the courage to speak. 'Our cola is not as good as American. I've tasted American and ours is a poor copy. Everything we do is worse. National cola. National jeans. National music. National cars. They're all ghastly.'

'Taste is a matter of education! You children are ignorant. Ignor-ant!' Prokovy glared at the teachers.

But the shiny-haired girl began again. 'But, sir, what *is* pizza? If we can't find out from you, our country's greatest experts, then we can't find out at all.'

Prokovy reddened and counted silently to ten. 'The answer is simple, young lady. This concept does not exist in our social conditions.'

'Write down this good answer, children,' said the headteacher.

'Why are there no fish in our rivers?' began Maxim Andreyevich again.

He could be imagined, Masha thought, fishing with pole and line for the rest of his life, looking for something really important. She liked him, whereas the older teacher was more afraid. Children for her were difficult these days, outspoken and unpredictable, where they used to be sweet-tempered and obedient.

'The People have shown a preference for frozen deep-sea fish over river fish. Our fishermen have therefore responded by trawling the seas.'

A nervous twitch showed through Prokovy's look of superiority, while Maxim Andreyevich closed his notebook defiantly. He wasn't writing down any more nonsense. 'I think it's because the fish can't breathe in our dirty rivers.' When Prokovy swished the pointer through the air, the boy bent his knees, drew in his buttocks and put out a staying hand behind, just in case.

Galina did her best to recover the situation. 'Is it true that they don't eat mushrooms in England, Prokovy Maximovich? Tell us about that.'

'Well! I'm glad you asked that. Here is a great historic nation, living on an island covered with damp forests, and yet they cannot tell a *boletus edulis* from a *champignon*. Perfectly true! The only thing the English are good for is big breakfasts. Hem and eks!'

Hem and eks! A little polite laughter restored the old order, while the children salivated. All this talk of food! By now they were really hungry.

★

As they entered Menzel's room, on the top floor, a gasp went up. The decor was fabulous. The black and gold border motifs of cockerels and arabesques round the red walls made visitors feel they were inside a magic box. For the first time too they saw food. Three long trestle tables were covered with white tablecloths and laid with sparkling glasses, bright cutlery and flowers. At every place invisible waiters had served a different meal, so that all national life was on display. A bowl of rich purple borshch with a swirl of cream suggested hidden depths to the satisfaction of appetite. A plate of golden pork and onion shashlik still on the skewer, with freshly quartered tomatoes and green onions, reminded everyone of a jolly evening out in a restaurant. A breaded veal escalope with gravy and carrots and potato purée was what you needed after an exhausting morning's schoolwork. An open sandwich of pink salami on black bread topped by a green gherkin recalled the unpredictability of airports and station buffets and the exciting business of being on the move. Boiled sausage with stewed cabbage was homely. Pancakes made late-night snacks with cream. Everybody loved them. The beef in cream lost its sauce to an absorbent mound of smoky buckwheat, but the diner lost nothing enjoying the gorgeous combination of flavours. Russian Camembert sliced and garnished with flowers of radish and carrot and cucumber and sprinkled with fine, feathery dill needed only vodka and black bread to make a feast. All this food gleamed. The colours blazed against the whiteness of the plates. But there was no heat and no smell. Everything was made of wax.

The shiny-haired girl cleared her throat of hungry juices. She said to the headmistress, who liked her, 'Our food never looks like that. How can they make models of things people never eat? Why do they do that?'

'Because,' said Maxim Andreyevich, 'this is a museum of things that don't exist.'

'Shsh! Children, children! We are here to admire Mr Menzel's art.'

'You know what?' whispered the prospective film star to the

girl who wanted a pizza, 'Before I'm twenty-one I'm going to *drown* in real cola!'

The children were impossibly noisy returning to school in the bus, and Galina went home with a headache.

The front office was so cramped that the four desks of the four old men formed one solid table. When they sat down for meetings, the bodies of Menzel, Prokovy and Andrei were so tightly tucked in they resembled children in highchairs.

'We must improve the exhibits, Prokovy Maximovich. The visitors' attention is not entirely captivated.' Andrei felt the genuine sadness of one who wanted to spread happiness but was not succeeding.

'Don't remind me!' Prokovy thoroughly disliked young people, with their poorly developed palates and lack of discipline.

'But I must remind you. Otherwise we won't get anything done.'

Prokovy sat twisting his lips.

Ivan burst in late. 'My friends, I have the answer to our prayers! There exists a truly new dish. I have not only spotted it but I have tried it. Mmmm! Delicious.'

'There's no need to shout,' said Prokovy to the half-deaf man.

Prokovy's puritanism made him resistant to all change. But there was something still more powerful that Ivan had to combat in all his colleagues, and that was experience, which invited scepticism. None of them had eaten or even heard of anything new to eat for years. Above all Menzel, whose face resembled a long thin white mask, showed no excitement. He had painted every foodstuff known to man. Probably the only challenge awaiting him before he died was this thing called pizza.

'What form does the new dish take, Ivan Gavrilovich?' he asked in his precise, mincing way.

'Round, Menzel, perfectly round, with a subtle harmony of colours and flavours.' Ivan breathed on his spectacles and polished them with his handkerchief, in the unconscious hope he was producing the most vivid description.

The very idea there might be something he could not cook goaded the silent, brooding Prokovy. He had worked without recipes ever since recipe books went short in the late 1960s. 'All right,' he said finally. 'Let's give it a try.'

'Come on, tell me what we need.' Andrei began writing on a scrap of squared paper in his shaky hand. 'Then I'll get off and see what I can find.'

The list he read through on the tram included vodka, beef, white flour, onions and salad leaves.

The vodka was his first consideration. With virtual prohibition, it was impossible to find vodka in the shops. He got off the tram closest to the hotel where he used to work and slipped in the back entrance. At a vast table women were chopping and boning scrawny raw chickens.

To a woman in white overalls supervising he begged, in her ear, 'You couldn't slip me a couple of bottles, Mila?'

'Papa, get out of here in your unhygienic state! I'll come over.'

Mila, who had followed Andrei into the catering profession, but found everything else about her father unexemplary, was even fiercer with him in private. She barked, 'What's it worth?'

He admired her thick hair, which ran in the family. 'An afternoon. You can have my flat for Saturday afternoon.' He could always play chess in the park or, if it was raining, go to a film.

Mila had a violent husband but a married lover who was much kinder. She softened. 'Done.'

Andrei left with three bottles in his nylon shopping bag, concealed under newspaper and tomatoes, in case he got mugged. Next day he rose early to make the remaining purchases at the private market.

Meanwhile, Prokovy set up a mincer, a chopping board, sharp knives, a mixing bowl and a frying pan, and for the first time since the merchant owned the house, the museum filled with the smell of real, hot food.

Prokovy removed his apron. Ivan, the waiter, scrubbed his hands pink and listened with approval to his gurgling stomach.

'Ready?' came a shout.

'Ready! Da-daaaa!'

All except Prokovy squeezed into their places. The cook set down two of his creations on the usual plain white plates.

'Aaaaaah.' Everyone was enthusiastic.

'Thank you, my friends, thank you. Here we have a simple new dish, of which it may be said that the unusually regular appearance is, er, unusually pleasing.'

Prokovy sat down, while Ivan poured vodka into the small fluted wine glass that traditionally set their proceedings in motion. Andrei drank the measure down, refilled the glass and passed it on. Someone shouted. 'Health and prosperity!'

'It's good.'

'You can say that again. How many did you make?'

They passed round the special glass again and again. The glass was the last relic from the wartime victory banquet, which Prokovy had secreted away in his pocket and kept all these years. They finished the excellent meal with glasses of strong tea.

Menzel cast the new dish in plaster overnight, painted the model with the help of a sketch made at the banquet and put it on display, garnished with wax pickled cucumbers.

'Now that really is beautiful,' said Andrei, the purveyor of happiness.

'Just one question,' said Ivan. 'How do you make it *so* lifelike?'

Menzel replied proudly, 'Liquid paraffin. You just wipe it over and everything gleams.'

Prokovy said, 'They should include that sentence in your obituary, my friend, followed by "He kept countless appetites whetted for the national heritage."'

'My art is to freeze reality at its best moment. Andrei's is to make people happy, Ivan's to make them well and yours, esteemed Prokovy, to teach everyone to appreciate our efforts.'

'Perhaps we should end our visits with that excellent summary. Or at least display it somewhere,' suggested Ivan.

'So long as we aren't indulging in the cult of our personalities,' warned Prokovy, noting how even with sixty years of practice, certain men could not stop the least praise going to their heads.

The sound of young feet galloping and trainers squeaking against the old wooden staircase rose ominously to meet Andrei.

'There he is! He looks as if he's guarding the mausoleum. He's guarding a bun that was alive once, but now it's been stuffed!'

Prokovy, bringing up the rear struggled to make himself heard. 'Shsh! Children. Respect, please. Today is a special day.' He extended the military-style pointer. 'Here we have a new dish.'

Two of the children tittered. The teachers looked embarrassed.

'But it's a Big Mac!' said one child.

'Bikmak? From Central Asia?'

'No, from Antarctica!'

'Who're you trying to kid, grandad? Can't you bring yourself to pronounce the word A-mer-ik -a?'

The children were roaring with laughter now.

'Tokens of The People's Labour.' Ivan tried to bring them back to order.

'Sources of national happiness,' Andrei reminded them.

'But we don't eat your horrid old food any more. That's why we've come to see your museum. So we can see how things used to be.'

'Oooh!' Prokovy groaned, clutched his chest and turned away.

'Museum's closed,' thundered Ivan.

'Heh, you, not so fast! That's not allowed under the new circumstances. We want our money back!' retorted the teachers. But Ivan slammed the door.

The fates of an artist, a teacher of happiness, a health instructor and a social co-ordinator hung in the balance.

But they bore up remarkably well. In the draught, slippery wrappers of crisps and chewing gum and chocolate blew across the floor.

'Andrei? See this? Can you get me one?' Such packaging Menzel had never seen.

'You bet.'

Prokovy too made a rapid recovery for the Tuesday meeting.

'Another addition? We shall soon be the museum of innovation!'

'I bought six. One each to eat. One for the modelling and, hell, one for the Devil. I couldn't buy five. The only problem is this item involves no cooking and needs no table setting.'

'We'll see about that!' cried Menzel.

When the time came, Ivan laid the tablecloth as always, taking a moment to wipe his glasses on the clean edge. He poured semi-sweet People's champagne into the communal Victory glass, which Andrei held up to the light. 'The colour of piss, just the right colour for health, so they tell me in the polyclinic. But oh, now look at this!'

Menzel the artist entered. He had pulled down the wrapper to midway along the bar, so a substantial chunk of chocolate was visible, smooth as dark skin, with a ripple of tight muscles.

'Oh, oh, sexy, s-e-e-x-y!' cried the old men, with one heart.

Each received an identical plate. The bar lay expectant on a length of white paper napkin. Little icing flower-heads in childish colours garnished the bed. Everyone clapped.

'So you understand my display?'

'Not half!'

Prokovy pulled up the wrapper on his bar, to a chorus of boos.

'Spoilsport!'

He laughed. He hadn't laughed like that for at least ten years. The new freedom and the new *materiel* of life were immensely enjoyable. 'No, I just want to read the name.'

'You don't need to know her name, you old puritan.'

'SNI-CKERS. What is that?'

'Shoes. Sneakers.'

'No, you fool. It's knickers.'

'Knickers!' they shouted.

Suddenly there was a bang, and the sound of glass shattering. A jar of pickled cucumbers landed whole on the table. Something small, flat and hard hit Menzel on the cheek. Another jar of cucumbers smashed, splashing Prokovy with pungent juice. His first thought was that he'd never stop smelling of the stuff. His second that they were clearly under attack from outside, and remained sitting targets, because of the cramped office. A tin of Bulgarian vegetable stew bounced off the side of Ivan's head, just behind his ear. He caught another blow in the chest from a packet of Hercules porridge oats. Half a brick fell out of the packet, which split on impact. 'SNICKERS!' cried Ivan dreamily. Glass from the office window tinkled down. Then silence.

'Oh, God.'

'It's no good praying now.'

Ivan, still wearing his glasses, had gone a strange colour and had no pulse.

'I'll go for an ambulance.' Andrei got up. 'Back as soon as I can.'

'Have you got contacts?' yelled Prokovy. 'They won't exactly hurry if you're nobody.'

After he recovered from the immediate physical shock of the attack, Prokovy took to the streets. Yes, with the freedom people spoke of and the new *materiel* of daily life, the food had changed. Foreign food, like this SNICKERS bar, was everywhere, in shop windows, but mostly being sold from tables in the street, or spread on a scarf on the bare pavement. He stopped to talk to a seller.

'How much?'

'A dollar to you, uncle.'

'Don't be silly, young man, I don't have dollars.'

'Go fuck yourself, then.'

Prokovy quivered. The heat rose to his cheeks. Everywhere behind him, beside him, in front of him, was this huge crowd of people showing no reverence, trading dollars and swearing. There no longer seemed enough space on earth to be of his People. Nor enough space to be Prokovy.

'How about *barrterre*?'

'What you offering, grandad? Your squalid little life?'

'Look, up there, it's the ghost of Little Father Lenin looking down on us. Can't you see? Up there!'

Prokovy grabbed three SNICKERS bars and surprised himself how fast he got away, blending into the dense crowd. He set up 'shop' fifteen minutes away, displaying his wares laid out on a clean handkerchief on the pavement. A greenback crossed his palm. He was in business.

Nor did Andrei ever go back to the museum, which was repossessed by the state and sold to a foreigner. In the hard times which followed the attack on the museum, Andrei devoted himself to his daughter's happiness, by becoming her shopping slave. In return he got his keep, and kept his flat.

It was, of course, Menzel, the star of the old museum, the icon painter of the material world, who triumphed. Menzel wiped the SNICKERS bar with liquid paraffin, put it in a clear acrylic box and knocked on his old front door. The foreigner who bought the museum had turned it into a smart restaurant, with a doorman and callgirls for foreign businessmen and Mafia types. The exhibit became the jewel in the new decor. Menzel's deification of the consumable transferred perfectly from one world to the next, and, as the commissions for frozen slices of the present, paid for in Deutschmarks, rolled in, he became astonishingly rich, which all goes to show that every revolution has its survivors, the ones who really controlled the previous life.

12

THE ETERNAL PROFESSOR

The garish shops, the balloons and the pop music of the Moscow airport called Sheremetevo shocked Victor Klein. He remembered that back in 1975 the old terminal was not much better than a tunnel you crawled through, so low was the ceiling and so oppressive the experience. Pasty-faced thugs and cruel matrons with pink lipstick stopped you with a jerk of the head. They unpacked your bags so you had to kneel down and repack. The suitcase, crammed with supplies for an underprovided land, wouldn't shut. You had to sit and bounce on it, and the whole ordeal which began with wordless undressing under a hostile gaze finally resembled some clumsy attempt at the sexual act, forced upon you in public. You never got a whiff of goodness. No indeed. In that old world language seemed primed to die out and along with it human kindness.

'Professor Klein?' A lovely blonde woman, though over-made-up, held out crimson carnations. Klein wore glasses, he had a moustache and his hair was dark and curly, but having never seen a photograph she recognized him by his quiet, slightly offended manner. No one else was likely to be the visiting professor. 'Welcome to Moscow. I am Valya. We are honoured.'

Valya thrust the blooms into his free hand. Of the flowers Klein thought not everything changed, but then a revolutionary smell of hamburgers wafted past.

'Are you hungry?'

'No, I –'

'Ah, I see you speak Russian, so you don't need me. Valery will take you to the hotel and I will collect you tomorrow at eleven o'clock. OK?'

'The honour is mine, of course,' he finally managed, caught in a no man's land between briskness and sentimentality and a foreigner's utter confusion. He made a faint stab at a wave and was irritated to find the flowers encumbered him.

'This way, Mr Klein.'

Confused, he must have stared after her, which was stupid, because there were plenty of attractive women back home. 'Valya *is* nice girl – ' the driver grinned into his mirror – 'but very busy. She runs a welcome and departure agency for foreign guests.'

'You don't say!'

Klein, transfixed by a dangling mascot of Madonna, sat sorting out his feelings in a Lada car that smelt of petrol. He bought time with his sarcasm, and, concealing his unaccountable hurt, he slid into sightseeing. The airport was ablaze with new neon, otherwise the darkness was pervasive, and the pattern of car and street lights sparse and unpredictable until the main highway began. He reflected that though the airport had graduated to international status, the area around remained a voluptuous wasteland.

'You smoke, Mr Klein? You have to be careful in Russia. They make many packs which look like American but which are not.' Valery, who had thick dull hair and a pimply nape, reached for the Stuyvesant packet lodged in the gear shoe.

Klein struggled to make himself heard over a head-blocking deluge of pop music and staccato talk. 'I gave up. I chew gum. It eases stress and it doesn't kill you. That's good enough for me.'

Klein was handed a packet of Wrigley's.

'Please.'

He noticed the surface of Valery's nails was riven, as if his diet lacked something. Klein had never thought of Russia as a healthy place.

They had been on the busy highway some five minutes when Valery suddenly braked. Klein jerked forwards. In the instant he realized there were no seatbelts and when blue flashing light illuminated the car he wondered if he was already dead. They sailed slowly past the militsia checking a vehicle on the hard shoulder. Klein worried about the smell of petrol. There was no money to service cars these days. If there were a crash, the whole damn thing would ignite in an instant.

'Stolen car, bastards. That's what's wrong with Russia. Nobody wants to work. If there are things they can't get now, they just take them.'

'I heard about the crime.' Klein leaned forward. 'Our newspapers compare 1992 Moscow with 1920s Chicago. I guess there's something in that.'

'*Maafia*. Everything *Maafia*.'

The driver sounded as if he was on Klein's side, the side of law and order, and reason, but the visitor wasn't sure. Russia, another civilization, had made Klein uneasy since he was a student. Now there was this new country.

'But no problem for you. The Institute looks after its guests.'

'They've been very generous.'

The driver shook his head. 'You write great books, don't you?'

Klein pressed his lips together. Even if he thought it, he couldn't say it. In any case, 'great' was probably an exaggeration. He stared out.

Multicoloured saloons queued bumper to bumper where not long ago bureaucrats' Volgas, filthy trucks and the occasional government Zil had seemed almost lonely on the road. At traffic lights pitched high in the sky, Valery shooed away two ragged windscreen boys. The culture Klein was most familiar with, and as a thinking person so despised back home, had seeped through every layer of this changed country, like water leaking through a roof. The obvious flood was on top, but no timber beneath escaped dampness. Klein sensed an inevitable natural event, not a human triumph.

'I couldn't find the hotel on the map.'

'That's because it was a Communist Party Guest House until last year. There! *Vot!* I wanted to show you the new museum to Aleksei Tolstoy just next door.'

A grand stone villa rose out of the darkness, with an ornate staircase lit by globe lamps. Klein didn't mind being treated as an upmarket tourist, except he was too tired to take in much.

'Did you read Aleksei Tolstoy at school?'

Valery moved the pimple constellation to one side. '*Net.*'

'Because he was a favourite of Stalin?'

'Exactly.'

'I never understood why he came back from France.'

'Oh, that's easy. He loved Russia. Now here we are. *Priyekhali.*'

Valery, sprightly in black jeans and trainers, set Klein's bags down on the white marble floor of the small foyer. The façade did not yet say 'Hotel'.

'By the way, you want some caviare? Only ten dollars. I can guarantee it's the best.'

Klein mouthed the Russian version of *ciao*, said he'd think about the caviare tomorrow, and made his way to Reception. '*Loved* Russia'?

The two girls in neat French navy suits and white blouses, one blonde, the other dark, as if they had been picked according to a formula for business success, spoke English with tortured efficiency. The even weighting of the vowels didn't come naturally and in the meticulously artificial way the language had been learned Klein detected repression. They had learned it from other Russians, at a vast distance from real America. He handed over his passport. The blonde registered every guest by hand, in beautiful old-fashioned flowing handwriting, like his mother's.

'The dining room is on the first floor and breakfast is from six a.m. Have a nice stay, Meester Klein.'

Room 107. Given a Cyrillic twist it looked like the word 'lot'.
'And the international phone?'
'Over there, Meester Klein. It looks busy at present.'
'Send the bags up, would you? I'll wait.' Tired from the flight,
he would call Marilyn, then sleep.

He passed the time with a local English-language newspaper,
another token of revolution. A foreign businessman who had been
stabbed in the stomach and kicked in the head was in intensive
care in Helsinki. Klein, not consciously patriotic, felt a tightness in
his chest as he read on. The man's unknown assailants took cash
and credit cards. His Russian woman companion was unhurt.
Well, yes, you could see how that might be. Kick the American.
Some people minded that America, so rich and powerful, had
won the game of the century. But it was outrageous to kick a man
half to death for that . . . symbolic business.

He strode across the mezzanine floor, past a language that
might have been Danish, towards the telephone. Two Russian girls
with rouged cheeks and the sour expressions of models on a
catwalk were eyeing a group of excessively well-dressed
businessmen from the half-shelter of a palm tree in a white tub.

'Marilyn? Honey. It's strange here. Spooky.' He retold the
newspaper story.

'I knew I should have come with you.' Marilyn's free hand
clenched. She didn't want her Victor hurt. She would have
protected him with her bare knuckles. 'Vee, if they jump you, give
them your wallet.'

'They can't even use the credit cards! You need your passport
here even to use a credit card. I guess I'll be OK.'

'Stop rationalizing! You make yourself all the more vulnerable.
They want your cards, Vee, are you listening to me? The credit
card fills a hole in the pocket where the Party card used to sit.
They feel nervous without some other hand-held entitlement to
a dream.'

Klein's wife was clever, probably cleverer than he was. 'That's
exactly it.' He felt grateful to be understood. His wife, who also
wrote, books about fairy-tales in her case, had metaphors at her

fingertips. He only had arguments. 'Look, I'll call again on Sunday.'

She didn't want to let him go. Damn the cost. 'Is it snowing, Victor?'

'Yeah, it's snowing money!'

'Go on!'

'Yeah, you wouldn't believe it. Like it used to rain propaganda. Everyone wants money and everyone's spending it. In case it disappears again. This hotel's awash in the stuff.'

'I'm going to change the metaphor. You make me think of Cinders going to the ball.'

A German built in the same vast mould as his country's chancellor peered in at Klein and tapped his fingers. The girls from behind the palm tree were now sitting with the businessmen, smoking ostentatiously.

'Hell, I don't know. I'll get a better feel for things tomorrow. Look, I must go, this phone costs eight dollars a minute. Bye, honey. Bye. I love you too.'

The German barely allowed Victor Klein time to manipulate his body round the concertina door. Moscow had become the world capital of briskness. The professor, feeling close to his wife, took the lift alone and found his room.

At 107, his lot, you could have broken into the loose and old-fashioned lock with a bent coat-hanger. Pushing the door open, he saw that the furnishings had not been changed since they last gave comfort to distinguished visitors from Czechoslovakia and Cuba, Angola and North Vietnam. The double and single bedheads and the table and the arms of the easy chair were made of dark veneer, scratched and scuffed, and the fabrics and wallpaper were neutral. The fixtures were cheap, the space vast. No one had thought it necessary to make every square metre of habitable downtown space pay its way in the old money-free life.

Klein snorted and shook his head. He hung up his clothes in the dark, capacious wardrobe smelling of fruitwood and mothballs and ran a torrential bath from old-fashioned upright taps.

Then he lay there, with the water fanning out the hair on his chest into a tree of life. If all this was Russia, and Russians, he did feel superior. Thus there was something disturbing about coming *here* to collect a prize for his life's work. And now the tap dripped it out, word by word. How Victor Klein wrote the definitive work on Dostoevsky and explained the quest of one Russian genius for authentic existence. Perhaps Klein resembled Aleksei Tolstoy returning from France, though not out of any love he recognized.

The morning dawned a bright whitish-grey. Klein pulled aside the nuptial gauze of the net curtains and gazed on a nineteenth-century stone building latticed with wooden scaffolding. Not so much as a crowbar resonated, despite an apparent intention to rebuild the ex-Communist city. He wondered for a moment whether it was not a statutory privilege of the area, this quiet which for years surely ensured the comrades slept in after a heavy night of official banqueting. If they slept as well as Klein, they must have woken day after day sure that their way of life would never end.

'How did you slleeeeep?' Valya's accent was more noticeable than had first struck him, and he disliked her limp handshake.

'Great. You're a great organizer, Valya.'

'Now I think you are being ironical.'

'Hell, no, I'm impressed by how quickly everything's changing. It must be difficult to find reliable people and ways of doing things.'

She set a lively pace. The morning brought the kind of freshness which anywhere in the world is a joy. Under a beige winter coat, Valya wore ankle boots, plain stockings and a skirt above the knee. When he fell behind, he especially admired the pretty curves of her legs from hem to boot.

'Here is Tverskoi Boulevard. You remember it was Gorky Street. Everything *is* changing. We rediscover the old names.'

'You're taking on some of our names too, by the looks of things.'

A large McDonald's, with the familiar red, yellow and white logo, waved at them like a flag from opposite the statue of the poet in Pushkin Square. A crowd of would-be breakfasters snaked back down the boulevard, where scaffolding bandaged and splinted the neighbouring building. The whole city was being rebuilt.

'Commercial kitsch is the price we pay for freedom.'

'Indeed. I wasn't being critical. By the way, where did you learn your English? It's wonderful. I almost wouldn't know you were Russian.'

'In the States. I was student at MIT.'

'Recently? '

'A couple of years ago.'

Her father must be someone, Klein thought. Perhaps someone in the American Institute.

'I had a boyfriend called Gideon Lightfoot. Do you know him?'

A woman like Valya would of course have a boyfriend wherever she went, but Klein felt shy to be told about it.

'Do I know him? Hey, Valya, America's a big place like Russia. I live right over the other side of it.'

'I just thought you might know him. He was in the same business. Just a graduate student, of course. He wrote a book on Dostoevsky.'

'Working on Dostoevsky?'

'Yes.'

'I've no personal recollection.'

'Maybe he's in your card index somewhere. He wrote an article but he couldn't get the book published. It annoyed the professors.'

Klein shook his head. 'I really don't know.'

They walked a few yards in the street to avoid more protruding scaffolding.

'Moscow is a beautiful city and you are a beautiful woman.' He saluted her and she gave a lofty nod. The Russians, unlike the Americans, he thought, had no god of modesty.

As they passed a small café a middle-aged man with a ravaged purple-grey face was alternately shouting and kicking the door. 'Eleven o'clock! Eleven o'clock! Why aren't you open? It's a scandal.' Flakes of new green paint collected on the pavement, like fragments of grass vomited by a cat. Klein sympathized. He felt that in Russia he had come up against the hardest surface he had ever encountered in his life.

A sweet unplaceable smell somewhere between cheap children's scent and domestic cleaning fluid wafted them into the Metro and they fell silent. Klein stopped to flick through a biography of Rasputin on a table selling hardcover books. The seller was a young boy in a leather jacket. 'You want porno, Mister?' As quick as a young animal he laid open the matt and fuzzy reproduction of a naked woman with her legs apart and a mouse running up her inner thigh. Klein ought to have laughed but he turned away in shame. Somewhere existed the glossy original from which this obscene mass of dots had been pirated, like a Platonic Idea, but a malign one. 'Loss of control of the belief system.' 'Collapse of the belief system.' Chunks of prose, labels from his casual reading, flashed up like autocues inside his brain. They were his thoughts, already packaged by some political commentator at home, but still they were his thoughts, and they were so vivid, he seemed to see them, as surely as he saw the mouse running up the tart's thigh. And by the way, Marilyn, this is surely post-midnight Cinderella.

'It is reaction against the past,' Valya announced, as if that were the sole fact.

'Sure.' He guessed the same went for the men and young women in white robes, standing beside a statue of Communist warriors and urging newly liberated passers-by to repent. Why, though? You haven't a hope in hell, kids. Your compatriots have just seen a world end – and the end didn't amount to much. Another world began.

'Attention! The doors are closing. The next station is Teatralnaya. Change here for Okhotny Ryad and — Gate.' Something he couldn't make out. Most of the central Metro stations had new, pre-Soviet names.

'We are through one,' whispered Valya, falling momentarily headlong into crazy, alien native thinking. 'The House of Pushkin.'

The Metro passengers had not forgotten their old habits, what Klein called Central Discipline. Voices were lowered as if in a gallery. Not a Walkman hissed. No feet soiled the blue plastic-covered seats. Men and women just rode silently, patiently, to their destination, through the dark tunnels interspersed with chandelier-lit marble catacombs. When against all probability the White Brotherhood did take over, they could make these tunnels their headquarters, for they suited each other.

A war veteran wearing his medals, sitting on the cold stone, blocked their path at the Metro exit. His left leg was missing below the knee. Everywhere Klein looked in Moscow there was a kind of second-rate moral poetry being enacted. The television news he had watched over breakfast had cut gleefully from champagne receptions for the new class of businessman to scavengers for mouldy bread on the city rubbish tip. This is what capitalism does, ex-comrades, it polarizes people. A few enjoy, a lot suffer. He was cross to hesitate at the sight of the beggar, but he couldn't help it. And now Valya heaped on the scorn, as if both men were acting. She prodded Klein. 'Come, we have to hurry, we are late.'

He handed the man a note. Minutes later they arrived.

A black shiny rectangular plaque with a hammer and sickle, and labelled in gold, announced the Institute and indicated the Soviet ministry to which it had belonged.

'To relabel everything is too expensive.'

'Sure.'

Valya added, 'The main entrance is at the side.'

'Of course.'

The ceremony took place in a large lecture theatre which, with its podium and wooden lectern and raked auditorium, might have been anywhere in the world subscribing to the value of an expert discoursing on his subject. The prize wasn't exactly new. Even as recently as Valya had been in the United States, it was known as the International Maxim Gorky Prize and went to obscure left-wingers. Yet as the Order of World Literature in a free world, it had been invested with new hope, like freely convertible roubles in the Pushkin Bank. That bank was now advertising its services on TV with a jingle from the poet's *Ruslan and Lyudmila.*

' . . . Our Hero fell at the old man's feet and in joy kissed his hand. The world brightened before his eyes. His heart forgot its burden. He came to life, yet suddenly again the woe showed in his brightened face . . . "The cause of your sadness is clear, but it's not difficult to drive away" said the old man . . . ' INVEST IN THE PUSHKIN BANK!

'And so, Professor Klein, I have great pleasure in presenting you today with the Order of World Literature. We hope with this new prize for a distinguished lifetime's work in Russian cultural studies to reunite East and West through literature, and especially today to join a free Russia with a free America in friendship and the promise of co-operation for years to come. Thank you, ladies and gentlemen. I do not intend to burden you with superfluous words in the Soviet style.'

The eminent writer and television personality had an ironic charm, which was fortunate, Klein decided, for with his waxy face and goatee beard he looked like a plumper, living version of Lenin.

Now it was Klein's turn to speak. He looked up. The first three rows were full of men and a few women, all about his own age. Valya sat alone a few rows further back, as if she were somehow directing the show. A television crew was stationed to one side of the podium. He stepped forward.

'*Damy i gospoda* . . . ' Once he began it was easy. Why had he for a moment doubted his sincerity and his power to convince? This recognition of his work by Russia as well as the West was indeed the culmination of his academic career. He knew what he believed. 'Ladies and gentlemen, I have had the privilege of writing and researching throughout my adult life in revered and respected intellectual freedom . . . I come from a world which vilifies fakes and charlatans . . . which lauds painstaking application because of the very link between patience, dispassionate inquiry and possible truth. Not Truth, with a capital T – I hope you understand me – but a commitment along its path . . . as if Truth existed . . . but without the pitfalls of absolute belief . . . Literature . . . pursued as a field of objective inquiry out of respect for human complexity and the desire to preserve sources of infinite renewal for humanity . . . a great honour to be here today and to accept this prize.'

The strung-out audience clapped and Klein clapped back. The TV crew, guided by a young woman with a clapperboard whose clothes resembled Valya's, caught the exchange of pieties on film, and then moved to the table where Klein's volumes were displayed, alongside a few single-volume Russian studies of Dostoevsky. Such a spontaneously curious crowd gathered round the table displaying Klein's six glossily bound and sewn volumes that the crew ran off another minute of footage. Klein wondered, amused, at the dubious prospects this table presented for good viewing.

'Allow me to present myself. I'm Stikh. I liked your speech.' The man who thrust out his hand was tall with large square spectacles and a high forehead. He looked Klein's age, mid-fifties, but was probably younger.

'Not Anatoly Gavrilovich? But I'm delighted. I'm such an admirer of your work.'

'And I of yours.'

Klein picked up a single volume in a green-leatherette binding from the display table. *Non-Belief and Verisimilitude: The Dialectic of Artistic Truth in Dostoevsky*. It was a clever title in Russian, something of a play on words, suggesting verisimilitude was a natural continuation or outcome of non-belief. Otherwise it looked just like anything else between hardcovers on sale in the street.

'Russian publishing is not so rich as in the US.'

Klein gripped his colleague's arm. The gesture was potentially hollow, but the emotion at meeting his counterpart after all these years was somehow real. 'My dear Stikh. It's the words that matter, we all know that. I must have a copy.' Stikh was a perceptive critic, strong on wit and irony, only he had not written enough to make his name internationally. And perhaps he had plugged the wit and the irony too strongly, because under his gaze the texts began to disintegrate.

'We can exchange books.'

'We sure can. Here.' Klein, opening his briefcase and taking out volume six, thought of the two hundred dollars it would cost his publisher to furnish Stikh with the complete set of volumes. He'd certainly ask. Stikh thrust the display copy of *Non-Belief* Klein's way.

'It is, how do you say, a token gesture. I feel my book exists just to . . . to keep your work company, Professor Klein. As it is my honoured job today to keep you company at lunch. Will you come this way? We will go by car.'

Valya reappeared. Klein wasn't sure he liked her, with her plastered-on make-up and her limp and deceitful handshake, yet evidently Stikh was pleased to see her.

She took over the talking. 'The Literary Institute has a deal at the Tsentralnaya. It's good for lunch. At your Marco Polo Hotel they charge seventeen dollars for a business lunch. You know that, Professor? Seventeen dollars. That's half a Russian professor's monthly salary.'

Klein whistled obligingly.

Stikh nodded, wanting to say and do the right thing today, realizing it wasn't going to be easy. His wife had recently described his personality as deeply recessed and it was true, he was perfectly aware of that wasteful withdrawal of himself from the community. But he could do nothing now, in established middle age, to produce more light in which others might bask. The awareness produced a perpetual dull, muted pain. He cursed whatever law meant a man could not quite die from the chronic consequences of self-censorship. Valya had once wept for him. Now she too, though so young, needed someone to weep for her.

Valery was waiting outside in the mustard-coloured, smoke-filled Lada. 'About that caviare . . . ' began Klein loudly from the back seat.

Everyone laughed. Everyone was in the same boat these days, trying to make a quick penny. Had Klein doubted it, he needed only look out at Tverskoi. Rows of amateur sellers had turned the main street of the capital into a jumble sale. The pavements were crammed ten thick with women in headscarves and men in fur hats and padded nylon jackets. Valya observed that the situation for ordinary people was desperate and Valery announced there would soon be a law.

'On what?' asked Klein, hoping it would stop the trade in fake caviare.

'Clearing the streets,' the driver replied through his cigarette.

'That's immoral,' said Klein.

Stikh struggled to agree. 'Maybe.'

'This mess is immoral,' said Valya.

Too much to tackle, decided Klein in the end. They drew up outside a three-storey building, which this time the black plaque said belonged to the Ministry of Food.

'The main entrance is at the side,' said Valya.

'Of course it is,' replied Klein and this time he laughed.

Marble Ionic pillars held up a fantastic neo-Baroque extravagance of moulded plaster, mirrors and chandeliers. The floor was shiny real woodblock parquet. On the cabaret stage at one end of the restaurant a huge silver and black backdrop had been left in place, suggesting a fairy-tale Russian village by night. OK, you win, Marilyn, I *am* in a fairy-tale.

'They have a floor show in the evening,' said Valya.

'The girls will come in to rehearse if we're lucky.' Stikh forced out the joke as they sat down. A *man* ought to take an interest in women, not dismiss them all as whores. At the table every one of forty place settings had three pink glasses with gold rims, one for vodka, one for fruit punch, one for champagne. Twin piles of black and white bread formed rectangles amid the rows of round white plates and the jugs of pink punch. Beside the table a series of curtained cubicles like railway carriages opened up the near side of the room.

'The *cabinets particuliers* of old merchant Moscow,' said Stikh. 'I love this place. You know, Klein, in the 1930s it was the home of the Comintern. The training ground for Communists the world over.'

Klein started. The information was too great for him to take in and would soon be washed away by the vodka a smiling blonde waitress with large firm hips was tipping into the small glasses.

Stikh got to his feet, raised his Devil's thimble of 40 per cent proof spirits and declared how happy he was to entertain Klein today. In the past this sort of occasion used to happen only with comradely colleagues, Czechs and Poles and Bulgarians. He still had in a display cabinet in his office all the souvenir red flags and ribbons and shields they brought with them as gifts. He paused for laughter.

'That's the sort of thing we Communists used to do. We gave each other useless presents, then we drank. Now we just drink. But we keep better company.' Stikh raised the glass again to Klein, then swayed it in the general direction of all the other guests, many of the men already inebriated.

Klein saw the long table slough off the bric-à-brac of the past like a gently writhing snake. He savoured the vodka and helped himself to red salmon caviare. The spirit had already dulled his nerve endings when he asked, 'Ladies and gentlemen, am I right in thinking with Dostoevsky that vodka cauterizes the weeping Russian spirit?'

'Whatever it does to the Russian spirit it's German now,' observed Valya, turning the label in Klein's direction. 'Russian vodka is not reliable these days.' Black caviare was also now impossible to find.

She droned on while the vodka ticked like a time bomb in the topmost compartment of his spine, as if waiting for permission to enter his brain. Gideon Lightfoot! Jesus. It was true, Klein had vetoed the book as fashionable rubbish. But hadn't he had every justification? Lightfoot's book began with the premise that biography meant nothing in the autonomous text, that nothing need be related to Dostoevsky's central experience of facing the fake firing squad, nor to his hard labour in Siberia. In his mind's eye, Klein saw the books on the table again, his and Stikh's. Gideon Lightfoot would have liked to see his book on such a table, of course. Jesus, the resentment that man must feel!

'Will they really put those dull shots of the books on the news, Valya? You know what I mean. You've seen US television.'

'It's true they are not exactly news. But we cannot have everything the same, Professor Klein.'

He hadn't wanted to suggest that. She twisted his words.

Stikh intervened. 'We used to be paid by the word, Klein. You would have done well here!'

Klein flushed, blaming the vodka.

Stikh was drinking steadily. All his working life he had imagined himself competing with the West, longing to know where their work was leading, in order to define his own task more accurately. Now, alas, he could be sure. He raised his glass again. 'The West has won, Professor Klein! Three cheers for the West!'

The American was embarrassed. He had feared something like this. 'In politics surely there can be no *moral* victory, my friends.' Klein nodded to every figure down the table where his eyes could catch some attention. Genuinely contrite, he might have been at the funeral of a friend he had not loved enough. And just as if they were at a funeral, he had a strong intuition of what should now be discussed, to strengthen and to comfort those who endured loss. He and Stikh shared their love of one writer.

'Dostoevsky had no sense of the erotic.'

'Oh, I cannot agree. What about *The Gambler*? Polina's wonderfully seductive long foot!'

Both men fleetingly recalled Valya's little ankle boots, somewhere under the table.

'The foot as object of desire. Only, Stikh, I suspect Feodor Mikhailovich borrowed that from Pushkin. Really I don't believe he had the erotic sense. He was too anxious, too aggressive.'

'He mainly wanted women to forgive him, it's true. But perhaps he had erotic feelings towards men. *The Eternal Husband* is such a strange story. You remember its White Nights. The drama of the season means two competing men cannot hide their night-time longing as they share a room floodlit by eternal day . . . '

'Their bond is an interconnected destiny, I grant you, and the mystery of that may be erotic.'

'Violent feelings bind them. Each fears violence at the hands of the other. They must always struggle against each other, even though one is predestined to lose. Into this relationship Dostoevsky put his deepest knowledge of the human heart, I believe. For once he did not try to soften that knowledge with religion.'

'It is a profound view, Stikh. I happen to be consultant editor on *The Journal of Dostoevsky Studies*. I reckon we would be honoured to publish such a paper. I hope you'll write it.'

But Stikh, drinking on, was moving towards the degree of intoxication which would soon dissolve not only self-respect but all respect, and he only said finally, 'You are safe in your university, Professor.'

'Safe?' Like all ugly people who are not coarse, Klein looked vulnerable.

'I mean that your seriousness is protected by the Constitution. Is that not what you were saying in your prize speech?'

Klein felt like a caricature of himself and wondered if that was what he had meant. 'I wouldn't say our seriousness — I take it you mean moral seriousness — is in any way *protected*. No, we're constantly having to redefine it.'

Stikh, instead of nodding politely, or answering, then did a strange thing. He got up, pushed back his chair and flapped his arms and clucked like a brooding hen.

Valya's face switched from sulking dutifulness to ecstasy. 'Bravo!' She turned bright-eyed and excited to Klein. 'Professor Stikh is very fond of acting out scenes from Chekhov.'

'Is it Chekhov? My ignorance, I'm afraid,' replied Klein, who decided nothing would be gained by taking offence.

The table had emptied because the German vodka was finished. Waitresses cleared plates. Stikh insisted Klein come home with him to meet his wife, and Klein, weakened by the little alcohol he had drunk, could find no reason to say no. Anyway, he liked Stikh.

The journey took forty minutes by Metro and was once again covered by Central Discipline, though Stikh said, 'Sleep if you like, Klein. I'll watch your wallet.'

They emerged in darkness out on to rough ground, ringed by a score or more high-rise blocks. Arm in arm they crossed a tram line, passed a row of closed kiosks and a provisions store like a concrete barn. A seemingly rural path made by constant human coming and going across a huge apron of scrubland led to Stikh's staircase, with the bank of letter boxes fixed to the cold stone wall and the brute stone stairs rising hopelessly out of the well. They took the lift to the twelfth floor.

Marina Stikh was not at home, and had no reason to be, not having been warned that her husband might bring Klein for supper. But the two-bedroom apartment betrayed her touch. It was neat and clean, with the slippers lined up in the hall, and the empty jars waiting in the kitchen to be returned. Under the low ceiling they passed through to the sitting room. Books in a huge piece of wall-to-wall veneer furniture lined the far side, with a wide shelf below for a few interesting objects in glass and carved wood. Opposite, an oil painting of a short-haired dark woman, invitingly dressed in the warmest blue Klein had ever seen, created, in the electric light, an instantly uplifting atmosphere.

'Is this your wife? She's a lovely woman.'

'Yes. When I come home and she is not here, I am always afraid she has left me. Excuse me while I check there is no note in the bedroom. Or the kitchen.' He returned, shaking his head. 'Vodka?'

'No.'

'As you like.'

They looked out over the estate, which resembled that desert of underdevelopment around the airport. Klein saw the path that led them from the Metro. It had lights, so it wasn't entirely improvised, only no one had got round to making a proper surface and now it wasn't necessary. The habit had become an institution. Carelessness, as much as anything, propelled life on here. To one side of the path some children had lit a bonfire.

'It's impossible to know where you are in a suburb like this without numbers. All the blocks look the same. And you can't see the numbers till you get up close. You see?'

Klein thought he did.

'I mean whatever happens deliberately in Russia is designed to confuse . . . Only, like that we make your meanings clearer. That is our Russian job in the world. Am I making sense? It is not really a paradox.'

Klein thought Stikh was unusually lucid for a man who had drunk so much.

'So now, tell me, what drew you to Dostoevsky so long ago? I suppose you were a student still when you made the choice . . . so much happens when we are so young. I remember making my choices.' Stikh paced the dining-cum-sitting room as he often did alone. Since his decision to stay in Russia he had grown perverse. A law as if of the natural world dictated that in intellectually unfree conditions he should become too detached, too ironic, too unconstructive to function. To converse with a man who still had belief took him back a long way. He begged Klein to answer as fully as he could.

'The problem of power concerned me . . . I found in Dostoevsky a message of love and humility . . . It seems to me even now his novels are among the few Christian books which retain any meaning in the modern world . . . '

But both oddly and rudely now, Stikh appeared not to be listening. He had walked over to the fitted furniture. There was a drawer beneath a green-glass vase and a mounted wooden cross. Out of it he took a red oblong box containing dominoes. He set out six on the small square dining table which divided the window end of the room from the sitting end. Beside the six close together he laid one apart.

'But six volumes! I cannot believe this! You want to take over the world through Dostoevsky, Professor Klein? I see your books and I know that in every human heart there is imperialism.'

Klein, letting the table edge pummel his abdomen, reminding

him this was really happening, stared at the dominoes. 'You've been drinking, Stikh. You're entitled to your view, but imperialism is a bad word all the same. It means domination.'

'Indeed. My view shocks me too. But I cannot change it for that. You, Victor Klein, who have enjoyed the privilege of an uninterrupted long life in a liberal society, have written a work inspired by the desire for a personal empire, is that not so? You have blocked students who do not agree with you. Your prose has got slower and duller over the years. Less than perfect reviews have so enraged you. You have complained to the press after every volume. You are compelled to dominate in your work because your life is too free.'

A wall of words toppled upon Klein. He could only fend off a few bricks at a time. One of them bore the name of Gideon Lightfoot. He took it in his hand, weighed it, felt its roughness and moved back to the window. From there he again looked out over the monotonous, endlessly self-duplicating estate. At first sight these horrendous godless towers dwarfed real people. In practice, though, Klein could see, the local inhabitants had simply become used to the tower blocks, and lived with them, as people did with ugly wallpaper.

'The point is surely that my opponents were free to defend themselves, to fight back,' the American said at last. 'And if they didn't the fault is only theirs. No one provided them with excuses for their inadequacy. There were no paper shortages. There was no censorship. Incidentally, you're not going to tell me that's why you have only written one book in your entire career, Stikh, because the State – the Communist state which demanded constant individual sacrifice – was short of paper?'

Stikh too stared out of the dismal window. Was a single volume all he had to show for his life? He was an easy target. Like many an outwardly fierce opponent, when challenged he suddenly shrank to nothing.

It was Marina they needed. When they heard the lock turn they gravitated like two lost boys towards a hopeful signal. They found her, hat in one hand, plumping up her dyed hair in the mirror.

Looking older than the picture, but bright-eyed and fine, she shook Klein's hand.

'We are drinking vodka, Marinochka, come and join us.' He stopped and started again. 'No, *I* am drinking. Because I am weak and I work slowly and I am Russian, *I* am drinking.' His words trailed after Klein, who found a seat unaccompanied on the sofa, beneath the portrait.

'Do your women disapprove of *vodochka*, Klein? They have to here. *Vodochka* is courtesan of the Russian spirit. She is their rival. A source of endless pleasure and relief.'

Marina, relaxed and alert, was utterly charming, Klein thought. How could Stikh ever prefer Valya?

Stikh had taken one arm chair, his wife the other.

She said, 'My dear, you will confirm our guest in his undoubted view that all Russians have an inferiority complex.'

Klein sat forward impassioned. 'No, that's not what I think at all.'

'You come to Russia at a difficult time for us. My husband's salary has doubled, but prices have risen twenty-fold. People are already wondering how they will survive next winter. It is likely to be even worse.'

'I know. I feel bad. It hurts. You can't know how much pain it is causing me to see this everywhere on the streets. I feel terrible guilt.'

Stikh watched them as if they were a pair of gambolling puppies.

'Marina works in the Kremlin. That's why we are all right.'

She made a face at Klein. 'The Historical Museum has an archive in the White Tower. I can take you in if you like.'

'I'd be fascinated,' answered Klein, knowing he really would be.

She disappeared and brought back German cheese biscuits, cucumbers and a plate of sliced salami and set them on the table beside the dominoes. 'Did I interrupt a game?'

'Not exactly.'

Stikh took the cheese biscuits and, returning to the armchair, ate them in greedy handfuls, as if scooping up the biscuits to feed to invisible birds. Then he fell asleep.

'He won't wake up till morning.'

The room was silent. Klein looked round. He was miles from anything he could be sure of and the sudden intimacy with Marina Stikh alarmed him. He cursed himself for being aware of it, but it was too late.

'Don't worry, Mr Klein, it's quite normal for Russian men to leave their women, by conscious or unconscious means, and to do so repeatedly through a lifetime. May I?' She slipped a few more salami slices on to his plate. She was too close. His eyes fell on the dominoes. The tart with the mouse pouted at him. He stepped back and found it hard to speak.

'I must go, Mrs Stikh. What time does the Metro stop?'

Marina looked at him. He had neither style nor beauty, but a reasonable mildness radiated from this American, as if he had firm principles, but saw no reason to invoke them except in an emergency. Now was an emergency.

'You have an hour. But you must take the bus first. I'm sorry, Professor Klein, my husband would have accompanied you, but as you see, he is like all Russian men, unreliable . . . He did not tell me you were coming as our guest tonight.'

'I understand, Mrs Stikh, believe me. I understand. You know, your husband's book really is wonderful. Russian studies would be the poorer the world over without it. And if he will only write this paper we were discussing, then I think his name will be made in the US.'

'You are very kind. I know we will meet again.'

Klein walked across the dark, numberless estate. Come on, you bastards, I'm here for the taking. You can do what you like with me, now it's clear what I've really been up to in my life. But Klein could not make violence befall him even walking in this wilderness. Central Discipline still applied. He felt then too free. He wanted to gorge himself on Marina Stikh's body. He heard her sighing. He started to run back. God, no! He took out a small fish-shaped penknife he kept in his pocket and jabbed at his palm until he cried.

The phone rang in the morning. He'd overslept. It was already past eleven. A man's voice spoke. Klein's whole body felt heavy and weak. At least it wasn't Valya.

'Can you give me ten minutes? I'll be right down.'

A grey face looked back at him from the bathroom mirror. Hah! I am like Nastasya Filipovna, the whore of Dostoevsky's creation, who wants to be punished. I resemble that lover of goodness whose greatest erotic desire is to be murdered! He washed the hand, tore a couple of handkerchieves into strips and bandaged it.

In the salt-mine foyer, where the palm tree stood bedded in giant eggs of grey-stone caviare, the face which loomed was that of yesterday's Master of Ceremonies: the television man, the one who used to be President of the Writers' Union, and before that was Lenin. Staying seated, he shook Klein's right hand as energetically as if he wanted to reconfigure him.

'But, my dear sir, did you hurt yourself?'

'It's nothing.'

The man gestured towards the coffee table in front of him. 'Beluga caviare, Veektor, just for you and guaranteed authentic.'

'Authentic, eh? How can I thank you?'

'Popov,' said the other. 'And my latest book.'

Klein wondered whether he had ever before seen a man so content with his lot. The book consisted of essays on the emergence of Russian writing from Communism.

'Wonderful. Would you sign it for me? I'm sure it should be translated.'

'I am sure too. The Americans do not understand Russia.' Popov had lovely handwriting, Klein noticed. He put away the expensive foreign pen. 'Professor, Veektor, if you don't mind my saying, you don't look very well.'

'Something I ate, I'm afraid. I had a rough night.'

Popov looked reproachful, as if this disingenuous account of the effects of vodka was not worthy of a grown man. Besides, it hardly accounted for the hand. But Klein, who had knelt beside the lavatory pan while his body rejected whatever had got inside him, and for an hour heaved and quivered in another parody of love, said firmly, 'It's true. And now I must pack.'

Klein disappeared into the lift. Popov snapped his fingers. 'Valery! Our Professor is not well. You must drive slowly.'

At the airport Klein was already checking in his bags, having thanked Valya for all she had done. The Departures side was never as busy as Arrivals. In Communist days the joke was that not everyone returned West who came East. So it was easy to hear a voice shouting and spot the body to which it belonged. 'Veek — tor! Veek — tor!' He saw Marina behind the barrier dividing landside from airside.

'I brought a present for Marilyn. Be careful! It's fragile.'

With his bags wedged between his feet, he ran his free hand down the bulky arm of Marina's coat. She was still a little out of breath and hot.

'It took two hours to get here on the bus. I was afraid I would miss you.'

'But you could have got to Frankfurt . . . ' He began a foolish comparison which wasn't worth uttering. Russia was a good place for wasting time. And wasn't that Valya, wasting some more of it, standing at a distance, watching them, as if they were acting out a departure for her entertainment? For God's sake! This place was driving him insane.

He held on to Marina's arm. 'Look, Mrs Stikh, Marina, if there's anything I can do to bring your husband over to the States and you with him, of course . . . '

'Veektor, no, no! I just came to wish you a good trip home!'

He stood, as if momentarily detached from his own fate. 'Yes, I am going home.'

Before the clock strikes midnight in Russia and the deepest things are made conscious a man must go home. For if he stays on there will only be darkness, and no Prince of Peace to guide him with love. Isn't that so, Feodor Mikhailovich? And if so, why did you not tell me before?

Klein was perhaps still feverish thinking these things, but when the plane was safely cruising at an international altitude, he at last saw everything more clearly. He had a home, but he no longer had a place in Russian studies. He would hand in his resignation on Monday.

217

13

SOFKA AND SASHA

Once in Russia we imagined human endeavour had gone underground; cells of good souls knitted together to fight the evil regime overhead. An American film mushroomed from this fantasy. Do you remember *Ghostbusters*? But in the country I knew the underground city was a recognized part of ordinary life. Tractors ran along empty rough-hewn corridors ferrying provisions to the rulers overhead. Off the tunnels were offices and storerooms, and thousands took lifts down to work in the tunnels every day, and joined the ordinary queues on the way home. The tunnel-workers lived by that electric light which was half of the official formula for perfect modern living: filing, ordering, storing and providing a comfortable life for others; they worked out of loyalty and ordinary human gratitude for a bearable routine. The only occasional rebellious thought was that if ever the important folk did move downstairs, in an emergency, they would dislike sharing their lives with rats and cockroaches. They would be out of practice and their eyes would take a while to adjust. You see, this story is about what really was achieved underground during the Cold War, though it is hard for us to recognize, being something like back to front, or the wrong way up, and because our eyes too are not accustomed.

Sofka, her face round as a clock, soft as a sponge, worked in the underground provision of the good life for thirty years. She was happily married, with a grown-up son. In her free time she helped out with a young people's group called Pioneers of the Better Life, and she watched television. She loved her stratified country with a speluncular passion and eyes weaned on blackness. This love was so intense that when the first Westerners arrived, liberators of the Cold War-torn land, door-openers of its unbroken network of prisons, Sofka, along with hundreds of thousands of other women, faced them with saucepans and spoons, and shopping bags for shields. They marched through the narrow streets behind Red Square, unleashing in their cause that supreme weapon, the wearyingly loud and consistently high voice of the Soviet matron. 'You are not necessary! Concern yourselves with your own motherland!' The liberators protected their ears and blamed anger and frustration for that punitive, autocratic tone. Of course, Sofka and her kind lost the battle against invasion.

On the long Metro ride home, she drank a last cup of chocolate from her flask. It was almost a mile home along half-made paths from the suburban station and the shopping weighed . . . well, there was a joke about volunteering to go into space, just to get away from the daily pull of gravity on your shopping bag. You could rest your other senses in space too. Here weeds grew up between the paving crevices and the concrete universal emporium stank and gaped like an empty fish hall. Sofka was usually merry, but the poor thing was tired tonight. Beside the *univermag*, in front of a closed side door, the man paid to keep the path clear of weeds waited with religious patience. Thirty to forty people kept him company.

Sofka scowled. 'Eh, citizen, we are all ashamed of you, you know, because you do no work.'

'Eh, granny, you know what you can do, gran, you –'

His words spun like a stalled whirlwind as he waited for more vodka. She threw her head in the air and strode on.

Sofka was a kind of dim, distant relative of Plato, I believe, now living unrecognized in Russia. With Pioneer songs in her head about sunshine and decency, she was one of those people for whom the rest of the world was indolent and decadent; an honest bureaucrat, she belonged among the few organizers who were reliable and good in a state which, alas, had false guardians. Her husband, Sasha, a mild-mannered silver-haired military colonel who did not drink and had therefore kept his health and good spirits, made an excellent team-mate.

They ate supper in the kitchen, after which the flat smelt of cabbage and hot oil. The interior lighting was uniformly bright, as were the colours of the furnishings and the shades of Sofka's clothes. The whole habitation revealed deficiencies in the official aesthetic, but it was indisputably comfortable. Sasha sat in a wooden-armed chair reading an approved classic in a leatherette binding: a translation of H. G. Wells's *The Time Machine*, approved because Wells long ago went to Russia, more to praise than to condemn, and certainly not, as now, to rescue. Wells wrote wonderful stories, Sasha enthused to Sofka. The anti-paradise of the Morlocks, the cave-dwelling ape people who had taken over the human race and reduced them to benign and pretty slaves, came over so vividly that he felt the Morlocks had become a problem in his own life. Like the hero of that story, he saw the possibility of people no longer defending their own moral worth, or each other's, and losing all reason for living except pleasure. Sunshine and material plenty would intensify the temptation to give up.

Sofka, her outdoor shoes exchanged for Turkish slippers, and the slippers now kicked off, was watching television in stockinged feet, some new comedy programme into which the political changes of the moment had introduced risqué jokes. A sketch showed some indolent men standing about, like the path-maintenance man, drinking vodka, getting no work done, advising their president on how to make their homeland a better place. She experienced a warm, piquant feeling of familiarity. Jokes about Russia were like jokes about marriage: fine so long as you stayed married. Then mannequins paraded across the screen in a talent contest. Each one from underneath her layers of make-up was required to describe her ambitions, avoiding any reference to the opposite sex, or winning another beauty contest, and she had to impress television viewers by speaking one or two foreign languages. At this satire on Western chic, Sofka rocked with laughter, lifting her stout calves in thick mud-coloured tights clean off the ground. 'Look, Sash, don't miss this . . . ' Her face crumpled, the eyeballs travelling skyward, the lower lip pursed over the upper one. But when her clear-eyed husband looked up, he was so engrossed he could only think that the mannequins and the idle workmen would be ideal prey for the Morlocks. 'Wells has convinced me. We must love and respect our neighbours. As we have love and respect for each other, eh, Sofka.' Many happy evenings passed like this.

One day, however, as was eventually bound to happen, Sofka met a Westerner, at what turned out to be the last May Day Parade. (It became one of the liberators' jokes. May Day – Mayday! – *M'aidez*! All through the Cold War all those people like Sofka stood waving in Red Square, asking to be airlifted out, and we never noticed.) The Westerner with the tiny-featured feline face, with downy skin and long eyelashes and breath never tainted by garlic and sausage, spoke to Sofka. They were neighbours among the spectators. At first Sofka pretended she hadn't heard the peculiarly unmusical version of her language. Then she turned. No harm in nodding. The speaker's dark lashes and high cheekbones and pretty little features were framed by a seductively soft collar of fake fur, so that she seemed like a sweet animal. A sentimental human being would have yearned to stroke her. Finally Sofka softened and said a few words. That she worked in catering. And part-time with children. And was a wife and housewife. Such was a woman's lot the world over, wasn't that so? *Sofka*. She repeated her name with a smile at the unintelligible difficulty. S-o-f-k-a. Toffee, said the Western woman's small son, brought along in American trainers and pale jeans and a red padded nylon jacket to watch the parade. The mother laughed too. 'Toffee. You know what that is – *karamel*!' And Sofka smiled.

'I shouldn't mind being called something sweet. And what is your name?'

'I'm Kate and this is Marcus.'

'Kait. Marcoos.'

Sofka was looking at these people, while the oompah of trumpets gave a musical frame to the picture and formations of fit young people marched across the square, holding flags and banners aloft. She was still happy when she suddenly realized something in life had passed her by. It wasn't travel abroad, but something else more frightening. She turned abruptly from the trumpets and the marching and the new friends. 'I wish you all the best.'

'No, wait! Won't you tell me how we can meet again? Where do you work?'

Weakened by a sudden insight into her deeper needs, Sofka did stop and write down her home number. But five minutes later she was, to her great relief, back underground, waiting for a Metro train.

Nearly four months passed.

'Hi, Sofka, this is Kate. Remember me? Won't you come over? My husband's dying to meet you. We're in that new high-rise block close to the American Embassy. Have you still got the address?'

Sofka called to mind the building site where the trams had passed. For two years passengers had smiled wryly at each other, thinking of the microphones installed in all blocks for foreigners. 'Both come?' she asked finally.

'Of course.'

'OK. Until next week. Have good time.'

Sofka put down the red receiver with the round earpieces. Sasha was in the kitchen, where there was just room for a table for two.

'That was that *foreignka* I met in Red Square. She wants us to go round.'

Sasha was sewing buttons on to a blue shirt. 'Why not? I should be ashamed to die knowing so little about the rest of the world.' He sucked the end of the cotton, trying to rethread his needle.

'Give it to me! There!' She stroked his thin hair. 'You're right. We should be interested.'

So they took the Metro, then caught a bus and arrived early. A stroll twice round the block brought them up to eight p.m., and on that stroke they stepped on to the cakewalk of another world. Kate was wearing a greenish-khaki shift dress in some textured material with a neat-collared black shirt beneath. Her legs had a balletic grace in matt-black tights and small high-heeled ankle boots. You could see immediately as she opened the door and gave her big white smile that Kate was in touch with a secret order of beauty.

Sofka sat flushed but happy. Sasha and Dan discovered they had no common language. Marcus ate up the entire bowl of mini-pretzels in two greedy handfuls, which he partly scattered on the carpet and partly spat out. He sat laughing loudly.

Kate served fresh tuna and *pommes dauphinoises*, but Sofka hardly ate, for it did not seem beautiful to eat. Dan tried to talk to Sasha about classical music by fetching him CD covers. It was a blessing that the au pair, a young American woman student of business, arrived home half-way through the evening and translated. Sasha asked about salaries in the West, and housing, and cars, and job security, and the prices of things, and Dan became quickly bored. Marcus did handstands on the carpet, had a lucky escape when he crashed legs-first into the glass-fronted case, and then entertained them all with magic tricks before refusing to go to bed. Kate and the au pair exchanged glances. While the off-duty au pair put the eight-year-old to bed, Sofka insisted on helping Kate clear the dishes. In the small super-modern kitchen, while the kettle boiled, Kate reflected on her difficult son, while Toffee hovered, blinded, and beamed. 'Children, *gospozha*! It's just a stage that will pass.'

'What did you think of him?'

The underground train home swayed them back and forth,

lights occasionally flickering. In the black window Sofka caught sight of herself as a bundle of human flesh and man-made textiles randomly dumped on earth, and felt the disappointment of the first human being who ever looked in a mirror.

'What do I know about banking! But interesting, a fine man. Sofka, we have so much to learn about their world. Sofka, you asked me . . .'

But his wife had fallen into a trance. She needed to dream. No state should deprive its people of dreams. Women especially. Especially Sofka needed, like Kate, to look at herself in the mirror and say 'Not bad!' That kind of dream.

Kate discussed it with Dan, then a week later rang Sofka. 'I hope you'll accept, Toffee. It's a pretty good salary, by Russian standards, but above all I'd love to have you work with me.'

'I shall have to give it some thought, my dear Kate.' Sofka was trembling. The plastic telephone felt disgustingly light and clammy, like a cheap toy, and the flat claustrophobically small. 'I will discuss it with my husband.'

'Love to Sasha then.' Sofka hung up. When she realized she had not herself sent reciprocal love to the unapproachable, immaculate Dan and to the excitable Marcus, she almost redialled.

Two more months of silence passed.

'I wondered whether you'd decided, Toffee . . .'

Kate loved being part of the age in which she lived. She loved the international life. Her passion for being up to date and adaptable made her in this matter of Russia extraordinarily patient, unlike her husband.

'Almost. Shall I come over and discuss the final details next week?'

Sofka too was helped to make up her mind by times changing. As of the New Year her country no longer existed. She and Sasha were orphans.

'Hi, Toffee!'

Kate embraced her, the stout Russian woman whose soft face threw her dark dyed hair into harsh relief. Marcus, ever more pale and freckled and wide-eyed, hung about while his mother and her guest had tea and little cakes in the room where they had previously dined. It was less magical in the afternoon, but in the full light you could see all the furnishings in the apartment were good quality, and its owners too. Half an hour was enough for Sofka to be sure. She now loved this delicate creature from the West. Loved her for her careless good taste and her cool organization and her pretty child. The power of soft femininity to transform and reconcile the harshnesses of the world radiated from Kate. Sofka fell into a half-trance again. Marcus somersaulted over the sofa-back, kicked over two cups on the table, burst into tears and cuddled up to his mummy like a baby.

'Mummy, I didn't mean to. Say I'm a good boy.'

'You are a good boy. Go and play now. If you're a good boy I'll get you a present.'

'Promise?'

'Promise.'

Now Sofka had Kate to herself. Her eyes crinkled as if she were blinded by sunshine. She loved the gentle life of tears wiped away and presents freely given and promises kept, and, wishing she could give something back in kind, she finally made a tribute of her labour. She gave up her tunnel job and went to work for Kate in a plate-glass palace as a sandwich-maker for Moscow's new foreign workers.

Most evenings after that her eyes closed in front of the TV, for she worked so hard and with such a will. As she sat back and snored, Sasha was touched at his wife's vulnerability and puzzled by her ambitions. Sometimes now she was so tired at weekends she couldn't find the energy to go with him to Sokolniki Park and watch the past being sold off as souvenirs. Sofka and Sasha were patriots, but there was something fascinating about the unpredictability of bric-à-brac stalls anywhere and since their country had deprived them all their lives of the joy of shopping, or even browsing, they had come to enjoy their Sunday excursions like children. The Sunday they did get to Sokolniki together, they laughed so much and so enjoyed their late lunch in the kitchen that afterwards they cuddled up on the sofa and Sasha kissed his wife passionately, a pleasure long forgotten. 'I am old and fat, Sasha. Don't try to argue with me.' And while she said that Sofka wondered how Kate was: graceful; beautiful; sensual; suntanned; like a body you saw on a film.

With the money Sofka earned they bought a few things. She ran a dollar purse as well as a rouble purse, for Kate paid her in precious dollars, and anyway the whole country had two currencies now. They gave things to their young married son, who lived in a communal apartment in Petersburg. It was like pouring water through a sieve but it didn't matter. Being well off probably wasn't a permanent arrangement, one shouldn't change one's life at the drop of a hat . . . And indeed, within six months Kate and her family moved to a new job in France. Sofka's hands flew to her face. 'Oh, Lord! What shall I do?' They had demolished the tunnels by then. But Sofka had her experience of working with Westerners and needed not fear unemployment. She was 'made' and took a job in one of the new hotels.

Kate did keep in touch. Some things like that happen. People feel guilty for good fortune perhaps, and feel they would do best to share it. Or they have a desire for symmetry and good workmanship in human affairs, which seems an equally moral impulse. The collapse of decades of Communist despotism also touched people in the West. They wanted to do something to help. How do you help people stand on their own feet? Use your contacts to give them a little money and a lot of knowledge? You can't just throw money at them. They have to learn to grow again. Try to help them. Anything's worth a try.

'Toffee, it's me, Kate . . . ' There was a pause while the voice bounced off the satellite and echoed down the line. 'How are you, darling? Toffee, come and stay with us now we're settled! We've plenty of room. We'll arrange it all this end and post you the ticket. You need to catch up on the world. Come and see us, please.' Why me, why all this good luck for me? thought Sofka, posing quite genuinely the question from which her neighbours and friends had extracted a year of envious gossip. 'If you want to go, Sofka, you should,' said Sasha with ideal understanding.

'Abroad, I mean the real abroad, not this near abroad the empire sentimentalists have just invented for us. Real abroad is something every human being should know about.' In truth Sasha did not know what real abroad was, if it was not the land of the hairy white Morlocks or their pleasure-glutted victims. But he wanted his wife to be happy.

'You must take care, of course.'

'Stop, Sasha, stop, I don't want to hear anything more about tunnels and people enslaved to hairy Morlocks.'

Already Sofka couldn't bear to think back. He was hurt. *The Time Machine* meant more to him than anything he could remember. It meant understanding. It gave a real clue to being a worthwhile person.

He gave Sofka long reproachful looks as she took ages in the bathroom every morning and added scarves and jewellery to her outfits. For the first time in nearly thirty years their marriage became awkward. 'Can't you understand . . . ' she shouted, but never completed the sentence out loud. He should understand. She hadn't had her turn.

They said six months for the visa. With the dollar purse Sofka reduced the wait to six weeks.

'Heavens, Sofka, that's bribery! You're going from being a slave in one world to a slave in another.'

'No, Sasha, in their way it's normal to do things with money. If you're in a hurry you can pay to speed things up. That's official, not under the counter, as it used to be with us. You see there are no sides now, I have learned. The great power struggle is over. There is only more or less money.'

Sasha shook his head, in fact his whole body shook, and he took his coat and boots and said he was going for a walk. Sofka shrugged and realized she had become embroiled in some great struggle. She prepared for her trip the way women everywhere in the twentieth century prepared for . . . independence! The struggle for women's independence made men afraid and unsure of who they were, and they drank or went out for long walks. Poor Sasha was suffering. He had been made redundant from an army that protected a country which no longer existed. Now Sofka made him redundant. She no longer watched TV in the evenings, but tried to learn French from a phrase book. She put herself on a diet and, as Sasha sat in his track suit and socks reading, he heard her stomach rumble in protest and felt angry she wasn't eating. She went to the hairdresser's and had her hair redyed too.

She wondered what presents to take. The problem was, nothing was available in the shops while the old system of provision was dying and the new one not yet begun. No point in taking smart Western people a substandard chandelier or a few bottles of vodka suited to the palate of a defective Russian park-keeper. But how about a tablecloth? In three months' worth of evenings she embroidered a small cloth in warm autumnal colours. You could never buy anything like that. And she would take something else homemade.

'Heh, Tanya, wasn't it you who said she had a cheese mould from her great-grandmother? Do you think I could borrow it for a few days?'

It was a beautiful antique from a nineteenth-century kitchen, made of smooth, light lime wood, in the shape of a pyramid with a flattened square top. It stood for a world of love and respect and no indolence. The four sides slotted together like paper cut-out models, with tags and holes. Each inner face was carved with a design: a rose, an Orthodox cross with two horizontals, another rose, and finally the letters XB, Christ is Risen.

'Vanya, was it not your son who became a carpenter? You don't think he could do me a favour?'

All these arrangements involved a lot of telephoning, a lot of the old bellowing and some handouts from the dollar purse. But finally Vanya's son made a passable copy of the beautiful mould and got stoned for a week on the proceeds. Tanya went shopping in the chic new mall that only a couple of years ago had been the dreary *univermag* called Tsum. One by one Sofka's friends and neighbours came to appreciate her position and redirect their gossip.

The time approached. Sofka collected the visa, took it to the airline and collected the pre-paid ticket. She couldn't eat that week and the sight of herself sideways on in the full-length mirror

228

inside the wardrobe door was almost bearable. She was wearing a skirt and bra, of course. She never looked at herself naked.

The suitcase lay open on the bed. She didn't know what the autumn could be like in Paris. She got out the atlas and checked where Paris was. Her ticket said she would fly to Paris Charles de Gaulle. Departure time 0920 from Moscow International Airport Sheremetevo 2. 'France France France France France. I'm going to France!' She packed her usual woollen skirts, the one she had on and another, and the violet jumper and the black leather coat, just in case the weather turned cold. The wooden mould and the tablecloth nestled among them. Sasha admired Vanya's imitation of nineteenth-century craft. He helped pack it. Already he felt better about Sofka's enterprise, for it left him with new practical ideas. Now he had a clear two weeks in which to consider his future.

Sofka's bulky, comic figure appeared out of the silver intestine walkway at Charles de Gaulle airport. She thought she was in fairyland. Little Marcus thought she resembled an ogress and Kate and Dan too started at her appearance, for her brown hair was now metallic red, not a happy match with the purple jumper, but they said nothing, other than that they were delighted to see her. Sofka stood childlike to attention as Kate kissed her on each cheek in turn. She inhaled her musky perfume, and felt the brush of her soft powdered skin. The most powerful erotic experiences come when we are reborn as someone else; as we follow our inspiration from air-conditioned airport arrivals halls to dark and chilly car parks and cannot see that it is also a new enslavement that lies ahead.

'This is Dan's new car. He's been made head of the bank.' Dan stowed Sofka's luggage in the boot of a green Saab, a boot which unfolded upwards at the press of a button. The beneficence on his face targeted the three loaded bags, too humble to be called suitcases, of which Soviet Russia produced none. They included a large shopping bag too full to zip up.

'It's brand new.'

'Oh no, it's old.'

'No, I mean the car. Our car. How do you like it?'

Sofka established herself upon invitation in the front seat. She half-turned, not quite catching Marcus, who was making faces at her from behind. 'We have cars too. Volgas and Ladas and Zils and Chaikas and Nevas. More makes than you.'

A smiling Kate sucked in the corners of her mouth.

The traffic was bad: thousands of cars with unsynchronized purposes criss-crossed the outskirts of Paris. But eventually they escaped into the semi-country and the tyres crunched the gravel. It was a mild, wet day which made the summer geraniums appear dementedly brightly coloured in their wooden tubs beside the front door. The house was dark brick, just two storeys high, with a wooden porch sheltering a front patio of rough stone. Beyond the gravel stretched to some invisible limit a beautifully tailored garden, with a stripy lawn, on which a layer of white drizzle had settled. Tall trees, probably elm, hid the house from outside eyes.

'Quick, inside! Don't get wet! Dan will bring the bags.'

From the moment of descent the lovely house fell for Sofka into the category of the great impersonal. It was like a hotel and a suite of state rooms and a monument and a dream. She marvelled at the pink-tiled bathroom attached to the guest room and the sheets with lace edges on her bed and the electric switch that closed the curtains.

'Settle in, then, if you like, and we'll have lunch at twelve.'

Sofka, reborn as Kate's friend, the friend of all delicate Western things, sat on the bed, which spread her thick legs to most undelicate proportions, and marvelled. Behind the bedroom door was a towelling robe for Sofka's personal use. She felt its thickness and looked forward to the moment she would wrap it about her damp, clean body, anointed with the oils and lotions that stood on the shelf at the head of the bath. So much wonderment filled Sofka's heart that it might have burst.

'Just like our houses! Lovely, comfortable, inviting places you can call home ...'

'Really!' Kate looked amused. 'That's not what I remember.'

'But you were a foreigner! How could you see the way we really were? So much in our country was disguised.'

Kate felt disappointment. Good workmanship in human affairs involves kindness to the past, but we are poor workmen. Sofka was making it difficult. She had brought the lost world with her and now she wore it like a mask. But it was Kate's problem too for succumbing to nostalgia. You go back to an old house, you take up with an abandoned child, you come across a garment you thought you threw away years ago, and you expect to love it as if time never moved, but in truth the injection of the past into the present is unwelcome.

'We're going to show you a world . . . '

'Like once I showed you Moscow.'

'We got to know Moscow pretty well.'

'But only as foreigners.'

They drove into Paris one evening in the new green Saab. Dan pushed it suddenly to seventy miles an hour in a rare space in the dense traffic. Marcus cheered him on. 'Hurrah! Well done, Pappy.' They passed the old Opéra and the Tuileries Gardens, and Notre-Dame on the Île de la Cité. In the distance the tip of the Eiffel Tower winked. The pavements were crowded, the department stores ablaze with light. Kate bought Marcus a huge bag of freshly popped popcorn.

'It's like Moscow, a second Moscow! How wonderful!'

They walked under the seventeenth-century porticoes of the floodlit Place Vendôme before settling on a favourite restaurant of Dan's in the Marais. The menu Sofka received had no prices. Anyway she couldn't read it. She stifled an almost overwhelming desire for curd cheese and cabbage fritters by saying, 'I'll have beef and champagne.'

Kate and Dan exchanged a glance. 'Anything to start? I know, we'll order you a surprise.'

'You can order me lobster!'

But on reflection Kate decided this would be a waste and told Sofka they didn't have any. She ordered her something with prawns instead. The seats were high-backed benches covered with green leather gathered into deeply stuffed diamonds. Sofka bounced a little on hers before looking around. 'No dance floor?'

'Dan likes quiet places, Toffee. You don't mind do you, or do you really want to go dancing?'

The waiter in a stiff collar and long black *tablier* brought Marcus a second Coca-Cola on a silver salver.

'I'm just interested in how people live.'

'Aren't we all?'

The meal arrived.

'What do you think? We think it's the best food in Paris.'

The Russian visitor waved her fork. 'We have beef too. Only different bread, as you know. So much refined bread is not good for the digestion. We have *shampanskoe* too. I am quite used.'

Kate sucked in her cheeks. She refused Marcus a second plate of chips and he threw all his cutlery on the floor. That was Saturday.

On Sunday Dan drove to a clubhouse beyond the *périphérique* and they took Sofka up in a balloon to survey all the loveliness of that saved corner of the world. The bright colder weather was just right. They gave her a hat and gloves and boots to wear and strapped her in like a child in a highchair. She didn't dare confess she was afraid. Lightly as a kiss on a child's forehead, the currents in the air caught them and changed their state from solid to liquid. Sofka marvelled, suspended, carried on the wind against her will, thinking of the annual excursions to the Moscow countryside and the spa holidays to the Caucasus which they used to provide for the tunnel-workers. How astonishing it was to discover that the world existed in duplicate! 'Yes we have all this too,' she cried, as they flew and flew, and eventually landed back on the ground, in a green field.

The bump finally knocked the lid off Kate's exasperation. 'You don't. You don't, Toffee, you're lying. When I met you you worked in a sewer. You led a miserable life.' Outside the clubhouse, as they walked back from the take-off field, she took Sofka by her plump shoulders and shook her.

'Mummy, don't fight! Pappy, Mummy's fighting!'

But Sofka just turned her eyeballs to heaven. She didn't understand half of what was said now Kate's Russian had deteriorated. It was just nice to be touched.

★

'I told you not to get involved.'

'You're the one who's always telling me to develop my interests.'

'But Kate, it was seventy years. This woman was born in the dark and has stayed there ever since. Never brought out until now. Ponies go blind. What do you expect of human beings?'

'That's very sad.'

'How many more days?'

'Ten.'

Kate didn't propose any more excursions.

That was the signal for Marcus to become curious, of course. Every day when Kate or another mother fetched him from school at two, his first question was, 'Where's Sofka?'

'In her room, resting.'

He knocked for the first time in his life on a door in his own house. She was lying, graced by the huge bed with the pink satin eiderdown, looking at the ceiling. 'I brought you this.' He waved a big picture dictionary, of the kind they used with the youngest classes at school. He had 'borrowed' it. 'Here's the game. We choose a picture. You say "Yes" if you like it, "No" if you don't. OK?'

She patted the eiderdown. '*Sidis*'! *Nachinai ty*!'

'Washing machine.'

'Yes!'

'Football.'

'Yes.'

'Aeroplane.'

'No.'

He shrugged. The limit of the Yes/No game was you couldn't know why.

Her turn.

'Bird.'

'Yes.'

'And me, yes!'

'That's cheating! It's not your turn.'

'But I bird, yes!'

'No! You can't answer mine too. You mustn't. Start again. Chocolate.'

'Yes.' She made him laugh by exaggerating her stomach. Her turn. 'Mummy.'

'Sometimes.'

She wagged a finger. 'Yes or No.'

'Pappy.'

He shrugged.

'Yes.'

She pointed to him. 'Markoos!'

'No!'

'No? Sofka, then.'

'Yes.'

'Ekh . . . ' She shook her head. 'Markoos? Yes!' She pointed to herself.

On Tuesday afternoon Kate had to go out. 'Homework?' she asked Kate in her own language.

'Feel free!'

When Markus arrived, dropped by the school run, they sat at a table in his playroom, which had a large picture window facing the lawn. He spread out his books. She noticed he wrote left-handed. He seemed too small for work, but she couldn't relieve him of his burden, so she spread what calmness she could in the room and stared out of the window. Suddenly there came a dull thump. Bird! Oh! Come on. They dashed outside without coats, keeping their eyes close to the ground. Eventually Sofka spotted the stunned blackbird sitting patiently under a bush waiting for death. Its beak was of a yellow to terrify all who approached: a last desperate intensifying of colour. She held Marcus's arm. With her hands she described something like a box with a lid; with her lips she suggested something to eat. He came back breathless, having tipped fifty wooden bricks on to the playroom floor at speed and thrown in half a baguette. They needed a cloth or a towel. A towel was too heavy. It was too difficult to describe. She went herself and took the tablecloth from her suitcase. Having been too embarrassed to give it in this house, she threw it over the injured bird and nudged him into the box. Marcus picked grass from the edge of the lawn which they scattered beside the rumpled cloth. Then they carried the whole into the playroom, where a jam-jar lid of milk in which they moistened breadcrumbs was added to the lifesaving equipment.

During the next hour as they sat trying to pick up the thread of the homework, the bird tweeted once. Marcus gave Kate a tour of the hospital when she returned, and went to bed in a state pivoted on excitement and anxiety.

The bird died in the night. Marcus banged on Sofka's door before he left for school to tell her. When he came back that afternoon they made a coffin with the cheese mould and completed a burial ceremony in the garden. A sad but companionable silence set in between them.

Marcus took the tablecloth indoors and spread it under his homework. After a couple of minutes he looked up. 'When I've finished you and I could watch TV together.'

'Yes, if you like.'

Sofka sat watching night slowly settle on the garden. The view of nature was entrancing; she felt she was born to watch over it. Which is what she was, an eternal guardian, for when Marcus turned on the TV in mid-evening, after Kate had come and gone again, Sofka found herself waving her hands. No! She positioned herself between the screen and his amused eyes; amused at her. 'Come.' She stretched out a hand and pulled him on to her knee. 'I teach you Russian.' He sat there, forgetting all his determination not to be babyish. She wrote out the letters of the alphabet for him to read. Next day in the town she bought him an exercise book in which to practise making the unfamiliar symbols. The ones he loved especially were Л and Щ, for they were letters with wings, betokening the bird.

The town was now, finally, where Sofka dared wander on her own while Marcus was at school. Having recovered from her first introverted shock at being out of Russia, she took a ten-minute bus ride into the prosperous human settlement where cars outnumbered human figures, and all the roads were paved and all the buildings made of concrete or stone. The town, called Igny, sat prettily on the River Marne, straddling an ancient bridge; moreover it was easily pronounced by a Russian, and other passengers were able to tell her, first time round, where to get off.

The shock, though, came not just from being out of Russia. She stared at each magazine in the newspaper kiosk, and at each picture advertising what was on at the small cinema, and at the adverts in the windows of the two pharmacies. Beautiful faces and beautiful skin, everywhere. It seemed all women were like Kate in the West; walking propaganda on behalf of sexual fervour and self-importance and health. In every magazine, on every street corner, on every screen, Sofka saw versions of Kate. She felt compelled to visit the town every remaining afternoon.

In the pink bathroom, meanwhile, she looked at her naked body in the mirror. In the best mirror she had ever looked in with no flaws, no distortions, she stared into her flaccid shapelessness, with the tyres round her middle, and her pudgy arms, and thighs like two long featureless faces, and shook her head. She hadn't always been like that, it just happened, what with the Moscow diet and no one caring. She ran her fingers through her hair before sitting down in the bath to wash it. Now that awful dye they had inflicted on her was fading with daily washes. Someone at the hairdresser's had been jealous of her trip to France and wanted to spoil it.

The lumps and bumps of Sofka's body took up different bodily stations when she sat down. She still found them despicable and spent all her holiday money on fragant oils and slimming massage pads which she applied morning and night. All the adverts in the pharmacy and the magazines said the undesirable bits of the body could be moved for ever. She massaged her hips and thighs standing up in the pink bath, side on to the mirror, and was shy of what she saw. She felt so very shy, as if she were getting married again.

When the morning of her departure came, Marcus wrapped himself in the tablecloth and refused to come back out of his room and say goodbye. So she shouted, 'Bird! Yes!' through his closed door, and heard him scream back, 'Yes! Don't go!'

Kate shook her head. 'He'll be all right. He's going through a very temperamental stage.'

Sofka laid a hand on her heart and Kate kissed her. It had in the end been much better all round to leave Sofka to do her own thing in France, not try to show her too much.

Dan shook the hand of his wife's guest at the airport, where he ran her out alone in the green Saab with the automatic boot. Lifting out the three bags, he smiled. 'Say hello to Moscow for me. I remember it fondly.'

'Me too!' She disappeared inside glass doors, wheeling a trolley.

Sasha brought red carnations to the airport to meet his returned time-traveller. His first happy glimpse was of her shouting at a man who took the baggage trolley from under her nose. Her hair was a mixture of colours, her face round and soft. 'Don't you understand good manners, citizen? You should travel abroad. At least they have good manners there.' And lots of free trolleys, she added silently, with a touch of guilt.

'Heh! Little Sofka! Over here! Give me your bags!'

'Sasha, it's you!'

Sasha had cool, smooth cheeks and his lips were soft and, so it seemed to her, childlike. He smelt bewildering foreign perfume on his wife, but also her own smell, which was good. He had been afraid she would get stuck in another dimension.

They walked across the Arrivals hall towards the exit and buses and taxis into Moscow. 'You know, while you were gone, I started a new *biznes* making wooden tools and dolls and traditional objects. In case . . . well, just in case.'

'Can you carve birds?'

'Of course.'

'Good, then make me two. You can set yourself up in the souvenir business and I will be your first customer. I place an order for export.' Sofka, clutching her husband's arm, took a deep breath of cold, heavy Moscow air and the fumes that always laced it. 'You silly-billy, little Sash, I really am glad to be back.'

14

POSTSCRIPT

Back in my own country, I was out of a job. I went to what used to be called the Labour Exchange and is now POWER TO THE PEOPLE. I chose an upmarket branch of P2P, assuming ex-Russia watchers might be more in demand in W1 than SW9. There was a queue as long as the daily wait for visas outside the American consulate, so when I heard and saw it was full of Russians I thought many of them had simply made that mistake. Grosvenor Square – Gross-venor to them – was round the next corner. Or perhaps it was a subconscious mistake. Russians had spent their lives queueing, so it wasn't surprising they couldn't kick the habit. The queue confirms the wickedness of the world and simultaneously represents hope. Who knows what you'll get if you wait long enough?

I stood among the troublesome time-travellers; unwilling disciples or former seductees of Vlad the Failure, upstaged by two smart women. The blonde wore a camel-wool coat over a tan-leather calf-length skirt, with brown boots and a gold-coloured brooch on her lapel, and a matching broad-brimmed hat. She scowled when a girl in leggings passed by eating a chocolate bar and dropped the wrapper. A van driver held up a finger to a cyclist, wound down his window as he sped past: 'Effing leftie!' People on their way to work wore blue denim and black leather. Several young girls had long ringlet perms. A male hand threw a lager can out of a speeding, overloaded, noisily souped-up Ford Escort. Two bedraggled young men with football shirts and coloured face make-up looked as if they had spent the previous night in battle.

'The proletariat has won anyway, Allochka. Our struggle to keep up bourgeois standards has been wasted.'

'Our good-for-nothing men will fit in here.' Alla, small, dark, and completely in black, cast sharp glances over all the males around her, as if she were scramming their faces with a flint.

The Russian men in the queue certainly wore their hair too long and their horrible apologies for grey suits appeared to be both vulgarly new and shabby, both baggy and tight all at once. My most generous thought was that Russian men's clothes were like demob suits after the war, not fitting the personalities inside them. As for their faces, well, even the one with a long prominent nose, a stream of shoulder-length grey and pepper hair, and artistic fingers, a man called Yegor, looked puffy round the eyes in a way that suggested rough insides. Though the one next to him, lean with thin straight hair, on the phone, looked better. Ivan Taranshchikov, who in England already called himself Eyevan Tarrant, and fancied his chances, kept stealing glances at Valentina. Then someone tapped me on the shoulder.

'Leather! Darling! I didn't expect.'

We stood on the clean solid grey pavement, with black taxis and red buses passing on their continuous, unremitting journeys yards from the neat kerb. Russia does not have the kind of neat kerbs and pavements Britain has had since Roman times, and as such appears to have no foundation for civic life. Leather looked good. He had been preening himself. No demob suit for him, only some dreadful grey openweave shoes with the brown socks peeping through. Valentina and Alla turned to eye Leather up and down with admiration. He had just arrived. Valentina lifted her nose higher as I kissed him very softly on one close-shaven cheek.

He smiled charmingly. 'Tell me, mistress, I come to London, but where is fog?' He held his smooth white hands up in the air. It was February but quite mild. No one needed gloves and many of my compatriots passing by were also without coats and showing too much pink-grey flesh.

'You're thinking of smog, Leather. We stopped making it.'

'Smog?'

'Yes, smog is deliberate fog. It's fog you can do something about. We began controlling factory and coal-fire emissions, when too many people choked to death one winter.'

His eyes glazed over at the word deliberate. He looked like a man acting the part of being in love. 'So you too believed in the mastery of man over nature, mistress? Aah, that is fine. You English stopped making fog.'

'No!'

But he was inspired by memories of the past. 'Ah, mistress, of our many half-hidden treasures, we had the technology to clear away the clouds and make clear blue days. Expensive of course, so we only used our science for special occasions. But everyone agreed that 1st May had to be perfect. On that day every year we manicured the universe. We gave her the works! She was dumb beauty at our disposal. Now we are out of a job.' Leather looked melancholy and untrustworthy and sentimental, and knew it was his most appealing expression. 'Make good advertisement, eh? "Defunct cosmetics company seeks world role".' He stared into my eyes. He was like a redundant monarch. 'I must get job, mistress.'

We shuffled on a few paces. 'Well, you're in the right place to get a job,' I said finally, with all the briskness I could muster. 'I expect you will.'

We were moving, but it wasn't clear people were getting inside the rather attractive brick building that housed P2P. Someone at the ground-floor bay window peeped through those kind of vertical fabric blinds which with one vicious hanging turn charming domestic buildings into impersonal offices, then vanished again.

Possibly still weighing my answer, Leather looked rueful, victimized and sweetly boyish. 'Mebbee I get one. *Bog znaet.*'

'God knows? If I were God I would have deserted you long ago.'

We fell silent, and the silence was filled with other people's chatter about shopping.

'No cockroach powder in any shop in all London, *forzample*,' said Valentina, who sent a monthly parcel to her mother.

'Ent no *kasha. Kasha* ensures inner beauty, but I think for these people the inner person is worthless.'

I knew where to buy the grains for *kasha* but I wasn't about to butt in. Valentina, I noticed, often touched her nose as a mark of discernment. The nose, well shaped without being beautiful or ugly or even characterful, twitched under a thick layer of matt-beige make-up. She took a lipstick from her leather handbag and twisted it up. 'The lipsticks, *forzample*, are good, but otherwise the people here suffer many shortages.'

Tarrant, still with the phone pressed to his ear, dissented enthusiastically. 'Is good place to buy bananas!' He was optimistic about the new life and had already put down roots, but because he was still most keen on Russian women he put himself in these queues regularly, to survey the newly arrived talent from the ex-motherland. Today the ampleness of blonde Valentina certainly recommended itself, but she found his drooling over bananas disgusting and turned away.

'Ent this —' Alla gestured towards a blue and orange sign on the lamppost behind Tarrant — 'is just not so different here. This Neighbourhood Vatch. Here they vatch you too. Only they put notice up and say so.'

I laughed quietly. Russians want too much. Leather was wanting God knows what, standing quietly beside me, smoking a ghastly Russian cigarette, while Tarrant, remembering the need for credibility, at last pushed down the aerial on the phone and put the whole toy in his pocket.

Then, as if we had been becalmed for days at sea and suddenly someone felt a breeze, our whole queue stirred. Hands pointed towards the P2P window, reaching towards a hand reaching towards them. Lacquered nails propped up a white card up on the sill, behind the glass. NO RUSSIANS THANK YOU. Fat letters, filled in with blue biro scribble.

I ran round to the front door and pressed the intercom. 'You can't do that! That's racial discrimination!'

They switched me off without replying.

'Mary and Joseph being turned away at the inn,' said Leather.

'You're too literate, that's your trouble. You'll never survive here.'

We stood, nonplussed. Valentina even looked across questioningly at Tarrant, wondering whether there was someone he could phone. Some in the queue began to drift away.

'Don't go!' I cried with frustration. Sheep were being lost.

A middle-aged woman with huge glasses on a string came out of the door.

'Can't we talk? What's your name?'

'Maggie.'

'Maggie, look . . . '

'*Chto?*' someone shouted. 'What?'

Alla had her own technique for winning sympathy. She slid up to the woman and stroked her jumper. 'Dear lady, if you could help me. I can see you are a nice person.'

But Maggie wasn't sorry, as Pilate wasn't sorry. She turned and walked off to fetch a pint of milk, leaving Alla and Valentina to make critical remarks about her balance on high heels. All eyes watched her pass a slaty-dull church with two propaganda boards in its modestly kept garden. One said St Saviour's. The other: JESUS IS OUR MIND, OUR HONOUR AND OUR CONSCIENCE.

'Our Christian Church has died like your Communist Party and we haven't even noticed.'

'That's because you didn't build any statues of your Jesus Christ,' replied Leather.

'Indeed. The Catholics who did have lasted longest.'

242

Alla, determined to survive, said, 'I know what we do now. We claim this "Benefit". They owe it to us, no?'

Leather nodded. "Strue. We died for your sins, mistress. Now you must pay us. I see people with collecting box in the streets here. Maybe now I take collecting box.'

Next moment the crowd turned in every direction. I saw them like a handful of spilt coins rolling away from me faster than I could catch them.

'Stop! *Podozhdite!* One pound a tale.'

'Done,' chorused just enough voices for me not to lose hope.

A tall, hairy-faced young man with round black spectacles upended his leather cap on the pavement, took a guitar out of an old case and tuned up. I threw a chunk of English gold into the hat. Matvei, or as he said, Methyou, played a few open chords, then fingered something familiar. People clapped and the atmosphere was transformed for a few seconds. Buskers change stations and pavements into churches, until we come to our senses and get on our way. '. . . we died and were reborn . . . ' Matvei sang with great tenderness.

'Bop Tylan,' whispered Alla.

'We died to save the soul of capitalism. Iss true,' nodded Leather.

> We are queing here to meet God
> free of fear but still so odd
> in this world where reason reigns.
> We stand like med*yee*val sinners,
> God's lost courtiers, soldiers . . .
> NOT WINNERS . . .
> in this world where reason reigns.

Matvei bowed. 'I sang this song in an Underground train between Camden Town and Hampstead. My song imprisoned the passengers, who hated me for it. They looked away and tutted. Only there was a blonde woman in a black suit with silk scarf. She gave me money. She was happy. She was getting married to a rich man. I sang to her slender calves in black nylon and she invited me home.'

'Phew-eee!' Tarrant shouted, and whistled. Valentina lifted her nose in the air. Others giggled and tittered.

'You're right. This is the place of sin in a reasonable world: to provide secret entertainment. The woman I sang to was a famous historian, and her mother was an historian before her and her grandmother before that. She came from a family in love with history and she loved my song because she realized a new era was beginning.'

'She'll name the era and become even more rich. Some people have all the luck,' I said.

''Strue, we Russians are just entertainers.' Leather put his arm round Matvei, who had pocketed the pound and put back the cap. Leather said goodbye for everyone. 'Matvei iss my brother. Iss lovely man.'

When we had recovered from Matvei's departure Yegor stepped forward, showing off his proud bearing. 'Some more music?' He had dropped his charity-shop black overcoat on the ground and was wearing evening dress. This outfit looked to be of the same origin, because the shirtsleeves were too short. He had a chest of championship depth and silver hair lapping his shoulders. 'I am also singer. I sang as a child and now I sing as a man. I went to school to sing.' He took a deep breath to cushion the outflow of memory. 'Two years ago I came here as guest artist. The West discovered we Russians had great talent and were cheap. So now I tell you what I learned about myself in the Albert Hall. I call this chapter in my autobiography "On first singing to *kapitalisty*"! I stood in the spotlight and felt the whole auditorium vibrate. That vast coliseum of cheering people, row upon row, tier upon tier, standing, clapping, cheering, stamping. I could bear all that terrifying spectacle so long as I acknowledged that the power of my music was something apart from me. Music was eternal soul, not just mine. It only used my lungs to appear human. But when

I realized that that applause was for me, I was immobilized. I just stood, transfixed until someone pushed against my shoulder and whispered, "Move over, Maximov, you vain bastard." It was the tenor Stefano Angelo, who wanted his turn. Eventually I stepped aside. The crowd threw flowers to him too. Only instead of just standing there, clutching them, as I had done, he plucked the flowers from the bouquet and threw them back to the crowd. My mouth tightened. My throat choked with envy. A newspaper photograph, alas, caught me at just that moment, looking like a sour, gauche Russian. The crowd had only admired me but they loved him. But, you know, my friends —'Yegor spread his arms — 'I was just sad, because it never occurred to me to throw back flowers to the people, and I blame our dark years. At music school no bows were allowed, and no clapping. We had the discipline and satisfaction of our art, they told us, and that should be enough. So I sought ways of putting all my feeling into art, while still hiding it, and I expected the audience to hide its feelings too. But when I came here, women screamed for me like I knew women screamed once for the Beatles. So I felt sad about myself, standing there in the Albert Hall, though of course it doesn't matter now. I have a great career ahead of me. I sing at their Glyndebourne this August.'

'You are vain, Yegor.'

'Get a new penguin suit before you go.'

Only Valentina was enthusiastic. 'You're worth it. False modesty is a waste of effort.'

'I do know,' he said, but someone handed him his coat, as if he really ought to cover up now.

Valentina shook her head. 'You just go on the same, Yegor Maximich. Just believe in yourself. I do!' She paused. 'Is everyone ready for me then?'

We formed a circle around her, while she applied a fresh coat of lipstick. Yegor stayed to watch.

'Until last year I was a train stewardess, a lowly creature. I used to man my wagon —'

'Woman your wagon!' cried Alla.

'Woman my wagon as far as Brest.'

'Women only to Brest!' giggled Tarrant.

'Comrades, are you listening? The train went on across Poland and I came back. Then one day I stayed on the train and no one asked me to get off. I went on making tea and handing out linen, only I insisted on being paid in hard currency. I arrived in Ostend with fifty dollars.'

'That's peanuts.'

'Call it bananas if you like. I don't care. I went to Harrods and tried things on. Because I couldn't buy anything and I wasn't a shoplifter –' Here Valentina shot a glance at Alla, who met her gaze unflinchingly. 'No, I wasn't a shoplifter, I was prepared to wait until I had money. But in Harrods' changing rooms I compared myself with other women. What did I see straight away? I see that I am bigger than other women. Now, I ask myself, how can I turn this to my advantage?'

Valentina handed the camel coat and hat to Alla and twirled, so all could see the advantage. Tarrant's eyes opened wider and wider. She was wearing a turquoise leotard, which matched, as she slipped out of the skirt and boots, her tights. A pair of gold high-heeled dancers' shoes drawn from the handbag threw her legs into heroic relief, and so she began her presentation.

'Now I turn from the waist very slowly to the right and to the left, ten times. Then I bend forward with my arms over my head, like swan. Next I hold bar – can be anything, kitchen sink, this brick wall – and slowly I lift each leg ten times. I make video for bee-eeg women to work out.'

Tarrant struggled to recover the power of speech. 'You're a genius, Valya.'

'Hear, hear!' the others chorused.

'I have genius because I have energy and courage. I sell my body and yet I still keep it for me. This is Russian strength. Double standards. Whenever I feel lazy I remember my modest friend Asya, who doesn't get out.'

'Bravo, Valya. You deserve success! We could maybe work out a banana diet together.' Tarrant cheered her again. 'I leave you my calling card, amazing lady.' He gave her a bunch of bananas, then, handing a camera to a tall man with round glasses, fell on one knee. Passing round the Polaroid a few minutes later, someone remarked that Tarrant must already be doing quite well for himself too. His eyes twinkled. ''Strue! I tell you, it all happened very quickly.'

'I sit in Green Park one day, watching the sad office workers have lunch. They bring their sandwiches in bags. The kiosk sells Mars Bars and ice lollies. Everyone looks bored. I think I will bring them something new. So I buy big bunch of bananas and go round the deck-chairs. '"Scuse me, sir, madam, you like banana? Not free but very cheap and very healthy. Give you good energy for the whole afternoon." If they ask I give my name as Rasputin. Some look afraid, some laugh. I sell all the bananas. Next day I go back with more, and also write speech on bananas, which I perform, and stick label to my front and back: RASPUTIN'S BANANAS. The man from kiosk chase me all the way to Mayfair. I say, "You stuck in prehistory with your nasty fattening snacks and is time for new ideas." He say, "You Commie bastard, this is my patch." But now I make banana ice cream, banana cake, banana biscuits all much better than his. Really modern!' Tarrant waved a whole pack of his bright yellow business cards at Valentina. 'Is growing business!'

'I get ten per cent.' The tall man with round glasses, apparently Tarrant's partner, spoke up for the first time.

Tarrant said, 'Leonid saved me by driving me away in a Rolls-Royce! Stylish, eh? I show him I am grateful. Capitalism with a human face.'

'Rolls-Royce?' Was Valentina targeting the wrong man?

'Oh, not mine! I am chauffeur in Mayfair. I wash cars, I drive, I do philosophy. I have best of all worlds. But none of them is *mine*.'

'Philosophy in Mayfair?'

'Lady! I observe the English do their best philosophy over

247

lunch. 'Strue, I was recommended to live in France, and maybe is better there, but I don't speak French.'

Leonid evidently construed as a failure of imagination my silent reeling in admiration.

'Wait! I paint a picture for you, of pretty old narrow streets, blocked by the fine cars of fine men. Is fact that fine men frequent Mayfair.' He exchanged an amused look with Tarrant. 'In Shepherd Market you will see many Russians lunching these days, having serious conversation. They know they are the best, so they go where the best go. Now I want you to picture it. One short fat man called Konstantin is saying, "What is to be done 'bout Russia?" Though he needs a book to sit on, because he is so short, this Kostya is handsome, and though he is fat his skin doesn't shine repulsively like the face of his bodyguard, Dima.

'Misha is a thinner type. In the old days you would have thought him the political commissar. While the others tuck into pasta with foie gras, which might otherwise cool too quickly in the air (for they are sitting outside, under the restaurant awning, to catch the midday sun), Misha reproaches Kostya. "Is awfully simple, Kostya. That is not Russian question. Question is, who is to blame?"'

Leonid chuckles. 'This is cue to raise glasses in compensation for communal misery. You know?'

Valentina and Alla nod.

'Including Dima, there are four more diners. "The President, our president," they cry, though their glasses are raised in self-preservation. Misha says, "Our President iss power-crazy. Iss megalomaniac. Iss tyrant."

'A dark-skinned waiter, wiry body, hair receding, doesn't care whether he interrupts. Between Misha and Kostya he slides a stiff white cotton arm to reach empty plates. He tops up the champagne glasses and sets the magnum back in its bucket. While the others light up, Kostya regains the initiative. "Gentlemen, you betray our Russian weaknesses. You indulge always in cult of personality, blaming one man. Cult of personality can be negative too. I say to you –" He bangs his knife handle on the table, and two Englishmen at the next table look at the Russian table. "I say to you what is wrong with our beautiful country is no one man, but the fact that we have no good tax system; the fact that our government is full of fiscal ill-leet-erates. Illleeterates!" He banged the knife again. "You understand? They cannot read the language of the human personality. They cannot create a system to encourage the best. They give the biggest tax breaks to the Church and all biznezmen become devout. President goes to church. Who can we trust? No one in our government. No one in our country." "The People!" said Dima the bodyguard. With the round face pink as well as shiny, and the blond hair curly and dry, Dima seemed born at such a disadvantage he needed the People to hide among.

'Kostya was outraged. "See, Dima, you've got to get an education. We must have leaders who seek the people's consent, as says the famous Eenglishman Dzhon Lok. But this not the same thing as having damn personality cult about the People."

'Misha's phone rang but he switched it off without answering. "Your Lawk didn't know Russia."

'Kostya began defending Locke.'

I interrupted Leonid's narrative. 'Locke: "The safety of the innocent is to be preferred." That's right, isn't it? Don't we *all* believe that now?'

Leather shook his head. 'Let Leonid go on, mistress, you're spoiling it.'

So the chauffeur resumed with what he had seen in Mayfair. 'Suddenly Dima leaps to his feet, scraping his chair. Under his napkin his right hand crosses to the left inside of his jacket. "Boss! Vatch out! *Vnimanie!* He cut your balls off, this secret agent."

'"Anything I can get you, sir?" inquired the waiter, working the lobster crackers.

'"Sit down, Dima! This is a peaceful, law-abiding country. You are fool."

'The neighbouring table of two was entertained.

'"Good appetites our old enemies have got." Michael Cairns was a small, shy, brilliant man who wrote leaders for a Conservative broadsheet. His desire to apply his mind to contemporary issues had driven him from Oxford, whereas Michael Myers was still there, just thinking. For years they had disagreed in their politics, but recently had found common ground.

"'It's all they have left at the end of History.'"

"'Do you accept that thesis?'"

"'History with a big H seemed to be about becoming a nation. What matters post-History is global business. The Russians represent a vast potential market.'"

"'You sure you're happy with mineral water, Michael?'"

"'Let me give you an example of globalization in a different sense, which I think is far more interesting. The great Russian soul, Rilke called it. Russians were prime examples in the old order of things of people who, when they ask you how you are, really mean it. Russians really cared. But now you can get those really caring souls in the States too. You can get everything in the States. Bottled. With or without bubbles.'"

"'Which means?'"

"'That certain thoughts, certain problems, certain misunderstandings, will always be present in the world, no matter who embodies them. As if the nations of the world were given different occasions to step up and explore one or other counter of the divine supermarket.'"

'You tell good tale, Leonya,' said Tarrant when he had finished.

'I still don't understand why they hang out in Mayfair.'

'Lady, they combine philosophy with property. Is quite decent, traditional, Eenglish thing, from time of Adam Smeet.'

'But —'

'Where did they get the money to buy the best property in London? They were Communists, looking after the People's money, when the people lost power. Now they keep it in *offshorny konto*. They live off rent from Immobility and pretend to care about Russian future.'

'You mean real estate.'

'No, lady, I mean rent from Immobility. Money for doing nothing, and calling it philosophy. Baah, philosophy should be like

250

cleaning a car. Keep cleansing the thoughts, looking for smudges in the reflection. But you see the way of the world. Is messy. Is scruffy. Oh, and one thing I left out: that stupid bodyguard. When the waiter bring the little stove to flambé the pancakes, this peasant throws jug of water over the whole table. Water drips off the table. Waiter has to mop up while they puff cigars. In fact, they all leave soon after that. And what happens but those two Englishmen move over from their table to Russian table, saying they like to be in the sun, and I notice they are looking for something, anything, like tramps rummaging in a rubbish bin.'

'Did they find anything?'

'Kostya left behind old book by Vlad the Failure which he uses to sit on. The Oxford one say Vlad is very good on Party organization and appealing to the People. The other one said the People is an elastic concept, not without worth.'

I shook my head. 'Don't tell me any more.'

There were five of us left outside P2P when a middle-aged woman with huge eyes and Georgian swarthiness dramatically took the floor.

'Aah, yes, philosophy!'

'No, no more, please!'

'Just one little thing, that explains my existence.' When she danced, she fed out her arms Oriental-fashion, like payropes endlessly releasing the ship of life from its earthly moorings. 'We did live in the most *philosophical* country in the world, which is why even our leaders took refuge in superstition. I made a good living.'

'Aha! And now?'

'Now I am out of a job! No palms held out for my healing advice, no tea-leaves saved.'

'No, I mean what do you predict?'

I had pressed a coin into her hand, but she held out for more. Tarrant matched my pound. She slipped the money into a purse ostentatiously held in her cleavage, and began to drag her forward-folded body backwards.

'I worry what will happen to the whole world, now that we do not have Russia as a conductor for bad things, like a rod for lightning . . . ' No one spoke. A passing cabriolet Mercedes treated us to a minute's rap.

I bowed my head. How could I let my refugees disperse? Yet how could I hold on to them? I walked away in no particular direction, as sad as the office workers in Green Park. A taxi driver swore at me for nearly confronting his wheels.

The fortune-teller ran after me, kissing my hands. 'I like you to be my friend. If only you could help me.'

I gave her my card, but the only Russian I kept up with personally was Leather. We met in a pub in Soho called the Sherlock Holmes which he liked because it reminded him of his childhood, and he could watch TV there and, a house speciality, detective story videos. The evening came when he announced he understood that the British people fought the metaphysical struggle between good and evil by telly-proxy. 'I write this for a newspaper, mistress. I psychoanalyse your British psyche. Which newspaper is it that your friend Roy Owedean works for? I need one that is more serious.'

'You'll be lucky.'

Leather shook his head 'So cynical, mistress.'

'What you should do is set up a replica of your old country and . . . '

He squeezed my cheeks, red with the heat of the bar. The next thing I knew he had tendered for Battersea Power Station.

'The Project needs backing . . .'

'Don't you want to marry me, Leather? I've given you this brilliant project.'

'*Iss* brilliant project, yes. But iss our Russian way to take your ideas and make them better.' Seeing me blink back a tear, he took a gentler tone, holding my cheeks again. 'Listen, mistress, I need a rich wife now. I am free man.' He looked at the Rolex on his wrist and then grinned and let go of me. 'If you are hard up you can be usherette in my park. Maybe even sideshow. Come and see me in the next century. See how I'm getting on.'

Leather spiked my drink and stole the contents of my wallet, though I guess he paid for the taxi. I woke up alone in my own bed, still woozy and with a real bender of a headache.

I had withdrawal symptoms. I cruised Mayfair looking for Leonid. All I wanted was a tale or two. I got one about Michael Cairns, who, with his friend Michael Myers, had actually been tailing Kostya and Misha, and eventually invited them for lunch courtesy of Cairns's paper. Kostya handed them a bag of rubbish about collectivity and community, which they ran away to sort like looters. All of which seemed just sad.

'Where's Dima the bodyguard?' I asked. So Leonid told this final story.

'He gets job in TV shop, because many Russians come to buy TV and hi-fi. He sees programme on memories of Gulag survivors. Dima's father was Gulag "survivor". Then this Michael Myers comes on and says, well, everyone knows KGB were not wicked, just inefficient. Poor Dima! He cries, in his own language, "No, no, this is lie. Bastard, you weren't there. How can you know." The manager, two sales assistants and a few customers: everyone looks. Maybe Dima is going mad. What's he saying? He is dangerous, living in the world of his imagination, especially when his hand goes to inside of his jacket and he points bloody gun at one screen and imagines blasting all twelve of them. Bam. Bam. Bam. Tshsh. Tsscch. Bam. Bam, Bam, Bam. Tinkle. Tinkle. Tinkle. Tsch. Tshshshshshshshsh. But he remembers. Dima, you stupid peasant. Get an education! This is country with good rules. He leaves gun alone, and the TV talks on.'

We count amongst those nations who seem not to be an integral part of the human species, but who exist only to give some great lesson to the world.

Peter Chaadaev, *Philsophical Letters* (1829)